Readers Love
Shira Anthony

Rainbow Awards Honorable Mention "One Perfect Score" 2012 for *The Melody Thief*

The Melody Thief

"This was an engrossing story that I was able to enjoy greatly without having read the first in the Blue Notes series…. the claim that it stands alone is one I can happily vouch."

"It's a story that holds your aggling story that I would definitely recom —(…Romanolics

Stealing the Wind

"The fantastic world Mrs. Anthony has created motivates you even more to understand and learn about the characters, and there is plenty of action, drama, suspense and adrenaline rush to keep you over the edge."
—Book Suburbia

"Refreshing new fantasy, with characters that grow on you… *Stealing the Wind* delivered what the cover promised."
—Pants Off Reviews

"I recommend this one for any lover of fantasy stories, mermen, or to those who simply want to enjoy the adventure. I'm looking forward to reading more about these two in book two."
—Hearts on Fire

By SHIRA ANTHONY

NOVELS

BLUE NOTES NOVELS
Aria
Blue Notes
The Melody Thief
Prelude

MERMAN OF EA
Stealing the Wind

With VENONA KEYES
The Trust

With EM LYNLEY
A DELECTABLE NOVEL
Lighting the Way Home

NOVELLAS
The Dream of a Thousand Nights

Published by DREAMSPINNER PRESS
http://www.dreamspinnerpress.com

ENCORE

SHIRA ANTHONY

Dreamspinner Press

Published by
Dreamspinner Press
5032 Capital Circle SW
Suite 2, PMB# 279
Tallahassee, FL 32305-7886
USA
http://www.dreamspinnerpress.com/

Encore
© 2013 Shira Anthony.

Cover Art
© 2013 Catt Ford.
Cover content is for illustrative purposes only and any person depicted on the cover is a model.

ISBN: 978-1-62798-248-1
Digital ISBN: 978-1-62798-246-7

Printed in the United States of America
First Edition
November 2013

In memory of David and all the other wonderful and talented men taken from us too soon, and to those still struggling with HIV and AIDS. Your fight is our fight.

Acknowledgments

Many thanks to my wonderful beta readers and editors. Without you, I really would be lost.

PART

February 3, 1971

IN A move likely aimed at cutting off supplies to North Vietnam via the Ho Chi Minh Trail, US and South Vietnamese forces have launched an attack on Laos. Although US officials are refusing to confirm or deny that an invasion is underway, reports from Japan's Kyodo News Service indicate that between four thousand and five thousand South Vietnamese troops have parachuted into Southern Laos, and that US planes and helicopters are assisting in the operations.

CHAPTER

Toledo, Ohio
September 1971

JOHN WOUND his way around gaggles of girls who blocked the hallway, turning it into a twisted obstacle course. He dodged a locker door here, someone slinging a backpack full of books there, and nearly got whacked in the gut by a kid holding a trumpet case. John's elbow connected with the hard fiberglass of the case as he pivoted to avoid the collision.

Shoot. That was going to make one big bruise. Not to mention it hurt.

He rounded the corridor and stepped inside the band room, relieved to find it empty. He leaned against the wall and took long, raspy breaths to try to calm his pounding heart. He wiped the sweat off his face, then rubbed his hands on his brown polyester pants.

"Hiding?"

"What?" John nearly jumped when he realized he wasn't alone. His voice sounded high and girlish to his ears.

"Are you hiding?" The speaker was a kid with wild brown hair and a hint of shadow on his jaw. He sat on one of the chairs by the podium, twirling a violin bow around like a baton. John hadn't seen the kid when he'd first come in, but it was clear the kid had seen *him*.

"I… n-no." Damn. Was he stuttering now? He hadn't stuttered this badly since elementary school.

The kid just laughed. "You new here?"

"Y-yes. Transferred last week."

"You got a name?"

"J-John. Fuchs." John's face was on fire as he croaked out his name. "Wh-who are you?"

"Roger Nelson." Roger ran a hand through his curly hair, which only served to make it stand up like horns. Roger reminded John of a devil, and it wasn't just the hair.

"N-nice to m-meet you, Roger." John walked over and offered Roger his hand.

Roger laughed and ignored the gesture. "Yeah." John could see his eyes were a deep green. Luminous. "Where'd you transfer from?"

"Saint B-Barnaby's."

More laughter. "So you're slumming it with us now?"

"I guess." He sure wasn't going to tell Roger about his parents' divorce, or about how they'd decided they no longer had the money to send him to private school one year before graduation. "I hear you've got a great orchestra." At least he wasn't stuttering anymore. He'd spent years in speech therapy in elementary and junior high school, but when he was nervous, it sometimes came back.

"We're pretty good," Roger said. John knew this was an understatement. His mother had done her homework—Marysville Senior High School's orchestra had won the state Division A championship the year before. "You play?"

"Piano. But I also play viola, trumpet, and flute." When Roger's eyes widened, John quickly added, "Not very well, though." John looked down at his feet and studied them intently. "I'm going to be a conductor."

When Roger didn't respond, John asked, "How about you?" He realized how stupid a question it was the instant he'd asked it. Of course the guy played violin.

"Concertmaster." In spite of the casual response, John thought he saw a hint of pride flash in Roger's eyes. "But *I'm* going to be the guy who hangs off the back of the garbage truck."

"Oh." What do you say to *that*? He had no idea if Roger was joking, but he sure wasn't going to embarrass himself by finding out.

Roger stood up and began to put his violin away. He was a little taller than John—who was now nearly six feet—with a lanky body and surprisingly broad shoulders. Good-looking too. John's face warmed once more.

"Is Mr. Constantino in his office?" he asked, mostly because he was having a really hard time not staring at Roger. He didn't really need to speak to the orchestra director.

Roger shrugged. "He was there a little while ago."

"Thanks." John waited for Roger to say something, but when he didn't, John made his way over to the office at the far end of the room.

BY THE time John had finished talking to Mr. Constantino, grabbed his books from his locker, and headed outside to the main courtyard, the sun was beginning to set. The air was cool, not surprising for late October in northern Ohio, so John set down his pack and zipped up his poplin jacket. The smell of fallen leaves mingled with a more pungent odor. Marijuana. He looked around and saw Roger seated on the low brick wall at the edge of the courtyard, smoking a joint.

"Hey." Roger inhaled and held his breath.

John swallowed hard, unsure of how to respond. "Hey." *Oh, that was great!* "Uh, h-how are you?"

Roger laughed and exhaled as John walked over. He held out the joint to John. "Want some?"

"No, thanks." He'd never even come this close to the real thing. "I've got to get going. Bus leaves in about five minutes."

A girl with hair down to her waist walked over to them. John was sure Roger was going to hide the pot, but instead he held it out to her and she took a long toke. Roger put his arm around the girl's shoulders and shot John a knowing look.

"Who's he?" the girl asked as she blew smoke in John's face.

John coughed and blinked.

"New kid. Orchestra."

"I'm John." John offered the girl a smile. He'd decided shaking hands was not public school etiquette after meeting Roger earlier.

The girl just stared at him, then turned to Roger and proceeded to kiss him. Not just any kiss. A french kiss. John felt sick to his stomach watching. He'd always thought kissing girls was gross. Now he was sure of it.

Roger kissed the girl back, then pushed her away before turning to John and asking, "Need a ride?"

The girl glared at Roger, who ignored her.

"I... ah... s-sure." John wasn't sure at all, but Roger was the only kid who'd acknowledged his existence since he'd arrived at Marysville and he figured it'd be rude to turn down the offer.

He and Roger walked in silence to the parking lot, where Roger led him to an enormous brown Buick. Small blue-and-pink spots dotted the exterior where someone had, he guessed, sanded off patches of rust in preparation for a paint job that never materialized. The windows were rolled down and the doors unlocked.

Roger grinned. "V-8." When John didn't respond, Roger continued, "This baby can outgun just about any car on the market."

"Groovy."

Roger's laughter echoed off the nearby building. "Jeez, what the hell did they teach you at St. Something?"

"St. Barnaby's," John corrected, feeling keenly awkward.

"Yeah. That place. Nobody says 'groovy' anymore."

"Oh." John's cheeks burned and he stared down at the blacktop, focusing on a weed that had forced its way through a crack and pushing it with his shoe.

"Get in."

The slippery fabric of John's pants propelled him over the vinyl bench seat as if someone had greased it. He stopped sliding about a foot away from where Roger was, key already in the ignition, his left hand releasing the parking brake. John looked around for a seatbelt. There was none.

"Always buckle up!" His mother's voice resonated in his brain, and for once, he ignored it.

"Where to?" Roger had started the engine, which roared to life, backfired once, then settled down to a noisy rumble. "This baby purrs, doesn't she?"

"I... er... yes." Then, realizing he hadn't answered Roger's first question, he added, "2430 Covington Drive."

"Fancy part of town, huh?"

Not for long. The Realtor had come by the other day, and John thought he'd seen her drool when his mother told her they needed to sell quickly. He wondered where they'd end up. Probably one of the duplexes closer to downtown—the places people moved in and out of on a regular basis.

He often walked the dog by the duplexes on garbage night, curious as to what ended up on the tree lawn after the latest renters left. He'd found an entire stack of LPs one night, including a boxed set of Tchaikovsky's greatest hits and a recording of the Singing Nun. He'd hidden them in his closet—God forbid his mother find out he'd been going through other people's garbage. She'd have a fit.

He hummed a bit of "Dominique" and smiled. He'd always liked that song. *Dominique, neekah, neekah....*

"What's that?"

Roger's voice brought John back to the here and now. "Nothing. Just a song."

Roger reached for the radio as they stopped at the light. The radio blared, and John winced inwardly. He didn't like loud rock music—it gave him a headache.

We're not gonna take it!

"We're not gonna take it," Roger sang along. "Gonna break it, gonna shake it, let's forget it better still." Roger looked over at John and grinned.

"Who's that?"

"The Who. That's who." Roger snorted, a look of smug satisfaction spreading across his face.

"Oh." John had heard of them, although he'd never heard their music.

"Cool, huh?"

"Uh-huh. Cool." John made a mental note not to mention the Singing Nun and to use the word "cool" instead of "groovy."

As they drove, John watched Roger. He wore a pair of off-white painter's pants with a half-dozen pockets and a hammer loop. John noticed how the pants pulled at Roger's crotch when he sat. Roger's shirt was a blue plaid flannel, unbuttoned to reveal a dusting of curly hair on his chest. John's mouth was dry, so he chewed on the inside of his bottom lip. He felt a pulsing sensation in his groin and shifted to accommodate his embarrassing erection. He prayed Roger wouldn't notice.

Disgusted with himself, he thought of his first and only discussion of homosexuality with his father.

They'd been sitting in the living room, watching yet another report about the war in Vietnam. It was pretty much the same thing every night—a daily tally of the number of American troops killed and the growing protest marches at home in the US. But this night, there was a story about a riot in New York City at a place called Stonewall.

"Fucking fluters," John's father said. "They should have shot them all."

John, who was about fourteen years old, just stared at the images on the TV. "What's a fluter?" he asked.

Jerome Fuchs looked down at his son and snorted. "Homosexuals. Fags. Deviants who prefer to spend time with their own."

When John just blinked in response, his father continued, "They don't like women."

"Why not?" John was genuinely curious.

"How the hell should I know?"

Six months later, after Raymond Lessor kissed him in the coatroom, John figured out what his father had meant. *He* was exactly the kind of man his father had been talking about.

"You okay?" Roger turned down the radio and looked at him.

"Yes. I'm great." He forced a smile and realized they'd just turned onto his street. "Oh, that's my house, about halfway down." He pointed.

Roger pulled into the driveway a minute later and John, backpack held in front of him like a shield, climbed out of the car. Slid, really.

"Thanks, Roger." John waved tentatively, feeling like a complete idiot.

"It's cool." Roger cranked up the radio and pulled back out of the driveway. He waved, then gunned the engine and took off down the street, leaving a cloud of white smoke in his wake.

John waved the smoke away and watched the car disappear around the corner. "Cool," he repeated as he swung his backpack over his shoulder and headed into the house.

CHAPTER 2

OCTOBER ARRIVED far faster than John expected. He'd expected a miserable first month at his new school. But he hadn't counted on Roger taking him under his wing and introducing him to the other kids in the band and orchestra. He also hadn't counted on the fact that all the band geeks loved Roger and welcomed John into their clique simply because he was Roger's friend.

"The last movement's too slow." Roger's mouth was full of food and he gesticulated with his fork, waving it in the air as if he were trying to spear an invisible something. "*Allegro non troppo* isn't a dirge."

"It means 'fast but not too fast,'" Nathan Zimmer agreed, his eyes fixed on Roger in obvious admiration. The other kids at the table—all of them orchestra or band members—chewed and watched Roger silently.

John speared a french fry and glanced around the cafeteria. The rattle of silverware against plates and the raised voices of the hundreds of students sharing the room were giving him a headache. He found it hard to focus on the conversation with all the noise. He also found it disconcerting to be around so many people—he'd never been good with crowds.

"What do you think, John?" Roger's voice brought his attention back to the table.

"Me?"

Roger made a noise somewhere between a grunt and a snort. "Yeah. You. You're the conductor, right?"

"I'm not a conduct—"

"Wannabe. What do you think about the tempo?" Roger's green eyes focused intently on him.

John found himself regretting having inhaled his fries. Something about Roger's gaze made him queasy. "I like it." Well, he *did* like the tempo. "It was meant to be a parody of the old Soviet marches. Big. Lumbering, like one of those parades in Red Square. Then, when it's just the strings with the melody, the tempo picks up. From there, it keeps building. It gives you that frenzied feeling so that when the trumpet line comes in...." John looked around the table and realized that everyone was staring at him. His face felt suddenly hot, his hands sweaty.

Great. Just great.

For a moment no one at the table said a word. Then Roger grinned his big sloppy grin and wiped ketchup from the corner of his mouth. "Keep going," he said.

John took a deep breath. "Well, I... Shostakovich wrote the symphony when things were pretty rough for him. Politically, I mean. He wanted to make a statement about Stalin and how miserable the Soviet people were, but he had to be careful. The dissonances are all about that. Suffering."

The sound of a crashing tray on the other side of the room and sniggers from some of the kids punctuated another long silence from John's companions.

"Cool." John hadn't realized he'd been holding his breath until Roger spoke. "I kinda wondered."

"Conductors need to be flexible," John continued, buoyed by Roger's response. "I mean, if you're conducting Bach, maybe the tempo is static. But the more modern repertoire is meant to ebb and flow."

John looked at Roger in time to see him smile. John shoved the last of the fries in his mouth in an effort to hide his discomfort. He nearly choked. Roger held his gaze a moment longer, then glanced back at Nathan and asked, "So what's the deal for tomorrow night?"

"Tim's parents are out of town." Nathan was clearly trying to look as though he were sharing a huge secret, although the way Tim had been talking up the big party all week, John guessed the only people who didn't know about it were kids in the next county over. "His brother's buying a keg. Thought they'd celebrate Halloween a few weeks early."

Tim's brother was a student at Marysville Tech and, John had heard, was a burnout who'd spent most of his senior year high on pot. A legend, Roger had called him. In spite of himself—because he was really nervous about his first "real" high school party—the thought of a party excited him. At St. Barnaby's, the only party he'd ever been to had been heavily chaperoned, and the only beer in sight had been root beer.

"You going, John?" Roger had perched his chair on the back two legs and was balancing with a foot against the edge of the table.

"Ah, sure, I guess." As if there was any question!

"Great. Because Sylvia's best friend, Tracy, is coming too. I told Sylvia I'd make sure she had a date."

Now John really felt sick. He started imagining illnesses he might fake to get out of it.

Get it together. You want to hang with him, don't you?

Yes, but not if it means french kissing girls.

"John?" Roger's voice interrupted his internal dialogue. He was sucking on a french fry and rocking back and forth now. There was something slightly obscene about the way Roger's full lips closed around that french fry.

Shit. What the hell was wrong with him that he was thinking about what those lips might taste like? "Sure. That'd be great." John hoped he sounded convincing.

THE NEXT night Roger picked John up to take him and their dates to the party. The two girls sat between John and Roger, making John feel even more uncomfortable. It was better than having to sit in the backseat with Tracy by himself, though. The girls giggled as Roger purposely took the turns too fast and they all slid back and forth on the slippery vinyl. John laughed at the look of mischief on Roger's face.

Twenty minutes later they were all seated on shag carpet in an enormous room on the top floor of Tim Miller's house. The house was on the border of downtown. Built around the turn of the twentieth century, it was nearly twice as large as John's house—stone, with high ceilings, pocket doors, a wide staircase in the entryway, and a carriage port on the side.

John guessed the room had been used as a ballroom, years before. Now, however, it was filled with kids, most with cups of watery beer in their hands, some standing, others sitting. Tim and a few of the audio/video geeks had set up a large screen at the front of the room and were busy snaking film through a gray projector Roger said Tim had "borrowed" from the audio/visual storage closet at the high school.

"*Psycho*." Roger waggled his eyebrows and grabbed John around the neck, pretending to throttle him. The girls giggled.

Tracy wasn't all that bad, John decided, as girls went. Tiny, with short black hair and large eyes. Funny too. Not that this changed his mind about kissing her, but at least she wasn't pawing him or anything.

Roger pushed John so that he fell back onto the carpet, laughing, Roger's hand pressing his shoulder to the floor. Their eyes met for just a moment, and John's face grew hot. Roger released John and shouted, "More beer, or I might have to slash someone!"

The girls giggled again as John sat up. One of the other kids handed Roger more beer, and he snaked an arm around Sylvia. Roger kissed Sylvia, causing John to look away out of embarrassment. Did they have to do that right in front of everyone? John looked around the room, but it was clear nobody cared in the least. In fact, there were other couples doing the exact same thing.

John turned his back to Roger and Sylvia only to see Tracy looking longingly at him and nibbling at her lower lip. He managed to smile back at her. There was no way he was going to kiss her, even though he was sure that was exactly what she wanted him to do.

John had finally relaxed enough to focus on the movie when Sylvia giggled. He glanced over to see Roger, his hand underneath her sweater. John forced his eyes back to the screen, but the movement in his peripheral vision drew his gaze once more. Roger and Sylvia sucking face. He turned his head the other direction and met Tracy's hopeful expression.

"Excuse me," he whispered to Tracy before standing and walking toward the back of the room.

The bathroom was occupied—he thought he heard heavy breathing behind the door—so he walked over to the small balcony cut into the roof of the house and slipped outside.

The air was still warm for mid-October. The moon was low in the sky, and John could see stars through the leaves that still clung for dear life to a massive oak on the back lawn. The distant rumble of cars from the freeway rose and died with the breeze. John leaned against the wooden balustrade and closed his eyes. From time to time, he heard screams from the partygoers inside and the sound of the movie soundtrack.

"You okay?"

He started and turned to look at Roger, who was standing in the doorway. "Yeah. Great. Good party, huh?" He tried to sound casual, but he was pretty sure he didn't succeed.

"Not a big party person, are you?" Roger handed him a beer.

"We didn't have a lot of them at St. Barnaby's," John admitted. He took a long swig of the beer. The first one had done nothing, but this one seemed to help.

"Don't sweat it." Roger leaned on the railing next to him. "You'll get used to it."

"Right." Plenty of time for him to feel awkward and uncomfortable. He took another drink.

Roger bumped John with his elbow. "We'll get the private school out of you before you leave this dump. Don't worry." His arm settled against John's and remained there.

John finished his beer and thanked God his T-shirt covered the beginnings of the tent in his pants. "Gotta try the bathroom again," he mumbled. "Busy last time." He didn't even look at Roger as he walked back inside.

THE PARTY broke up around one. Roger, John, and the girls piled back into the car. John's fear that Roger had drunk too much to drive was dulled by the beer and the sinking feeling that he'd never fit in at Marysville.

Roger dropped the girls off first, although that didn't stop him from spending a good five minutes on Sylvia's front porch with her arms wrapped around him. When Roger hopped back in the car, his face was flushed and his lips a bit rosier than they had been.

"You like Tracy?" Roger asked after they'd driven in silence about half the way to John's house.

"Sure. She's nice." He told the truth. She *was* nice.

"Cool."

"Thanks for inviting me." John kept his eyes focused on the road in front of them. He didn't really want to look at Roger. Well, he did, but he knew better.

Neither of them said much as Roger stopped in front of John's house. "I figured I wouldn't pull into the driveway," Roger said as he put the car into park in front of the tree lawn. "Wouldn't want to wake your mother."

"Thanks." He didn't bother telling Roger her bedroom faced the rear of the house.

Roger gestured to the For Sale sign. "You think it's gonna sell?"

"Yes."

John had overheard his mother yelling at his father over the phone the week before: "Not even a year more, and he could have stayed in this house until graduation. But no, you and your fucking lawyer need the settlement now. Screw your son, right?"

"Bad, huh?" When John just looked back at Roger, uncomprehending, Roger added, "The divorce."

John stared back at him. "H-how d-did you know?" Shit, he was stuttering again!

Roger shrugged. "One of the other kids knows someone at St. Barnaby's."

"Oh." John looked down at his hands, which were now clasped tightly in his lap.

"I know a bunch of kids whose parents are divorced. Major bummer."

"Yes." John couldn't think of anything else to say.

"They say it gets better." Roger's mouth was set in something between a smile and a frown, his eyes sympathetic and a bit sad.

"Thanks."

"No problem."

John slid over to the door and opened it. "See you Monday."

"See you."

CHAPTER *3*

December 1971

ROGER LEANED against the door to the band room as he listened to John play the concert grand piano at the bottom of the stepped room. From his vantage point at the top of the built-in risers, Roger was pretty sure John wouldn't see him, which he figured was a good thing. John didn't like anyone to hear him play, but Roger had discovered John's secret: he would practice in the early morning before most of the band and orchestra kids came to drop off their instruments.

He wasn't sure what piece John was playing, although he guessed it was Bach. The melody was crisp, deceptively simple, and John's playing reflected the clean Baroque lines. John was a far better pianist than he'd ever let on. Not that this surprised Roger—in the four months since he'd met John, Roger had learned that John was not only shy, he was modest to a fault. It didn't take a seasoned musician to hear the delicate grace of John's Bach. Then again, he'd listened in on several of John's "secret" practice sessions, and Roger had heard the same depth of understanding of the music when he played Schumann and Brahms.

The piece ended and Roger waited patiently for the next. Instead, he heard John say, "You might as well come inside."

Startled, Roger poked his head into the room and grinned like a kid caught with his hand in the cookie jar. "You knew I was there?"

"You mean today?" John asked. "Or the last three weeks?"

"Shit." Roger climbed down the levels to the front of the room and leaned against the piano. "I didn't think you noticed me."

John shrugged and shuffled some music around on the piano. "I don't mind if you listen."

"You're really good, you know. Have you thought about a senior solo on piano? I bet Mr. Constantino would—"

"I don't want to perform." John blinked and looked down at his fingers on the keyboard. Roger couldn't tell if John was just being his usual shy self or if he was lying about performing. "A good conductor needs to be able to play piano."

Seemed reasonable enough. John was usually pretty honest, so Roger figured he probably wasn't bullshitting. "My mom forced me to take piano lessons when I was four." He sat down on the piano bench next to John. "I only stopped about a year ago. I guess she finally realized I really was a better violinist."

"I didn't know you played piano."

"Yeah. I'm okay, I guess."

"Want to play with me?" John flickered his gaze around the room, and Roger could tell he was a little embarrassed to have asked.

"Sure." Well, why not? "But I'm nowhere near as good as you." Roger tried to pretend it didn't make him nervous to play with John. It wasn't like he was nervous playing violin in front of him. Why would he care if John heard what a shitty pianist he was?

John's entire face lit up and his pale cheeks pinked. Roger also pretended he hadn't seen John's pleasure, although it was hard not to notice how John's eyes looked like melted caramel this close up. "So what are we playing?" Roger asked in an effort to hide his embarrassment. He needed to say something or he might blush like John.

"Schubert's Fantasy in F Minor. It's a four-hand piece. You know, two pianists sitting at one piano." John dug some music out of his backpack, set it on the piano stand, then opened it. "Which part would you like to play?"

"Which one's easier?"

"Probably the lower part."

Roger got up and John slid to the right. "Works for me. You want to take a minute to look it over?"

"Nah. I'm an okay sight-reader."

"Great." John was grinning now, although Roger thought he felt him shiver when their hips touched on the bench.

"So… let's see… I start like this." Roger played the opening chords. Dark and brooding, setting the scene for the haunting upper hands. John joined in a moment later with the melody, and Roger could see the grin fade as John's focus returned. Focus and pain—as if John felt the heartache and longing written into the notes. The smooth skin of John's jaw caught his eye. Roger noticed the hollow of John's cheek, noticed how John's eyes had closed much as someone might close his eyes to a lover's kiss.

"Roger?"

John was frowning at him. It took a moment for Roger to realize he'd stopped playing. "Oh, crap. Sorry. I got a little distracted."

"It's okay." John smiled at him and Roger's face grew hot.

What the hell is wrong with you? He swallowed hard, then said, "Try again?"

"Sure." John, too, looked a bit uncomfortable.

They played through the piece, this time without stopping.

"I suck," Roger said, mostly because he felt uncomfortable after what had happened before. He knew he'd actually played the piece pretty well.

"You're pretty good." John's eyes were bright, and the smile on his face made Roger feel at once happy and painfully embarrassed.

"Thanks." Roger looked at the clock. It was just about time for class. "I'd better go. Mrs. Marsten gets really mad if I'm late." He shot John a grin. "Of course, I'm never late."

John laughed. "Never. See you at lunch?"

"Sounds good. Share your fries?"

"Don't I always?"

Roger waved back at John, then climbed the levels to the door and walked quickly into the hallway.

"Hey, Roger!" Laura Willis was leaning against her locker, putting on some lip balm. She wore a white blouse with a green vest over it, buttoned over her full breasts. Her hair was teased and curled, and her eyelids were painted with eggshell-blue shadow. *Nice.* Roger pushed all thoughts of John aside as he walked with Laura to class.

CHAPTER 4

February 1972

ROGER GRABBED a handful of fries off John's plate, stuffed them into his mouth, and sighed contentedly. John, who'd been staring at the snow as it fell in heavy clumps outside the cafeteria windows, turned back and shot Roger a scathing look. "You could ask, you know. I'd share."

Roger laughed. "More fun this way." The words were muffled as he chewed.

"Gross." John shook his head and looked over at Nathan, who just shrugged. It had become a running joke amongst the band and orchestra kids how different John and Roger were. Roger was the slob, coming to school most days wearing a ratty T-shirt, with his hair sticking up, uncombed, and John the super-tidy kid with the perfectly pressed button-down shirts and the neatly styled hair. Inseparable, in spite of their obvious differences.

"You coming to the mall after class?" Roger asked as he finished John's fries without even a hint of guilt.

"Sure. As long as you can give me a ride home. I've got my advanced theory class in the morning at the music settlement, and I need to do some homework." He also didn't want to brave the snow and the biting February cold at the bus stop.

"Homework on Friday." Roger snorted and bits of half-chewed fries flew across his tray. Nathan laughed. John was beginning to wonder if Nathan's hero worship might be something more like a crush. He wasn't sure the thought was comforting.

"That's really gross, you know." John shook his head and fought off nausea. Between the greasy cafeteria food and Roger's disgusting eating habits, he was pretty sure he was going to vomit. He looked away and took a deep breath.

"Sorry." This time Roger looked slightly remorseful as he wiped his face. A moment later he grinned and continued, "Meet me by the car when you get done with class?"

"Okay." At least Roger never asked Nathan—or any of the girls he always seemed to be making out with in the courtyard—to come along with them. The mall was *their* time. Time to be stupid kids and blow whatever spending money they had on the biggest Orange Julius they could buy or shot glasses with sayings like "Never Drink Water" or "Hangovers are for Amateurs" printed on them. John loved hanging at the mall with Roger. It made him feel cool. Not that *he* was cool, but Roger was cool among the music geeks. John always felt as though he was someone with Roger. Everyone liked Roger. At least all the band and orchestra geeks did.

THE LAST bell rang, and John made his way from the top floor to the lockers by the band room. A few of the kids hanging around—band kids he didn't know very well—whispered to each other and waved at him. In his office, Mr. Constantino was hunched over some papers, although he didn't seem to be reading them. John decided he wouldn't interrupt to say good-bye. He'd quickly learned it wasn't cool, anyhow, to tell your teacher to have a good weekend.

He put a few of his books in his locker and retrieved the flute he'd borrowed from the pile of school-owned instruments. He needed to practice over the weekend. Not that he hoped to be the next James Galway, but if he was going to get that scholarship to the University of Michigan, he needed to be better than the next kid. Good SAT scores weren't going to help him get money for music school.

Most of the cars were already gone from the parking lot by the time he made his way outside. You didn't hang out after class on Friday, so most of the kids scattered like cockroaches at the final bell. John made his way over to where Roger's car was supposed to be, but the spot was empty. It didn't take long for him to realize that Roger's car wasn't in the lot at all. John walked back over to the school, figuring that Roger might have decided to pull around and meet him out front. Roger wasn't there either.

Weird. Roger had never stood him up before. Whatever you could say about Roger, when he said he would do something, however insane, the guy followed through.

John shifted his backpack to his other shoulder. He'd stopped wearing it on both shoulders after Roger told him it wasn't cool. He walked back into the building and over to the band room, figuring he'd ask someone.

"Fuchs."

"Oh, h-hi, Mr. Constantino." John hoped he wouldn't get into trouble for coming back into the school without permission. "I'm sorry. I was l-looking for Roger. Have you seen him?"

The teacher frowned. "You two are pretty good friends, aren't you?" John just nodded and chewed on his lower lip. "Come into my office."

He *was* in trouble. Other than the day his mother had taken him to school to fill out the transfer student paperwork, John had only been in the office once: the day he'd met Roger. His heart pounded as he tried to think of what he would tell his mother. Would he get a suspension for this?

"Sit down, son."

John did as he was told, set his backpack down on the floor, and tried to remember to breathe. "Sir, I—"

"There's no easy way to say this," Mr. Constantino said, apparently oblivious to John's discomfort. "I knew him, you know. Marc. Good kid. Talented fiddle player too."

Marc? John struggled to understand. Roger had an older brother named Marc, but why would Constantino bring him up? Marc was in Vietnam.

"I got the news this afternoon. Terrible tragedy, really. Your friend's going to need someone to talk to."

"I... sure... I mean... what happened?"

"Roger's mother called after lunch. Told me what happened and asked if I could pull Roger out of class. Said Marc's platoon was ambushed.... Came under heavy fire.... They just got word."

"Was Marc hurt?" *Oh please let Marc be okay.* He'd heard of some guys who'd made it home even when they'd been badly hurt. Not that he wanted Marc to have been hurt, but that'd be better than not coming home at all.

"He was hit pretty bad. They flew him to a field hospital. He died during surgery." Mr. Constantino's jaw tensed and his Adam's apple bobbed as if he were struggling to control his emotions. "Marc's dead."

CHAPTER 5

THE SUN had set by the time John arrived at Roger's house on the edge of downtown. He'd called his mother to tell her he'd be home late and hopped on one of three buses that would take him from the school to the working-class neighborhood with its boxy houses and tiny lawns.

John had been here at least a dozen times, but he always found himself fascinated by the number of variations on a theme: a brick house, a stone exterior, followed by a house with white aluminum siding, each with shutters painted in different colors, some with dormers, others with bay windows that looked out onto the street.

He chewed on a fingernail. What did you say to someone whose older brother—whose *only* brother and the apple of his parents' eyes—had been killed in a firefight with the Vietcong? It didn't matter, he decided. He needed to come. It hadn't even occurred to John that Roger's family might not be home until he saw Roger's car parked in the driveway. The small detached garage behind the house was empty—Roger's parents' car was gone. Other than the light in the living room, the only other light on inside was in the right rear bedroom. Roger's room.

He waited a few minutes after ringing the bell, listening to the dog announce his arrival with barks and growls. "It's okay, Roofster," he said in his most reassuring voice. "It's just me." The dog continued to bark until the front porch light illuminated and John heard the deadbolt slide open.

Roger peered out from the partially open door. "Oh," he said, his voice overly nonchalant. "It's you." He paused for a moment, then added, "Sorry about standing you up this afternoon. Something came up."

John stood there, unsure of what to say. He chewed the inside of his cheek for a moment, trying to gather his thoughts. Whatever he'd expected, he hadn't expected Roger to be so, well, so damn *calm*. "I... I heard about your brother." Better just get it out before he exploded or melted into a puddle of stupid right there on the front step. "I'm really sorry."

Roger shrugged. "You want to come in?"

"I... ah... I don't want to intrude."

"It's just me and the Roof man." John noticed the dog poking his head between Roger's thigh and the doorjamb, wagging his tail to see John. "Folks flew out this afternoon. They wanted to meet the body. They won't be back until tomorrow night, maybe later. Depends on how long it takes to arrange stuff. Someone needed to stay to keep an eye on things."

"Oh." John followed Roger and the dog into the living room. John's eyes watered at the strong smell of cigarette smoke.

They sat down facing each other on the sofa and love seat. As he often did, John ran a hand over the flocked green fabric, tracing the outline of the fleurs-de-lys with his fingers. The fabric was slightly worn, much like the matching drapes with their heavy gold tassels, but John liked the warm feel of the small room. The living room wasn't off-limits to kids like it was in his own house. It felt lived-in. Comfy.

"Are you okay?" John asked after a moment.

"Yeah. Why wouldn't I be?" Roger's eyes shone with a silent challenge.

Oh, I don't know. Maybe because you're not supposed to be? John wasn't sure how to respond. Roofster put his paw on John's knee and gazed up at him longingly. "Hey, boy." John scratched under the dog's muzzle and fidgeted.

"You want something to eat?"

"Sure."

Roger got up and motioned John to come with him to the dining room, where several large trays of food sat, untouched. "Neighbors brought them by." He snagged a piece of rolled ham from the tray, pretended to play it like a trumpet, then shoved it in his mouth and began to chew. "Not sure what it is about someone dying. They always bring food. Did the same when my grandma died a couple of years ago."

Did Roger even care that his brother had died? It didn't make sense. He was acting like it didn't matter, but he talked about Marc a lot.

"It's really Marc's car," Roger had admitted when he'd driven John home a few days after he and John met. "Marc is fixing it up. He's going to paint it when he gets back from 'Nam. I'm going to help. He said I could drive it while he's gone." The pride and hero worship had been obvious in Roger's expression. John remembered wishing he had a brother like Marc. Or just a brother, period.

John wouldn't ask Roger about Marc, though. He just nodded and snagged a piece of swiss cheese. "Good cheese." He smiled at Roger.

Roger laughed, sending some of the contents of his mouth flying. "It's okay, man," he said as he grabbed some turkey breast. "It's just me. Not like anything's different or anything."

John finished his cheese. "I know. It's just... I don't know... I mean what happened and all. I just—"

"You wanna watch some tube? They've got reruns of *F Troop* on channel sixty-one right now." Roger didn't wait for John to respond but piled some food onto a paper plate and headed back to the living room. A moment later he pointed the remote at the console TV, clicked it a few times, then sat down on the floor with his back to the couch.

John filled his own plate and sat down next to Roger on the carpet. Roofster came over, and Roger tossed him a few pieces of meat. "Don't tell my mom," he whispered conspiratorially. "He's supposed to be on a diet. Vet says he's getting fat."

"I promise I won't tell." John smiled back at Roger, relaxing for the first time since he'd arrived. Still, it felt weird, with Roger acting as though nothing had happened. The photograph of Marc still sat on the mantle where it always had. John thought Marc looked a lot like Roger. Handsome in his uniform.

John focused on the TV. He'd never seen the show before—his parents didn't think much of TV. The only TV when he was small had been a tiny black-and-white portable that came on for *Masterpiece Theatre* or Walter Cronkite and the news and went back to its place in the basement when his parents were done watching.

"You like this show?" Roger's mouth, as always, was full of food.

"Uh-huh." Well, he did. At least, he did now.

They watched without speaking, and *F Troop* morphed into *Get Smart*. John hadn't seen that one either, but he got the reference to the James Bond movies. Those, he'd seen at the movie theater with his dad. He remembered thinking how sexy James Bond was.

Roger shoved food into his mouth, pulled off his shoe, and spoke into it like the shoe telephone on the screen. "Hello? Is this Mrs. Fuchs? Your son's a dweeb."

John pulled off his own shoe. "Hello? Hello? Is this Mars? I think you left one of your aliens when you blasted off. He can't seem to eat without making a pig of himself."

Roger laughed and rolled onto his back, clutching his stomach. "You're weirder. *Way* weirder."

"Screw you, man." John felt oddly exhilarated, swearing at Roger. He'd never really sworn before, and he decided it was kind of fun. Dangerous, even. He lay belly down, looking up at the TV, propped on his elbows.

"Marc loves this show." The words seem to come out of nowhere. "Loved." Roger's voice grew quiet with the last word.

John swallowed, his throat suddenly dry, the laughter gone as quickly as it had come. He stole a quick look at Roger, who was staring up at the ceiling. Tears slid silently down, falling into his ears.

"Hey." John sat up and looked down at Roger. "You okay?"

Roger hunched over his knees, his back to John. John reached for Roger's shoulder, hesitating just above it, unsure of himself. He took a deep breath, then touched him.

"I'm really sorry." He felt like crying too. His eyes burned. Not that he'd ever met Marc, but he felt as if he knew him, just having listened to Roger talk about him. He didn't really think about it, he just wrapped his arms around Roger and held him while he cried.

CHAPTER 6

March 1972

"YOU DON'T like girls, do you?" Roger was lying back on the bed, hands supporting his neck.

The question took John by surprise. The orchestra members had all gone back to their hotel rooms after dinner, laughing to each other about how Mr. Constantino and the orchestra parents were going to tape their doors. They'd performed at a high school right outside Toronto that morning, then spent the rest of the day sightseeing before eating dinner at a supper club that featured a comedian and live music.

The orchestra went on tour every other year. Up until a few years before, they'd gone every year, but then the levy had failed and the school district stopped paying for part of the trip. They'd sold enough fruit, lightbulbs, and chocolate bars to make up some of the difference, but it hadn't been enough for yearly trips. John was just happy the trip landed on a year when he was able to participate. Happier, even, that Roger had asked him to share a room in spite of the fact that Nathan Zimmer had asked Roger first.

"Huh?" John figured he hadn't heard right. At least he hoped he hadn't.

"I said," Roger said as he rolled over onto his side and looked at John across the gap between the two beds, "that you don't like girls much."

"I like girls."

"You know what I mean."

John hoped the heat in his face wasn't translating into something visible. "No, I don't."

"Justine drooled all over you at lunch today. Man, she was giggling with Mary Lee afterward. Didn't you notice?"

Of course he'd noticed. He'd just ignored Justine like he ignored all the other girls who flirted with him. "She's not my type."

"I'd be cool with it… if you didn't. Like girls, I mean. Wouldn't bother me."

John weighed his options. Tell the truth. Lie. Obfuscate. Definition according to Mrs. Patterson: to make obscure or unclear. Maybe if he kept talking about how he liked girls?

"You don't have to answer if you don't want to."

Thank God.

"Have you ever kissed another guy?" Roger was watching John carefully.

So much for getting out of it. He should have known Roger would never let it go. John chewed on his cheek but did not answer.

"I thought about kissing a guy once."

It was the last thing John expected. "You… *what?*" He sat up and stared at Roger.

"Gotcha!" Roger laughed.

Great. John considered strangling him but then thought better of it. He was, after all, supposed to play the Mendelssohn Violin Concerto the next day. Mr. Constantino probably wouldn't appreciate it. He kept his mouth shut instead, his jaw clenched.

"But seriously…."

"When the fuck are you ever serious?" John wasn't sure where the words had come from, but for once he couldn't stand the smug look of satisfaction on Roger's face. John had never used the word "fuck" before, but Roger making a joke of things? That made him mad.

Roger flitted his gaze about the room and finally let it rest on the harvest-green lamp on the desk by the TV as if it held great interest for him. "Sorry," he said after a moment. "That was pretty lame of me, wasn't it?"

"Yes."

"Sorry." Roger sounded genuinely contrite.

John didn't say anything. He wasn't sure why, but he wanted Roger to stew. He'd never done anything like that before—call someone out—

and he was half-tempted to apologize a moment later. He didn't. Something told him he shouldn't. Not this time.

"I really *am* sorry. I shouldn't have yanked your chain like that."

For the first time in their friendship, Roger had backed down and apologized to *him*. That was a revelation. He hadn't told John to go screw himself, and he hadn't given John any flak. He'd just backed down. "No, you shouldn't have," he agreed. "And just for the record?"

Roger shot John a look of surprise and genuine anticipation. "Yeah?"

"Girls are fine." John repressed a smile. Maybe not exactly obfuscation, but it worked. Roger dropped the subject completely. Well, at least until the graduation party at Olivia DiMarco's house.

CHAPTER 7

June 1972

JOHN ARRIVED at Olivia's later than he'd intended. His grandmother had flown in for graduation, and he'd eaten dinner out with his family to celebrate. If you could call it a celebration: it was more like someone's funeral. His parents barely spoke during the meal, and his grandmother just glared at them both. John had done his best to keep the conversation going, but he'd spent more time than he wanted just looking at his food. When he finally left the house in his mother's car, it was nearly ten. Well, maybe ten fifteen, since his mother insisted on reminding him not to drink or drive and, to his great mortification, gave him a handful of condoms. "You may be eighteen, but you wouldn't want to ruin your life by getting a girl pregnant on the night of your high school graduation." As if *that* would ever happen!

"Hey, John." Olivia was a round-faced girl who played oboe in the orchestra and had dated Roger a few times. Nobody went out with Roger more than a few times, and nobody seemed to mind much either. He was just, well, Roger.

"Hi, Livvie." John's face was hot as she pulled him inside and handed him a cup of something that looked like fruit punch. Cherry red, like Jell-O. "Thank you for inviting me."

She giggled and he kicked himself for being so formal. Embarrassed, he took a long drink. It wasn't punch. Or rather, it was punch, but with enough alcohol that it burned going down. He managed not to cough, but he was sure his face was bright red.

They walked through the living room, where several couples were making out on the sofa and love seat, then headed down to the basement by way of the kitchen stairs. The room was full of people, most of whom he knew or had seen around the band room. The place smelled of pot and cigarettes, and loud music blared from a double set of speakers placed in each corner of the room. "Smoke on the Water." He'd heard the song before on an eight-track cassette Roger loved to play in the car.

John spotted Roger in the corner, talking to a girl John recognized, a tenth grader. She was watching Roger with the kind of breathless lust that made John feel slightly sick. That, and jealous, although he wouldn't dignify the emotion by giving in to it.

Roger saw him and waved. John forced a smile and made his way through several groups of people, accepting another cup of the alcohol-with-a-little-red-stuff before sitting down next to Roger.

"Hey, *John*." Roger laughed as if John's name was suddenly funny. His eyes were bloodshot, and John guessed he'd been smoking weed nonstop since he'd arrived. Several empty plastic cups littered the floor beside him. *High and drunk.*

John finished his own drink in about five minutes, doing his best to ignore the burn at the back of his throat. The stuff was horrible, but it did the trick. His shoulders and neck already felt like jelly—raspberry jelly, he decided as he eased into the sensation—and his mind was blurring rather nicely. Better that way when it came to dealing with Roger and girls.

Someone cranked the volume on the stereo and the tinny speakers crackled. John was glad he was buzzed or the sound would have hurt his ears.

Roger said something to him, but John couldn't hear it over the music. John pointed to his ears and offered him a shrug. Roger laughed and leaned over, effectively cutting off Miss Tenth Grade from the conversation. "How was dinner?" he asked, his words slurring.

John tried to answer, but Roger rolled onto the floor and nearly into his lap, and he forgot what he was going to say.

"Need more weed." Roger grinned up at him. "You in?"

"You know I don't—" John began, but Roger had already gotten to his feet and was pulling him up by his arm. John followed, only vaguely aware of people moving out of their way to let them through. Roger pulled him through a doorway, then closed the door behind them and locked it.

"Don't wanna share," Roger mumbled as he pulled a joint from his pocket, lit it, and inhaled.

There was a mattress on the floor, a tiny black-and-white TV propped on a plastic milk crate, and a bunch of psychedelic posters stuck to the wall. John stared at them, trying to decide if they were crooked or if he was just trashed. *Probably both.* He felt a little dizzy following the swirls around in circles. But maybe that was the pot. The smoke was thick enough that he didn't think he needed to take a toke to get high.

Roger handed him the joint, mumbling, "I'll share with you." He grinned as John took it. "Go on. Try it. Feels good."

John took a long drag. He smiled at Roger, then began to cough. "Crap!"

"S'okay. Gets better. Try again."

John blinked away the tears at the corners of his eyes, then drew in more of the smoke. It still burned his throat, and he coughed a little, but he held it longer than before.

"See?" Roger grinned at him and took the joint back, then set it down on an ashtray that was overflowing with cigarette butts.

John nodded and looked back at the posters. "I like the color," he said to himself. "Like one of those pictures of a nebula or something."

"*Star Trek*," Roger agreed.

John lay on the bed. There was another poster on the ceiling, but it looked blurry, so he just closed his eyes and sighed.

Roger fell back on the bed with a thud, then giggled. John wasn't sure he'd ever heard Roger giggle. He turned to look at Roger, who was looking back at him with a serious expression. "What?" he asked.

"Nothing." Roger kept staring at him.

"Come on. Do I look like an alien or something?" He was still thinking about *Star Trek*, imagining what Leonard Nimoy might look like without the blue uniform top. Pretty good, he guessed.

"Nah. You look good."

John's face warmed, but he didn't say anything. He was too busy eyeing the patch of Roger's abdomen visible where the fabric of his shirt had scooted up. Roger would look better without a shirt than Spock. Definitely.

Roger rolled onto his side, then pushed himself up on an elbow, his face above John's. Roger's odd expression made John feel strange. Horny too. Normally he'd have been mortified for Roger to see him with a boner, but for some reason he didn't care. He felt really good. Warm and fuzzy and something else: happy. He smiled.

Roger took another toke on the joint, then handed it to John as he held the smoke in. John inhaled, and this time he didn't cough at all.

"Good stuff," Roger confirmed.

"It is." John couldn't think of anything else to say.

"I'm glad we're going to college together." Roger was watching him with the same strange expression as before. It reminded John of the way Roger looked at some of the girls. Dreamy. Kind of sexy.

"Me too." John hadn't told Roger just how relieved he'd been when they'd both gotten their acceptance letters to the University of Michigan. They'd only talked about how they could avoid the draft, at least for a few more years. But John had been thinking about more than that. He didn't know what he'd do without Roger to talk to. And when Roger had asked if he wanted to room with him, John had been even happier.

"You know what I asked you about girls when we were on tour?"

John wasn't sure how to respond. Of course he remembered it, but he didn't really want to get into that whole discussion again. "Yes" was all he said.

"I've kind of been thinking about it."

"Why?"

Roger moved closer to him. The joint sat forgotten on the ashtray. "I know this is going to sound weird." Roger made a funny face—kind of like a slow-motion grin. Or was the pot just making it look that way? "I wasn't really lying when I said I thought about kissing a guy once."

John shook his head. "Don't bullshit me, Roger. I'm not falling for that one again."

"I'm serious."

"Fuck you." John hoped maybe Roger wasn't bullshitting. Then again, Roger always bullshitted, didn't he?

Roger leaned closer. Close enough that John felt his breath on his face. Then Roger's lips met John's and John bit back a moan. Roger's lips were warm and slightly moist. Soft too.

Holy crap! John kissed him back. This close, Roger smelled of weed and red punch. Something else too. He smelled like Roger. The thought made John giggle.

"What?" Roger looked a little worried, as if he thought John hadn't liked being kissed.

"You smell like you. I mean, you smell good."

John could see relief on Roger's face. He kissed John again, and this time he put some of his weight on him so John could feel Roger's erection against his own. John had started to wonder if he was imagining the whole thing, but he was too wasted to care. Besides, in his imagination, Roger had now slipped his arms underneath him and rolled them both onto their sides. Sometime after that, they'd taken their shirts off.

Definitely better than Spock. John touched his fingers to Roger's chest and traced circles around one nipple, then the other. Imaginary Roger murmured something that came out sounding like "Mmmm... nnnn... uuhhhh." John decided he wanted to do more than just trace those hard little nubs. Not that he'd ever touched another guy's nipples before, but he'd sneaked into a gay porn flick once when he'd been on a class trip to New York City, and he had a pretty good idea of what you were supposed to do.

"Fuck, John. What're you doin'?" Imaginary Roger was grinning, so John figured he was doing okay as he rolled a nipple. After a few minutes, he decided he wanted to taste it. "God. Oh, fucking hell. You're making me harder than nails."

They both laughed until Roger undid the top button of John's pants. He was still wearing his scratchy polyester pants, having come right from the restaurant. Something about that thought made him wonder if he'd have imagined the entire thing with him wearing dress pants. Wouldn't he have worn something really cool, like painter's pants or Levi's? Something like what Roger was wearing?

"What are you doing?" he asked.

"No idea." Roger grinned up at him. "But I've been wanting to do this for a while now."

Maybe he needed another drink or something, because he was beginning to think he had this imagination thing backward. John had imagined making out with Roger before, but this time it felt *real*. He didn't have time to think much more about it when Roger kissed him again. He was absolutely *sure* it was real when Roger unzipped his pants and pushed them down with his underwear. John just watched Roger, transfixed. Then Roger took the rest of his own clothes off and John's heart began to thud hard against his chest.

Roger lay down next to him and ran his fingers from John's shoulder to the slight indentation of his waist. "Your skin is really soft. Like a girl's. It's really nice."

Heat burned John's cheeks. He was positive this was real now, because he knew he wouldn't blush in his dreams.

"Can I kiss you again?" Roger asked. He had that dreamy kind of look in his eyes that the girls in the car commercials had. The thought made John giggle again. God, why did he have to giggle like a girl? Then again, Roger didn't seem to mind.

"Yes. Please."

"Always polite." Roger laughed, then pulled John on top of him and kissed him.

The vague thought that what they were doing was wrong faded as Roger pressed his tongue between John's lips and John finally understood why kids liked to make out. It had been gross when he'd watched Roger kiss the girls he dated, but this was amazing. Roger traced a line over John's teeth with his tongue, then snaked around John's tongue in something like a dance as he slid his hands down John's back to cup his buttocks and squeeze. Tentatively, John began to imitate Roger's tongue, and Roger responded by moaning.

The kiss finally broke, leaving both of them panting. Roger's hard-on pressed against his own.

Oh God! John was pretty sure if Roger moved at all, he was going to shoot all over. John wondered if Roger felt the same, because a moment later Roger sat up and broke the contact. John's relief mingled with disappointment at not feeling Roger's body anymore.

"Turn onto your stomach," Roger said.

John did as Roger told him and rested his head on his arms. The next thing John felt was Roger's hands on his shoulders, kneading at the tension there. "Feel good?" Roger asked.

"Wonderful." John hoped he didn't sound like an idiot. His head was starting to clear of its fog, and the realization that this was Roger—his *best friend* Roger—massaging him made John feel self-conscious once more.

"Cool. Mary Beth says she likes this." Roger proceeded to draw circles on John's back.

John's eyes drifted closed, and he tried to push the image of Roger massaging Mary Beth Foster from his mind. It only took a moment more to forget how incredibly nervous he was. All he could think about was how good it felt.

John heard Roger's slow breaths grow more ragged as he continued downward and reached the slight indentation of John's waist. Roger kissed his lower back, along his spine.

"Roger." John hadn't meant to speak his name, and he blushed once again, happy Roger couldn't see him.

Roger paused, then kissed lower. John fought not to wiggle under his mouth. It tickled, but it also felt incredible. John had almost forgotten to be embarrassed. Almost, but not quite. He shivered as he remembered whose mouth was touching his ass.

Roger squeezed his cheeks and laughed. "You've got a nice ass, you know."

"You're high."

"Yep." Roger sounded pleased with himself. "You wanna stop?"

"No." No way did he want Roger to stop.

"Good."

He squeezed John's ass again. Then John felt Roger's cock between his cheeks. Roger's breaths grew rough as he rubbed back and forth. "Damn. You feel good."

John couldn't find the words and just nodded. Roger stopped, then turned him over so they were face-to-face again. "You okay?"

John nodded. He was more than okay. He was wonderful.

"I don't know what the fuck I'm doing," Roger said with a sloppy grin.

"Feels good to me." As if he knew anything more about this than Roger!

"I want to touch your... you know." Roger's cheeks flushed at the admission.

For the first time that night, John realized Roger was nervous. Maybe even a little scared. He felt better knowing he wasn't the only one. He nodded again.

Roger took John's cock in his hand, pressing it against his own. Holding them both together, rubbing them. John bit his lip. He wouldn't come yet. He wanted this to last. Roger leaned in and kissed him again. John fought back another wave of dizziness. Or maybe that was just the alcohol. Maybe it was Roger. It was just too much. "I can't hold back anymore," he moaned.

"Then don't." Roger spoke the words against John's neck, causing him to shiver.

He loved how Roger just spoke his mind and never seemed to worry about things. A moment later, John felt a tingling at the base of his spine and he came with a shout. He should have been completely mortified, but it felt so good that the thinking part of his brain seemed somehow disconnected from his body.

"Oh, fuck!" Roger squeezed them both harder, and John knew he'd come too.

John rested his head against Roger's chest. From the slow rise and fall of Roger's breathing, he guessed Roger was asleep. The sounds of the party ebbed and flowed outside the basement room, but John was only vaguely aware of them. The enormity of what they'd just done was too overwhelming for him to think about anything else.

I just had sex with my best friend.

What now? Would Roger even talk to him in the morning? What had he done?

He must have fidgeted, because Roger wrapped his arms around him and said, "It's cool."

Startled, John said, "What?"

"I said it's cool. This. You and me. Weird, but cool."

"I'm sorry."

"What are you apologizing for?" Roger sat up as he said this. His eyes were still a bit bloodshot, but he looked sober.

"I don't know."

Except John *did* know. Roger seemed to understand it too, because he said, "You didn't make me do anything. I wanted this." He scrubbed his face with his hand. "Honestly, I think I've wanted this for a while now."

John had no idea what to say to that. He knew what he wanted to ask, but he was afraid to. He just chewed his lip and stared at the wall.

Roger lay back down again and pulled John against him. "I know it doesn't make any sense," he said. "I mean, I like girls." He took a deep breath and hugged John a bit tighter. "But I never liked them like this."

Again John was silent.

"You okay?"

John nodded.

"I'm not going to date them anymore." Roger kissed the back of John's neck. "I want to date you."

John struggled against his tears.

"Unless you don't want that, I mean." Roger's voice was tentative now, and John realized it was his fault for not answering.

"I want that," John said. And for just a moment, he really believed it was that simple.

CHAPTER

October 1972

ROGER ROLLED over to avoid the light streaming in the dorm window and groaned. The sheets they'd tacked up as curtains didn't come close to blocking out the sun. He worked open an eyelid just enough to catch the numbers on the flip clock on the desk: 10:15. Just one time, he wanted to sleep in on a weekend. Maybe until noon. Was that too much to ask? He was a college student, for fuck's sake!

Roger reached for the second pillow, pulled it against his chest, and inhaled deeply. It smelled good. Like John. He loved the scent of John's aftershave—some expensive European brand John's aunt had sent and which Roger couldn't pronounce the name of. The smell made him horny as hell. As if he needed another reason to wake up to morning wood.

John was already in the practice room. He'd taken on a job as a rehearsal pianist for one of the voice teachers to help pay for tuition, since his parents couldn't seem to agree on who was supposed to pay for his school. Roger was pretty sure that together, John's parents had enough money that he didn't need to work as hard as he did, and they were using the dispute over his tuition as a way to take swings at each other. The divorce had gone through right before Roger and John left for the University of Michigan. The extra work was taking a toll on John, although he'd be the last one to complain about it.

Roger had wanted to call John's parents and give them a piece of his mind. He didn't, mostly because he knew John would be mortified. He also knew John's father hated homosexuals, and he knew John worried his father would figure out he and John weren't just roommates. Not that

Roger's own parents were overly fond of John either, and Roger sometimes wondered if his mother had guessed at his secret.

Roger closed his eyes. *Hey, Marc. How are you doing?*

God, he was an idiot! What the hell was he doing, talking to his dead brother as if he were really there? Roger was pretty sure his brother had been straight, but he'd also been pretty cool about things. He'd have understood. He might even have run interference with their parents. Roger imagined Marc would have understood about John.

What would you do, Marc? Roger laughed. *You'd tell the Fuchses to get their shit together and do what's right for John. And you'd tell Mom where to take it when she treats John like shit.* He silently wished he'd done a better job of standing up to his mother.

"You spend too much time with him, Roger," his mother had said the last time Roger called them. "You should be dating. I married your father right after graduation, you know. How are you going to meet girls if he's attached to you like glue?"

He'd been tempted to tell her they were attached a bit more intimately than that, but he'd kept his mouth shut. His scholarship paid his tuition; he needed his parents' help to pay for room and board. Someday he'd get up the nerve to tell them to go to hell, but not yet.

Screw them. What did it matter what they—any of them—thought? This was his fucking life, wasn't it? He wasn't Marc. Perfect Marc. His parents' golden boy. The war hero who had died pulling one of his buddies' bodies out of the line of fire. The straight-A student. Roger had loved his brother. He'd looked up to him, wanted to be just like him. Sometimes he wondered if his parents would care about him at all if Marc were still alive.

Fuck this. He stretched out on the bed and scratched his chest. The door opened and he grinned up at John, who quickly closed the door behind him. "Morning, sunshine."

"You were supposed to clean the room." John's smile belied his admonition.

Roger yawned and glanced around. The extra bed—neither of them ever slept in it—was covered with piles of books and music. Roger's violin sat atop the open case where he'd left it the night before when he'd finished practicing. Next to the bed was a pile of dirty clothes that spilled out of the tiny closet, fragrant and begging to be washed.

"The RA doesn't come to inspect until tomorrow." They'd need to take the crap off the extra bed so it looked as though one of them actually slept in it. Roger patted the bed. "There are much more interesting things to do than clean."

"I'm saving a practice room. I really should get back to it."

"It's already got your name on it. Everyone knows it by now. You practically live there." He patted the bed again and rolled onto his stomach to make sure John got a good view of his bare ass. Why should he play fair?

"Shit. Roger." John locked the door and pulled the Rolling Stones T-shirt over his head. "You know you're making me nuts."

"Good." Roger glanced over his shoulder to admire the smooth skin of John's chest and let out a contented sigh.

"But we really need to practice." John was smiling now, giving Roger that look Roger knew meant John wasn't really serious. John was also biting his cheek—he did that when he played hard to get.

Roger rolled over and hopped out of bed. He knew full well John was watching his naked body, and it turned him on even more that he knew how to read John. "Okay," he said as he brushed his calloused fingertips over John's soft skin. He knew John liked the feel of the skin made rough from the violin strings.

"Oh...." John's voice sounded like a sigh.

Roger couldn't help but grin. "Still thinking we need to get to the practice room right away?"

John shivered as Roger traced the outline of one of his nipples, drawing smaller and smaller circles around it until the bud hardened and puckered. "I... I... it can wait."

"TIME TO practice." John kissed the base of Roger's neck as they lay in a sweaty tangle of limbs half an hour later.

"You're not going to let me off the hook, are you?"

"Concerto competition is next week. You're a shoo-in." John nipped his way over to Roger's jaw and Roger groaned.

"You're not helping, you know."

The corners of John's mouth edged upward. "Just giving you a taste of your own medicine." He sat up and swung his legs over the side of the bed.

"I love it when you talk dirty to me." Roger tackled John and pulled him back onto the sheets.

"Stop."

"Nope." Roger kissed John and wrapped his arms around John's waist.

"I'll buy pizza tonight. And after, you can do whatever you want."

"Seriously?" Fair trade, really. He could wait, and the added incentive of pizza instead of gray mashed potatoes and Salisbury steak that looked like a cow pie and smelled only slightly better, sounded like nirvana.

"Have I ever lied to you?" John stood up and, this time, made it over to where he'd left his clothes in a pile on the floor.

"Nah. You're good for it."

"Tchaikovsky, then." John pulled on his clothes. "Meet me in the practice room?"

"Fifteen minutes." That would give him enough time to shower and brush his teeth. Roger watched as John walked out of the room a moment later with a casual wave back in Roger's direction.

He leaned back on the bed for a moment and smiled. Life was good. Weird, but good. He hadn't really thought about things with John except that he was pretty happy they were together. All the other shit about being gay or whatever the hell they called what he was—if he still kind of liked girls, did that make him gay?—didn't matter. At least not here at school.

CHAPTER 9

"HEY, ROGER." Elizabeth Bates waved at him from the other end of the hallway to the practice rooms.

"Hey." He couldn't avoid her. The room—John's usual practice room—was past where she was standing.

She walked over to him, swinging the tiny case that held her flute. Her long hair swung in tandem with each movement. She was pretty. The kind of girl he might have asked out only a year before. Before John.

"I heard you're a finalist in the concerto competition." She swung her case again and let it settle behind her back, where she clasped it with both hands.

"Yeah." He set his own case down on the floor.

"That's cool." She smiled to reveal a set of straight white teeth. Her lips were shiny with gloss. Roger caught a faint whiff of something. Watermelon? Lip gloss. All the girls in high school loved the flavored stuff. He'd always hated it.

"Listen, Elizabeth. I'm supposed to be rehearsing with John. I wouldn't want to—"

"Roger?"

"Hmm?"

"I was wondering if maybe you'd like to see a movie on Sunday afternoon. I heard *Cabaret* is supposed to be good." Another smile. Shit. He'd always been a sucker for smiles like that.

"I really can't. Sorry."

"Oh." Her smile faded, replaced by a tight, thin line where her lips met.

"Look. I gotta go." He shifted his weight from right foot to left, then back again.

"Okay." She turned to leave. "I'll see you later."

"Later." Roger headed down the hallway.

"Roger?"

"Yeah?" He turned back to her. He'd only made it about four feet toward the practice room.

"I… I know it's probably none of my business," she began, case swinging once more, faster this time.

"What?"

"You… I mean…. Are you and John… uh…. Are you… gay?" She fixed her gaze somewhere over his shoulder, as if she were afraid to meet his eyes and learn the answer.

"Me?" *Shit.* He ran a hand through his hair. "No. Of course not."

She let out an audible breath. "Great." Then, perhaps thinking better of it, she added quickly, "I mean, it'd be okay if you were, you know. But…."

"No problem." He laughed and shook his head. "A lot of people think that." What the hell was he saying? *They think it because it's true.* Even if he weren't gay, he was with John, wasn't he?

"Yeah." She giggled, then blushed. "Maybe we can do a movie some other time, then."

"Sure. I'd like that."

"Okay. See you round."

"Yeah. See ya." Roger watched her leave. With each swing of the case and her hair, his stomach seemed to knot up even more tightly than before.

What the hell did you lie for? What would John think if he knew? But he didn't need to know. It was all bullshit, anyhow. He and John were together. What did it matter if she thought he was straight? He wasn't going to go out with her anyhow.

Of course, he knew the answer: it mattered because being with another man wasn't natural or normal. At least that was what he'd spent his life believing. And he was doing a pretty crappy job of handling things while pretending he was something else. He felt like shit. He felt guilty.

He pushed these thoughts from his mind and opened the practice room door.

ROGER LEANED against the curve of the piano and closed his eyes as John repeated the opening melody of the Tchaikovsky violin concerto in the accompaniment. The piano was a workhorse Yamaha that had probably been sitting in the same practice room for a decade now. The surface of the case was pitted and scarred from years of abuse, but the way John played it, Roger could almost imagine a Steinway grand. He loved to lean against the wood and feel it as it vibrated, much as the violin vibrated against his chin and shoulder.

He'd told Roger more times than he could remember that he should consider a career as a pianist, but John had laughed and responded with some self-deprecatory comment about how he wasn't an instrumentalist. Then he'd add in a soft voice, "I want to be a conductor." As if he didn't believe he could, but he wanted it more than anything.

Now, as Roger set bow to string, he let his mind go. He forgot about Elizabeth, forgot about his parents, and forgot about everything but John and the music. He closed his eyes and stopped worrying about the runs, about making sure the harmonics in the upper register of the violin resonated. He didn't think about the notes themselves but let them well up from his heart. It didn't matter that he knew with every fiber of his being that the romantic music sang with his own passion, that it wasn't "cool" in any sense of the word. He just let his soul shine without trying to pretend he was something he wasn't. He leaned on John's musical presence and gave himself over to the expression, unconditionally and with every ounce of emotion he had to offer.

"Roger?"

"Shit. Sorry. I missed my entrance, didn't I?" Roger's face felt warm as he realized how carried away he'd gotten.

"You could say that. But it was stunning."

Roger's laugh came out as a snort as he tried to disguise his continued embarrassment. "You *sound* like a conductor when you talk like that, you know."

John just glared at him over the piano stand, his lips pursed. If he hadn't been playing the piano, his hands would be on his hips right now. Prissy. One of the kids back in high school had called him that. Hell, the kids had called John worse than that. Yeah, John was prissy. Roger thought it was kind of cute. Even the polyester pants were kind of cute. Not that John wore those anymore—he'd finally managed to talk his mother into letting him buy his own clothing now that he was a college student. Roger had helped him pick out his first pair of painter's pants.

"I think we were at letter *B* in the score," John said as he played a few chords.

All business. John was always all business in the practice room. Outside, he could goof off. That was kind of cute too, in a twisted sort of way.

Roger looked over the piano stand to see where they were.

John huffed softly.

"Come on. You didn't think I had the rehearsal numbers memorized, did you?"

"I'm waiting." John raised his eyebrows and blinked.

"You look like an old geezer when you do that, you know?"

"Shut up and play."

Nope. Nothing ruffled John in the practice room. But it was far too much fun to try to get John to lose it. Roger repressed a smirk and shoved his violin back under his chin.

"WE SHOULD apply for a summer program next year," Roger said as he pressed his cheek into John's back that evening. "Aspen, maybe?" They'd decided on sex after dinner instead of homework. Roger figured they needed to get out of bed at some point, or maybe they would just do their coursework in bed. *Sex. Music theory. Music history. More sex.* It worked for him.

"Tanglewood would be nice."

"Someone said Marlboro in Vermont is the best for chamber music. You could go as a pianist and maybe we could find a cellist. There's some great piano trio music."

"They're all really competitive," John said with a sigh. "I'm not sure I'm good enough."

"Shut up. You're more than good enough. And maybe if you go as a pianist, you'll get to know some of the conductors and coaches. Might help get you some conducting gigs."

"Thanks." John's voice was an undertone.

"What are you thanking me for?" Roger kissed John's back.

"It means a lot that you think I'm that good." John sighed. "I wish I was as sure of myself."

"We'll both get in," Roger reassured John. "I promise."

CHAPTER

One week later

"I'LL GET us a few beers," Roger told John after they'd settled onto one of the threadbare couches in what had probably been a living room before the house was sold to the frat.

"You don't need to. I can come with you." John looked uncomfortable. He always did at frat parties, although he never complained when Roger dragged him along.

"No. It's better you save us the seats. Otherwise we'll be standing out on the grass watching someone puke their guts into a bush or something."

John's face grew paler than usual, and Roger wondered why the hell he couldn't keep his mouth shut sometimes. "Verbal diarrhea," one of the cellists had called it. Probably a good description. It was worse when he was nervous, and even though he wouldn't have admitted it to anyone, parties made Roger nervous. More so now that he and John were together, since people always seemed to ask questions about them.

"Roger!" Valerie Thomas waved at him from over near the keg. She was blonde, with legs that wouldn't quit. Tall and thin. A flautist. They were in the same music theory class.

"Hey, Val." He pulled a couple of plastic cups from a stack on the floor next to the keg. The whole place smelled like beer. Maybe the keg had leaked when they'd rolled it in, or maybe someone had spilled a cup or two nearby.

"Where's John?" she asked with a brilliant smile.

Shit. She was interested in John. He could see it in her eyes. John didn't handle women all that well.

"Over by the door." He pointed to the couch where John sat, legs crossed, back straight, looking more uptight than usual.

"Great. I wanted to ask him something. See you around, okay?"

"Sure. See you." He started to fill the first of the cups, then set it down where he hoped it would be safe while he filled the other. He'd get over to John and rescue him from Val as soon as he could.

"Roger?"

"Oh. Hi, Elizabeth. How're you doing?" Another complication. Music geeks rarely went to the frat parties—it was part of why Roger preferred them. Anonymity. Most of the kids were too trashed to figure out that he never left with any of the girls and always left with his roommate. Besides, he and John were freshmen. Nobody expected them to make out like bandits with the chicks. At least Roger hoped they'd buy the excuse.

"Good." She hiccupped, then blushed.

"More beer?" he asked.

"Sure."

He put his cup down and filled another, then handed it to her. Their fingers brushed.

"So how's practicing coming? For the concerto competition?" she added when he just looked at her blankly.

"It's good. John's been coaching me. He's really good."

"That's what I heard. One of the french horn players says John helped him with a piece he's working on."

"Do you think he'll be able to make a living conducting?" Elizabeth asked.

"Of course." No hesitation. He might not be sure of a lot of other things, but he was sure about that.

"He's lucky to have a friend like you." She blushed again and took a long drink, leaving a beer mustache on her upper lip when she finished. She giggled and wiped her mouth with the back of her hand.

Roger glanced over to where Val had just joined John. John got up when she sat down—the guy was over-the-top polite sometimes—and then proceeded to fidget when she moved to close the gap between them.

"Listen, Elizabeth," Roger said. "I gotta do something. Maybe we can talk later, okay?"

"Sure." She didn't look very happy.

"Maybe we can have coffee sometime," Roger offered. He felt a little guilty stranding her there, but John's face was obviously tense and his cheeks were pink with embarrassment.

"Sure." She brightened. "How about Monday after music history?"

"I… ah… sure." Crap. He hoped she'd just forget or that he'd be able to weasel out of it. "Look, Elizabeth, I really need to go."

"WHAT WERE you talking to Elizabeth about?" John asked as they walked across campus to the dorm. "She looked really happy."

"Nothing really. She just wants to have coffee with me after class."

"Why?"

"I don't know." He grinned at John, hoping to cover his own discomfort. John wasn't buying any of it. Roger knew he should have realized John would see right through him. John knew Roger worried people would figure out they were together, or at least Roger was pretty sure he did.

"It's okay if you want to do stuff with her." John's face reddened and he added quickly, "I mean having coffee." They turned down a narrow walkway, and John walked in front of him.

"Oh." Roger wasn't sure he liked how comfortable John seemed with it. He'd kind of wanted John to be more possessive. Jealous, even.

Neither of them spoke until they were back in the dorm room, and then it was just dumb things like what homework they had to do when they got up in the morning and what time the RA would be by to inspect their room. By the time they settled into bed, Roger had the definite impression that he'd hurt John.

"Hey," he said after they'd turned off the light.

"Hey." John's voice was a soft monotone.

"You mad at me?" Roger was pretty sure John wouldn't tell him if he was.

"No."

Roger rolled onto his side, propping himself up on his elbow. "I'm sorry."

"Don't apologize."

"I like being with you, you know." He kissed John and tried to ignore the guilt that made his gut do backflips. "I really do."

"I know."

CHAPTER 11

"ROGER."

"Mom?" *Shit.* What the hell was she doing here, standing outside their dorm room? She was supposed to be at home. He heard movement from behind him—John shoving all the crap off the other bed and climbing under the sheets—and he smiled at her. He hoped the twitch he felt in his cheek wasn't totally obvious. "What a surprise. It's great to see you."

Right.

"Let me just get some pants on and then I can let you in."

She frowned and crossed her arms over her chest. Roger thanked God or whatever part of the universe was looking out for him that he was at least wearing boxers. He closed the door, doing his best not to slam it shut and piss her off more, then scrambled for a pair of jeans.

John shot him a questioning what-the-hell-is she-doing-here look. At least they were both on the same page. Shock and awe, Miranda Nelson style. Roger just shrugged in response as he buttoned his fly.

"Sorry it's such a mess," he said as he let his mother inside.

Miranda Nelson looked through her glasses and down her nose as she took in the room. "I'm not sure 'mess' truly covers it." She stopped her appraisal of the room and her gaze landed on John. He offered what Roger knew was supposed to be a smile, but looked more like a grimace. "Miranda scares the shit out of me," John had once told Roger.

"It's past noon. Why are you both still in bed?" she demanded.

John's lips moved, but no sound issued from them.

"Late night practicing," Roger lied.

"Nice to know you're so studious." She clearly didn't believe a word of it.

Roger's gaze flitted around the room and landed on the bottle of lube by the pillow on his bed. He managed a smile he hoped looked more convincing than John's and scooted sideways to block her view of it. Then he turned and began to make the bed, surreptitiously slipping the lube under the pillow. A single pillow. He'd need to thank John for having the presence of mind to grab it when he switched to the other bed.

"Your father's downstairs waiting," she said when neither he nor John spoke.

"Oh. Great." He caught John's eye, at a loss as to what to do, but John just stared blankly back at him. It wasn't as if Roger's parents showed up unannounced on a regular basis.

"We're taking you to lunch."

Fucking hell. What had he done now? "That's cool. Why don't you give me and John a couple of minutes to get dressed and—"

"Just you, Roger."

"Ah… sure."

John didn't say anything, but he didn't look particularly happy. They'd talked about driving over to the IHOP for pancakes.

Miranda glanced over at John, then back at Roger. "We'll be downstairs waiting," she said before turning to leave.

"Okay," Roger said to the door as it closed.

John was silent.

"What?"

"Nothing." John pulled his knees up to his chest and wrapped his long arms around them.

"Come on. Something's bugging you. You know I can tell."

"You can?" John bit his lower lip.

"Yeah. Always. Like an open book."

"It's nothing. Really."

Roger sighed and went to sit beside him. "I'm sorry about her. How she treats you."

"Like I said, it's nothing. No big deal."

Roger leaned in to kiss him. "I don't give a crap what she and my dad think."

John managed another of his tight smiles but didn't respond.

"I mean, who the hell are they to tell me what to do?" They weren't really telling him anything, he realized. They were just *doing*.

"They're your parents. You're their only son." John didn't add the word "now"—they both understood.

"I'm never going to take Marc's place." He'd said it, so it was true, right?

John put his hand over Roger's. "You don't have to be him. Not for me." This time John's smile was more genuine, causing Roger to swallow back a wave of emotion. "I mean it." John squeezed his hand.

Roger hopped up from the bed, unsure of what to say. Why did John have to be so nice about his parents' shit? "I better get dressed. Don't want to piss off Miranda again." He always called his mother that when he was with John—it just felt better. Easier. As though somehow he was an adult and not the kid who always seemed to be getting into trouble.

"Sure."

"We can go for pancakes tonight, after rehearsal."

"Okay."

Roger leaned down and kissed John. "Thanks," he said.

"Sure."

ROGER HEADED down the dormitory stairs. John had told him it was okay at least two more times before he left. If it was okay, why did his stomach feel as though it was twisted like a pretzel?

Miranda waited outside, smoking a cigarette. Roger hadn't smoked since he'd come to college—John hated it—but the smell made him long for it. She took a drag and looked him over, then dropped the half-smoked cigarette on the concrete and smashed it under her foot. She'd leave it there. She always did. John had once pointed out all the cigarette butts on the ground around the small pond on campus. Since then, Roger saw them everywhere, and they reminded him of the back patio at his parents' house.

"Your father's waiting." She gestured to the parking lot, where the Chevy Chevelle wagon sat idling at a low rumble. The gold paint sparkled in the sunlight and the chrome bumpers were pristine. His father loved that car. He'd let Roger drive once to test out the V-8, but Roger was pretty sure his father didn't trust him to drive the speed limit with the tricked-out engine. After that Roger's brother had bought his own V-8 and let Roger drive it. Marc's car wasn't as nice as his dad's, but Roger didn't drive the speed limit with it either.

"You going to stand there staring?" his mother asked him. She made no bones about the fact that she hated the car. Roger wondered if she was jealous of it—his father spent more time detailing that car than he did with her.

Roger opened the rear door. "Hi, Dad."

"Hello, son."

That was usually the extent of their conversations. Richard Nelson was a man of few words. Roger slid onto the vinyl seat and closed the door.

THE HOWARD Johnson's was quickly filling up for lunch. Roger had been listening to his mother drone on about relatives he wasn't even sure he remembered. "… and your great-aunt Margie is having surgery next week for polyps." Roger didn't want to ask where the polyps were and ruin his meal. "I'm sure she'd love to hear from you. Maybe a card or a letter?"

"Sure, Mom."

"Of course you hardly write to us," she added, her lips pursed. "We'd really like to hear from you more often, wouldn't we, honey?" She looked directly at his father, who just nodded.

"So how are your classes?" Roger's mother asked as the waitress brought them their meals.

Roger had ordered the fried clams and coated them with cocktail sauce as he avoided his mother's gaze. "Fine. I'm pretty busy."

"Were you able to schedule the introduction to accounting class we talked about?"

"Couldn't manage it with my schedule." He wouldn't tell her there was no way he was going to take accounting classes. She knew he wanted to be a musician. Why did she keep hounding him about accounting? Okay. So he knew why: Marc had been an accounting major. Suddenly the fried clams made his stomach turn.

"Really, Roger. You know how important it is to keep your options open. It's all fine and dandy to have a dream, but music isn't exactly the most stable career choice."

"There are plenty of people who make a living as musicians." They'd had this conversation a million times, and Roger knew she'd never be convinced. He'd told her he'd be perfectly happy playing in an orchestra and maybe teaching on the side, but she didn't listen.

"Your father and I just want to be sure you don't put all your eggs in one basket." She lifted her cup of coffee in his father's direction and received the obligatory nod in response. "You're so good at math. Almost as good as Marc was. Isn't he, Dick?"

Roger's dad nodded, then picked up his soda and drank.

Now Roger really felt sick. He took a clam and dunked it in the sauce, then turned it around in the small metal cup, just staring at it.

"So have you met any nice girls?" his mother asked as he continued to swirl the now-soggy clam around.

"Sure. There are lots of nice girls at school."

She did that thing she always did when she didn't believe him: she raised an eyebrow and cocked her head to the side. His stomach roiled. He glanced over at his father but found no help there.

"You and John spend too much time together, Roger." Her face was set in a frown as she put a cigarette between her lips and lit up. "We've talked about this before. How can you meet girls if you spend all your time with him?" She leaned in and lowered her voice to add, "There's something not quite right with that boy. He's just so"—her voice grew even softer—"effeminate. People will talk."

"He's my best friend, Mom. I don't care what people say about it."

"You know I only want what's best for you, sweetheart," she said on a puff of smoke. "I wouldn't want people to think you're... well... a *homosexual*." This last word was barely audible.

"I don't care what people think." *I don't care what you think.* He knew he was lying to himself.

"Roger." His father scowled at him.

"Your father's right."

Roger wasn't sure what his father was supposed to be right about. Had he even been following the conversation? Roger said nothing. It just wasn't worth arguing about. They'd be gone in a few hours and he would get back to his life—the life *he* wanted.

"Tell him about the summer," his mother prompted.

His father, who had a mouthful of hamburger, blinked and wiped his face. "Huh?"

"The job, Dick."

Roger fidgeted in his seat. He'd hoped they'd let the whole accounting career thing go. No such luck.

"Right."

"Well, tell him." Miranda stamped out her cigarette in the plastic ashtray.

"I've got a summer job lined up for you at the office," his father said.

"It's working for the accounting department at Midwestern Insurance," his mother added. "It pays. You can live at home and commute with your father."

"I'm applying for summer programs, Mom." He'd told her at least four times how he had applied to be a counselor at National Music Camp in Interlochen, Michigan. He hadn't told them John had also applied. He figured that was best left unsaid. "*Music* programs."

"This is a great opportunity for you." His mother's voice carried throughout the restaurant, and Roger wanted to disappear into his chair. "Marc spent the summer at Fisker his first year of college. They still ask about Marc, don't they, Dick?"

Roger's dad nodded again.

"So it's all set, then," Miranda continued as if she hadn't heard a word of what Roger had said about summer music programs. "You'll spend the summer at home and work with your father at Fisker."

"Mom, I explained that I—"

"You don't have to give your father an answer now." She glared at him and he knew she wasn't going to let it drop this time. Better to toss her a bone.

"If I don't get into a music program, I'll do it. Okay, Mom?"

She continued to look at him through narrowed eyes for several minutes, then huffed softly and lit another cigarette.

One hurdle down. A million more to go….

CHAPTER 12

"HOW WAS it?" John guessed it hadn't gone all that well. He could smell the cigarette smoke on Roger's clothes and his hair was a mess—no doubt he'd run his hand through it a dozen times over lunch.

"Fine."

John hated what Roger's mother did to him. Her visits—which blessedly didn't occur more than once a month—always left Roger on edge and irritated with the world for a few days following. John was pretty sure he knew why Miranda hated him. And after the little slip with the bottle of lube, he was sure she'd be making their lives a lot more difficult in the future. He'd been so stupid not to have noticed it!

"What did she have to say?" He wondered if he was pushing Roger too much, but he figured he'd better know what he was up against.

"She wants me to work at my dad's company this summer." Roger screwed up his face and shook his head. "As if. I'd be so bored I'd probably shoot myself."

"What did you tell her?"

"Nothing. Just that I'm applying for music stuff and that if I don't get it, I'll take the job. Seemed to satisfy her. At least she stopped bugging me about it after I told her that."

John tried not to react outwardly. "Sounds good." Truth was, he wanted to agree with Roger that Miranda was a pain in the ass, but he couldn't quite get past the idea that she was also Roger's mother. He could never say anything bad about her just like he could never say anything bad about his own mother.

Roger sat down heavily on the bed and let out a long breath. "Do you ever feel like you can't do anything right?" he asked, sounding dejected.

"Sometimes." Sometimes John felt as though he made Roger's life so much more difficult. He knew Roger worried about what people thought of them. He'd heard the rumors. And even though music school kids were more accepting than most, he also knew it was much harder for Roger than him. He'd spent most of high school and a good portion of junior high hearing the taunts. John moved closer to Roger and rubbed his shoulders.

"I know they mean well." Roger leaned in to John's touch. "But why the hell can't they leave me alone?"

John wished he had an answer.

"I know I'm a fuckup."

"You're not a fuckup." That one was easy. Roger might not be what his parents wanted, but he worked his butt off and he was a really good musician.

"Then why do I feel like shit?"

Because you care what they think even though you don't want to. "I don't know. You shouldn't." He offered Roger what he hoped was a sympathetic smile, then combed his fingers through Roger's hair to smooth it.

Roger just leaned into him and sighed. "Promise me you'll always be my friend."

That was easy too. "I promise. Always."

CHAPTER 13

One month later

ROGER LOOKED up as John raised his baton. He knew John was scared to death, but it didn't show. John's eyes were intense, focused on the score Roger was pretty sure he didn't need. For a split second, their eyes met. Roger was one violinist out of about twenty, but he knew he'd done well to volunteer to play with the orchestra. John needed his support.

"I've wanted to conduct for so long," John had told him as he chewed a fingernail. They'd stayed up talking the night before, John unable to sleep. "But really doing it… I'm not sure I can."

"What's different from the rehearsals?" Roger asked. "I mean, I know there'll be an audience, but really, when you think about it?"

"I know." John's voice was barely a whisper.

Roger put his arm around John and pulled him against his chest. "You're really good. You've worked your ass off studying the music. The rehearsals went great. You're gonna be fine."

"Thanks."

Now, as Roger raised his violin and watched for John's downbeat, he was absolutely sure it *would* be fine. Better than fine. He'd known plenty of people who'd dreamed of difficult things—being an astronaut, a rocket scientist, a doctor—but John really had the stuff. He just hadn't realized it yet.

John cued the orchestra and the sounds of Mozart's Jupiter Symphony filled the concert hall. Students who had been fidgeting while they waited now sat still, their eyes focused on the stage. The clear sound of the violins enveloped Roger as he and the other musicians followed John's bright and thoughtful baton. Maybe Roger had heard more polished interpretations in recordings, but the promise of John's talent was there for everyone to hear. With each new phrase, Roger felt John's music wrap itself around him, lift him outside of himself, and make him want to play that much better. John's music made him want to give everything so John's musical voice could soar.

Roger glanced to his left and caught his stand mate's eye. She smiled back at him with obvious approval in her gaze. He knew she felt it too. He saw the flush on her cheeks and the wonder in her eyes.

You're going to be a star someday, John. The thought left him a bit breathless. Sad, even, although he wasn't sure why.

THE CONCERT ended around four, and the musicians retreated to the band room for cookies and punch.

"Great job, John," Ralph Wicker said with a clap on John's back. He was one of the upperclassmen who had initially balked at having a freshman conduct. "You gonna do another next semester?"

"If Professor Walsh can find a spot for me." John glanced downward and shifted from one foot to another, appearing at once pleased and embarrassed at the compliment.

"He'll find a spot," Cathy Volker chimed in. John hadn't even noticed she was looking at him with newfound respect. And something else: lust. Yep. Roger knew that look, even if John never noticed. He'd once thought John was just ignoring it, but he'd long since realized John really *was* clueless. He liked that about John—liked that John looked at him in a way he didn't look at anyone else.

"Hey, Roger." Elizabeth smiled up at him, swinging her flute.

"How're you doin', Elizabeth?" Roger caught John looking at him, his smile fading.

"Great." Her cheeks pinked and she looked down at her feet for a moment before looking up again.

John had turned his back to Roger and was talking to one of the professors. "Look, Elizabeth, I can't talk now."

"No problem." The look of disappointment on her face belied her words. "Talk to you later, Roger."

"Sure."

"YOU LIKE her, don't you?"

"Who?"

John frowned at Roger and went back to washing his face. "Elizabeth. The flautist."

"Yes, of course. I mean, she's cool."

"That's not what I meant." The words weren't harsh, but Roger fought the urge to cringe.

"Look. John. I've told you before, I'm not interested. Why would I be?" Roger did his best to keep his voice even, but he was having a hard time of it.

"It's really okay, you know. If you want to hang out with her." John picked up a brush and began to run it through his hair. Roger saw the hurt in John's face.

"I don't want to hang out with her." Well, it was half-true. He liked her, but he didn't want to *date* her. He might have if John weren't in the picture, but he was.

"Okay. It's just that I know your parents hate me."

"They don't hate you." Of course it was a lie, but he didn't want John worrying about his parents on top of everything else.

"They do. I'm not blind. And I understand. They want what's best for you. I'm not exactly—"

"I don't give a crap what they say."

John sighed but said nothing.

"You were great tonight, you know." Yes, he was changing the subject, but he really didn't know what else to say.

"Thanks."

"We should get some sleep." They climbed silently into bed.

"Sure." John rolled onto his side, away from Roger. Roger rolled over and wrapped his arms around John's waist, then kissed the back of his neck. "Good night."

"Night."

One week later

"CONGRATULATIONS," JOHN mouthed as he caught Roger's eye through the crowd of people. Roger grinned back at him.

John headed over to the refreshments table for something to drink, nearly colliding with Roger's parents. He'd managed to avoid them for the duration of the concerto competition finals, which had lasted most of the evening.

"Good to see you, Mr. and Mrs. Nelson." He did his best to appear polite. Miranda intimidated the hell out of him.

"John." As always, Miranda was barely civil.

John smiled, then waved good-bye—he was sure he looked like a total idiot—and slipped through the crowd into the hallway outside the theater. He'd wait to get something to drink until he got back to his dorm room.

"Hi, John."

Great. Cathy Volker again. He really didn't want to talk to her. She always seemed to stand too close to him, and it made him feel uncomfortable.

"Hi, Cathy."

"Roger was incredible, wasn't he?"

"Y-yes."

"That was nice of his parents to come up from Ohio, wasn't it?" As always, Cathy stood a bit too close. He stepped back from her, then forced a smile.

"Y-yes. V-very nice."

"I didn't know Roger and Elizabeth were going out," she said offhandedly, flushing as she said it.

"Going out?"

"Yeah. I heard him tell his mother they were dating."

"Oh." When had his stomach fallen to his feet? "That's nice." *It's okay*, he told himself. *He's just keeping up appearances.* Still, he wished Roger had told him he was going to lie to his parents. "Look, C-Cathy," he began. "I'm k-kind of tired. I think I'm g-going to head b-back to the room. It was good talking to you. M-maybe we can t-talk more another t-time."

At this, her eyes widened in obvious surprise. Perfect. Now she thought he was talking about a date. "I'd like that. Maybe next weekend?"

"I… ah… m-maybe." Or maybe not. He was going to be sick as a dog next weekend. He and Roger could plan something. A cold. Maybe the flu?

"Sounds great. See you later!"

"Bye."

John closed his eyes and took a long, slow breath.

"WE DIDN'T have to go out," John said quietly as they drove back to the dorms a few hours later. Roger had spent an hour trying to track John down at the party but had finally given up and headed back to the dorms.

"I figured you needed time with your folks. I didn't want to be in the way," John said when Roger had walked into their room.

Anxious to smooth things over with John and too antsy to hang around the dorms for the evening, Roger had said, "Let's go out. Grab a few drinks. Just hang. Without my parents, I mean."

"Sure." John hadn't sounded convinced. Now, headed home from the bar a few hours later, Roger was sure John was angry with him. Or at least upset with him. He hated how John stared out the car window, not meeting his eyes. He'd been like that since they left the bar.

"I wanted to go out." Roger hadn't particularly wanted to go to the bar. Not that he'd minded it, but more than anything, he felt guilty about how horrible his mother was to John. He also felt guilty about Elizabeth and what he'd told his parents about dating her. The bar would be just him and John, and he could reassure John that they were still okay.

Roger squinted at the headlights of an oncoming car and jerked the wheel to the right. The car rumbled over the shoulder at the overcompensation.

"You sure you're okay to drive?" John looked at him with concern. Roger could see he was gripping the door handle with his right hand.

"I'm fine." He'd only had a few beers. Or at least he only remembered having a few.

"Okay." Roger saw John's jaw tense.

They drove in silence, and with each passing minute, Roger tapped his left foot against the floor a little faster. He could deal with a lot of shit, but he couldn't deal with John's silence eating at him. "What's bugging you?" he finally asked.

"Me?" John raised his eyebrows. "Nothing. I'm fine."

"Like hell." Roger spoke the words under his breath and immediately wished he hadn't said them out loud. He had a hard enough time keeping his mouth shut; it was ten times worse when he'd been drinking.

"What was that?"

"Something's bothering you." Roger looked at John for a long moment.

"Watch the road!"

Roger turned his focus back to the road. He'd strayed into the opposite lane without even realizing it. Maybe he had drunk a little more than he should have. "Sorry."

John said nothing.

"Look"—Roger kept his eyes trained straight ahead of him—"I know you're mad at me."

"Do you?" John spoke in an undertone.

"You're mad because of Elizabeth." Best face it head-on.

"No." John now had his hands in his lap and was twisting them around. Roger had a hard time hearing him over the growl of the engine. "It's not that."

"I'm not dating her. You know that."

"I know."

"I'm not even interested in her. It's just that my parents are so—"

"I know you wouldn't cheat on me. You don't have to explain. I understand."

Roger pulled his gaze back to the road and took a deep breath. His heart was beating hard and his palms were damp against the steering wheel. At least John knew he wouldn't cheat. No matter what, he would never do that to John. So why couldn't he just be himself? Why did he care what other people thought? Because no matter what he said, he *did* care. "So what is it, then?"

"It's nothing."

God, he hated it when John clammed up and wouldn't talk to him! "Don't bullshit me."

"Let it go. It's not worth it."

That *really* pissed Roger off, although he wasn't sure why. Maybe because he was so goddamn scared of losing John and equally as scared of what being with John meant. "Not worth it? What are you saying? That this... us... we're not worth it?"

"Watch the road." John was staring out the window again, but Roger saw his shoulders tense.

"Fuck the road. Tell me why you're mad at me."

Another car drove by them in the opposite direction, and John clutched the door once more. "We can talk about it later. We're both tired. And you should be celebrat—"

"Dammit, John. Just tell me I was a shit and get it over with!"

"You're not a—"

"I was a shit. I treated you like crap and I don't even have a fucking excuse." *Except that I'm scared of losing you.*

John was still staring out the window.

Roger reached over to put his hand on John's leg, but John had slid to the far end of the seat, as far as he could get from him. Roger glanced at the road, then back at John and said, "Please. Say something."

John turned and glared at him. "Fine." His voice sounded tight, like an overtensioned piano string, ready to snap. "You want me to tell you the truth?"

"Yes." Roger's voice sounded shaky to his own ears. He'd never seen John get angry before.

"Yes, I'm angry." John raised his chin and pursed his lips. "I'm angry because—" John hesitated, as if he was afraid of what he might say or how he might say it. "—because you're so full of shit."

Roger knew his mouth was hanging open, but he couldn't help it. He'd never heard John say anything like that before, and he wasn't sure he'd ever seen him genuinely angry. "Full of shit?"

"Yes." John sat up straighter and turned his head to look directly at him. "Full of it." John, too, seemed surprised with himself.

"Why?" John had a ton of reasons to be mad at him. Roger didn't expect what John said, though.

"Because you're embarrassed to be with me."

"I'm not—"

"Yes, you are," John interrupted. "Because you don't know what the fuck you want." John blinked, as if he'd also surprised himself by swearing at Roger again. Roger knew John didn't like to swear.

"I want you." Roger glanced back at the road.

"Do you? Because I'm not so sure. I think you *think* you want me, but that would mean you're gay or something, and you don't want that."

"I don't care what people think."

"Bullshit." John's voice was low but charged with anger. "You *do* care. It's why you told your parents you're dating Elizabeth, and it's why you tell everyone we're just friends."

"Come on, John. I can't just tell them we're fucking each other, can I?"

"Is that what you think this is? Fucking?" John's voice rose an octave. "And no, of course I don't expect you to tell them we're together like that. But you don't have to flirt with every girl you meet either. Sometimes I feel like you really don't want to be with me."

Shit. Had he been that bad about things? Yeah, he had. "Of course I want to be with you." It was the truth. At least underneath all the other shit floating around his brain. "The stuff with Elizabeth... you know it's all bull."

"I know you don't want to sleep with her."

"Of course I don't!"

John sighed and shook his head. "I know you need to keep up appearances. But it just feels bad sometimes. I worry that you'll get sick of sneaking around and you'll just leave."

"I won't leave." Okay, now *he* was angry. Not with John but with himself. John was right: he deserved better. He looked over at John, who was flushed with anger and hurt, and he knew it was all his fault. "I *won't*. I want to be with you. I know I'm an asshole sometimes. I know I don't deserve it, but I really do want to be with you. Hell, John, I—"

"Roger! Oh my God! The car!"

Roger growled and turned his attention back to the road just in time to see the oncoming headlights. With only one hand on the wheel, he overcompensated again. The car swerved onto the shoulder and slid on the gravel as he tried to wrangle the steering wheel.

The last thing Roger remembered was a dull thudding sound as the front of the car plunged into the ditch.

CHAPTER 14

Two days later

"ROGER?"

Roger struggled to open his eyes. "Mom?"

"Oh, thank God."

He blinked a few times before she came into focus. "Why are you here?" His voice sounded scratchy.

"You don't remember?"

He shook his head and tried to swallow, but his tongue stuck to the roof of his mouth. "Water?"

She stood up and held a paper cup with a bent straw in front of his lips. He drank the contents and she refilled it for him. "Better?"

He nodded and noticed for the first time that he wasn't in his room at home. Or in the dorms. A yellow curtain was pulled halfway around the bed. "Hospital? Why am I in the hospital?"

She looked down, then up again. "There was an accident." She spoke the words in a hushed whisper.

A tiny flicker of memory stirred at the back of his mind. The bar. Too many beers. He tried to sit up, but it hurt so bad, he barely got an inch off the pillows. His body ached. "Where's John?" he said as his heart leapt into his throat. If anything happened to John, he'd never forgive himself.

"He's fine. He went back to the dorms yesterday. They kept him overnight for observation."

John went home yesterday? Did that mean he'd been unconscious for more than a day? *Shit.*

"They took you into surgery." Her voice faltered and her eyes filled with tears. "We… your father and I… we got a call. We… I couldn't go through that again." She was crying now. He'd only seen her cry once, when Marc died.

He closed his eyes and clenched his jaw. His face was about the only place on his body that didn't hurt. His left arm and his left shoulder hurt like a beast. He took a few deep breaths, then opened his eyes again and glanced at his arm. A cast ran from above his elbow and onto his hand, ending at his knuckles. His forefinger and middle finger were taped together and attached to a piece of metal.

"Surgery for what?" He could barely get the words out.

"Your arm." She still wasn't looking at him. Why wasn't she looking at him?

"What about my arm?" *Please. No.* He swallowed again. Or tried to.

"It was broken in a half-dozen places. And your fingers…."

The violin. He'd play the violin again, wouldn't he? She must have guessed at his silent question, because in response, she just shook her head.

ROGER STARED out the window into the night. No moon, and the bright lights from the parking lot hid the stars. His mother and father had been by to see him after dinner. Not that he'd eaten anything. He felt sick.

Dr. Farthington had checked on him. "Your folks tell me you're a lefty," the surgeon said. "With a little physical therapy, you'll be able to use that arm to write."

Write? He'd forgotten about writing. He didn't give a shit about writing. "What about my hand? My fingers? Am I going to be able to play the violin?"

He was glad his parents weren't around, because when the doctor told him he'd never regain full dexterity in his hand, he cried. Sure, he waited until the man had left, but he cried all the same.

John. He needed John. Needed to see him. Talk to him. See that he was okay.

CHAPTER *15*

"EAT." MIRANDA hovered over Roger and waved a forkful of something gray in his face.

"You don't need to feed me, Mom. My right hand works fine." He wished she'd just go away. He hated how she hovered over him like he was some sort of fucking invalid.

"You're not eating enough. The nurses said so."

He wasn't hungry. Three days had gone by, and he'd been sitting in this fucking bed feeling sorry for himself and missing the hell out of John. Three days and he still hadn't seen him. Not once.

He's probably pissed at you.

"Have you seen John?" Roger asked, trying to sound as though he didn't really care.

"John?" She said the name as if there were some question as to which John he was talking about.

"John Fuchs, Mom. You know who I mean."

"Oh, of course." She offered him an expression that was a cross between a smile and a look of sympathy.

"You hate him, don't you?" He didn't care if he sounded pissed off. He was.

"Darling, I don't hate him." More of the same expression, but this time with a bit of the long-suffering parent thrown in for good measure. "It's just that he's so... clingy. And now that you won't be going back to school...."

There. She'd said it. The thing he'd been dreading. The reality of it all. Of course he couldn't go back now. Even if he proved them all wrong and got his hand back into shape, it wouldn't be in time to finish out the semester. Hell, he'd be lucky to get the damn cast off by the time finals rolled around. The realization hit him like a Mack truck. He sank down into the bed, feeling defeated.

This is all your fucking fault, Roger Fucking Idiot Nelson. All of it. If you're lying in shit, it's your own.

She took his good hand and patted it. "I know how hard this must be for you, sweetheart. But it'll be fine. You can move into the basement. It'll be like having your own apartment. You can start at State in the fall and study business. You were always so good with numbers."

"I don't want to talk about this, Mom." His gut clenched. He was a violinist. It was in his blood, in his bones. *Fucking broken bones.* His music was everything. The *only* thing he had.

"It's going to be all right. I promise. I know that right now it seems like it's the end of the w—"

"I really don't want to talk about it right now." Couldn't she give him a few days to be depressed? He'd fucking earned the right.

When he met her gaze once more, her mouth was tight and she sat a little straighter in her chair. He hated it when she tried to do things for him, make them better! He felt like a little kid—a little kid who got into trouble and needed his mommy to fix things for him. *Fuck this!*

When she spoke again, Roger could hear the hurt in her voice. "We only want what's best for you, your father and I. Obviously you can't stay here in Ann Arbor. There's no one to take care of you."

Of course she was right. John wasn't even speaking to him. Besides, even if John wasn't MIA, Roger couldn't ask the guy to play nurse, either. He wasn't even sure how he was going to take a bath on his own with the cast.

"I'm sorry, Mom. I know you just want to help." He stared out the window at the cool blue sky and thought of John.

"YOU'LL BE going home tomorrow. Isn't that wonderful news?" the nurse asked as she took his blood pressure and checked the line of sutures that ran from his shoulder to just under the cast.

"Sure." At least his parents had left early tonight. His mother wanted to go by the dormitory and pack up his things. She seemed almost cheerful about the task.

The nurse left a few minutes later and took his half-eaten meal with her. He rolled onto his side, facing away from the door. He didn't want fucking cheery candy stripers checking in on him tonight. He wanted to feel like crap. He deserved it. All of it. And John.... His eyes burned. Nearly a week, and John hadn't even called. Not that Roger blamed him. But he missed him so much it hurt more than his shattered arm.

Hey, Marc. Yeah, it's me. I fucked up big this time. Can't fucking play and the one person I need isn't talking to me. Mom's about to smother me, and I'm not sure I can handle going back home.

Another nurse walked into the room, smiled at him, and handed him a few pain pills and some water. She lifted the bandages and checked the stitches in his arm and shoulder, took his temperature, then tucked the covers around him before leaving again without a word.

He dozed off. Morphine was nice that way. Faster than booze or pot.

"HI."

"John?" Roger smiled through the haze of painkillers. He was glad for them if it meant he could dream about John.

John brushed a hand over Roger's cheek and Roger let out an audible sigh. "How are you feeling?"

"Better now. Really good. But I'd be better if you'd kiss me." He shivered as John brushed his cheek with his soft lips. *This is a great dream.*

"I can't stay long. Visiting hours are over."

"If it's my dream," Roger wondered aloud, "why do you have to leave?"

"Mr. Fuchs? Mr. Fuchs?" The nurse's voice was like an irritating gnat Roger wanted to swat away. "Time to say good night."

"I need to go."

"Stay." He was starting to get irritated with the dream.

John kissed him on the lips this time.

"I like that."

"I need to go. You take care of yourself, okay?"

"Not fair." None of this was goddamned fair. Not the dream, not reality, not anything.

"I love you, Roger." Another soft kiss, and the dream was gone.

CHAPTER *16*

JOHN WAS dozing in a sitting position, back against the wall, a pile of music spread out around him on the bed, when he heard the lock click and the door opened. For one fast moment, he thought it was Roger, but the glimpse of dyed blonde hair immediately told him otherwise.

"Oh, hello, Mrs. Nelson." His voice came out as a half croak. Damn, he was so tired! He'd barely slept since the accident—he couldn't sleep without Roger—and the worrying was killing him slowly.

Had she come in without knocking? Even if she had Roger's key, it was still his room, after all. Of course, he didn't say anything. Things were bad enough without making Miranda angry.

"John." She smiled at him.

"How's Roger doing?" He'd been hoping for a chance to talk to her about seeing Roger. When he'd called the hospital, they'd told him Roger was not to have guests without his parents' permission. That permission didn't include him. John was pretty sure they couldn't legally keep him away—Roger was an adult, after all—but he also wasn't going to argue with the nurses.

"As well as can be expected, I suppose." She propped the door open with a shoe and dragged a metal trunk into the room. Roger's trunk.

Of course he'd known Roger couldn't stay at Michigan. Still, seeing the trunk made it seem so much more final somehow. *I won't cry. Not in front of her.*

"Do you need any help, Mrs. Nelson?" The last thing he wanted was to help her pack Roger's things, but if it got her out of the room sooner, he'd gladly do it all by himself.

"No. Thank you."

"Oh. Okay. Just let me know if—"

"There's no need," she said as she began to go through the closet and pull some of Roger's clothing out.

John's gut clenched as she folded Roger's tuxedo. Less than a week ago, Roger had worn that tux and played. And now.... "I'm really sorry about what happened." He wasn't sure why he felt the need to apologize to her.

"It'll all be fine now," she said as she shoved Roger's clothing into the trunk along with his books and papers. She looked almost happy, the usual dour look on her face replaced by a peaceful expression. "His father and I will take good care of him."

"That's good." He meant it. He knew Roger needed his parents now.

"It's better this way, you know." She was folding some of Roger's T-shirts and setting them lovingly into the trunk.

John watched her, and with each passing minute, he saw himself losing Roger. The finality of it all made him feel light-headed, and the omelet he'd had for breakfast suddenly sat like a lead weight in his stomach. It was too hot in the room. He had to get out. "I'm sorry," he whispered. "I'm not feeling very well. Please excuse me."

"Oh dear," Miranda said as she pulled Roger's underwear and socks out of one of the dresser drawers. "I hope you're not coming down with something."

He got up off the bed, ran out of the room, and arrived at the bathroom with just enough time to vomit into the toilet. He shoved the door closed with a foot, leaned against it, and slid down to the cold tile floor. He shivered and pulled his knees to his chest.

Roger. I'm so sorry. Please forgive me.

JOHN MANAGED to convince the night-duty nurse that he wouldn't hurt Roger. God, had Roger's parents told the hospital staff he might? Miranda hadn't said anything else to him when he'd come back to the room as she was finishing up packing, but she didn't have to say anything for him to understand she didn't want him anywhere near Roger. It wasn't as though the other kids from school were banned from Roger's hospital room—Elizabeth had told him she'd visited just the other day.

John had barely gotten up the nerve to come, finding the strength only because he knew he needed to tell Roger he was sorry. He'd taken the bus from campus to the hospital and waited until he'd seen Roger's parents leave for the evening before going inside.

Roger's eyes were open when John got to the room, although he didn't immediately seem to notice John standing in the doorway.

"Hi." He hoped he wasn't being too loud. He'd waited nearly a week to see Roger, and the last thing he wanted was to be kicked out.

"John?" Roger's smile was goofy. Goofier than usual. He looked a little like he did when he'd been smoking pot.

John walked over to the bed and stroked Roger's cheek. He wondered how badly Roger's arm must hurt. It looked bad enough, and his fingers were swollen and bruised. John sighed.

"How are you feeling?" *Dumb, dumb, dumb! Of course he feels terrible!*

"Better now. Really good. But I'd be better if you'd kiss me."

John hadn't expected that. He'd meant to tell Roger he was sorry, but Roger didn't seem to be interested in apologies. In fact, he didn't seem angry with him at all. John hesitated just a moment before brushing his lips over Roger's cheek, afraid to do more in case someone saw him. He didn't even want to think about what Miranda would do if she saw them.

"I can't stay long. Visiting hours are over." He wanted to say so much more, like how sorry he was that he'd upset Roger. Or how much he missed him. Or how it broke his heart each time he realized he'd never hear him play the way he had when they'd played together.

"If it's my dream," Roger said, slurring his words as he spoke, "why do you have to leave?"

"Mr. Fuchs? Mr. Fuchs?" The nurse hovered in the doorway, looking at her watch. "Time to say good night."

"I need to go." He looked at the nurse and nodded. She left a moment later. Maybe she'd understood he needed another minute alone with John, or maybe she had to get back to her station.

"Stay." Roger screwed his face up in a scowl.

John kissed Roger on the lips this time. He didn't linger, even though he wanted to. He wanted so much more.

"I like that." Roger had that silly look again.

Definitely stoned. John wondered if Roger would even remember that he'd been there. "I gotta go. You take care of yourself, okay?" He wouldn't cry, he told himself. Not here, at least. Why was he such a girl at times like these?

"Not fair."

No. It's not fair. None of it is fair.

"I love you, Roger." *Always.*

John managed to make it back to the dorm room—*their* room—before he really lost it. He'd never felt so alone.

CHAPTER *17*

Summer 1973

"JOHN?" MARTHA Fuchs peered into John's bedroom. "Aren't you eating breakfast?"

"I'm fine, Mom," John told her. "I'll get something in a little while."

"It's almost lunchtime, sweetheart." She frowned in that way only mothers can frown, with just a touch of concern written between the lines on her forehead.

"Really, Mom. I'm fine. Promise." He offered her a smile he hoped would set her mind at ease. He couldn't eat. Not now. Not before he saw Roger.

"All right. But I'll leave some of the pancakes out. You can warm them in the oven in case you want to eat. I won't be back until dinner." He'd forgotten she was working today. She had gone back to work to make ends meet, and he hadn't wanted to ask about alimony. He wasn't sure she was getting any. He only knew that his dad had paid for the small house near downtown. The rest, he figured, wasn't any of his business.

"Thanks."

"It's good to have you home, even if it's just for the summer," she said. "I missed you."

"I missed you too, Mom."

Her face lit up at these words, and she backed out of the bedroom and closed the door. He waited until he heard her pull out of the driveway, then took a shower. It took him nearly another hour to decide what to wear. Too dressy and he might make Roger feel uncomfortable. Too casual and Roger might think he didn't care. Then again, he didn't want Roger to think he cared too much, or Roger might feel bad about telling him to take a hike. Not that he wanted Roger to tell him that, but they hadn't talked at all since the accident. He finally ended up with a pair of Levi's and a T-shirt that read "Old musicians don't die, they just decompose."

After the accident, he'd wanted to call Roger, but he'd lost his nerve. So he sent Roger a letter before Thanksgiving break and told him he'd like to see him. When Roger didn't respond, John sent him a Christmas card and said he'd be staying with his mom for the holidays. But Roger didn't call or write back then either. At first, he'd figured Roger's mother had intercepted the letters, but after months passed and Roger didn't write or call, John wondered if Roger was still angry with him for causing the accident. Even when he got home from school at the end of May, John still wasn't sure what to think, but he knew he needed to see him, if only to accept that things between them were over.

It took John ten minutes to take a look at the bus schedules and realize he'd get to Roger's place twice as fast if he just rode his bike, though he still vacillated: his old Schwinn wasn't exactly the kind of cool ten-speed his friends rode around in Michigan. He could leave the bike at the side of Roger's house, maybe hide it by the garage, even, so Roger wouldn't see how pathetic a bike it was.

What is wrong with you? This is Roger. Your best friend. He tried to silence the voice within that added, *The guy you're so fucking in love with you can't even think straight. The same guy who hasn't called or written in seven months and probably doesn't want to see you.*

In the end, he left the bike chained to the rack in front of the drugstore about three blocks from Roger's house and walked the rest of the way. It was pretty hot for mid-June, and the humidity made it feel like August. By the time he got to Roger's house, his underwear stuck to his skin underneath the heavy jeans, and he had a large sweat mark under each arm.

Lovely.

He was relieved there were no cars in front of Roger's house. He'd planned on waiting if he needed to, just to make sure Roger's parents weren't around. The last thing he wanted was to run into Miranda. Of course, Roger might be gone too. So when the dog barked and he heard footsteps from inside, he was happy. And scared to death. He'd thought about this meeting for so many weeks now, run it over and over again in his mind, that he was suddenly terrified he wouldn't know what to say when he actually saw Roger.

He needn't have worried.

"Hey." Roger looked genuinely pleased to see him as he pushed Roofster behind him to let John inside.

"Hi." John didn't look Roger in the eyes—all of a sudden he felt the need to check that his feet were moving one in front of the other.

Roger locked the door behind them and motioned John into the living room. Everything was as he remembered it. John wasn't sure that was a good thing—it just made him remember everything they'd done here, all the conversations they'd had, the afternoons spent watching tube. All of it.

John sat on the flocked couch and ran his hand over the fabric as he'd always done. He glanced up at Roger, who was looking back at him. Roger seemed distracted. Tired. Maybe even a little uncomfortable. He'd so rarely seen Roger look uncomfortable that it took him by surprise. Then again, he knew it was only his fault that Roger was uncomfortable. If he hadn't—

"Just got back from school?"

Roger's question brought John back to himself with a start. He nodded and met Roger's eyes very briefly, then looked back down at his hands, which were now clasped in his lap and felt slightly sweaty.

"How long you back for?"

"A week. I'm working at Interlochen this summer."

"National Music Camp?"

"Uh-huh." John wasn't sure how Roger would take the news, since they'd applied together before the accident. It had been John's idea that they both go, since he'd spent a few summers there in high school before his parents' relationship had taken a nosedive and money became scarce.

"Cool." Roger smiled.

John relaxed a bit to see Roger's reaction. "I'll be an accompanist for some of the teachers. Maybe even the operetta. You know, Gilbert and Sullivan? They do one of those each summer. They said I might be able to conduct a rehearsal or two."

"Cool."

"So what are you up to?" He realized too late he probably shouldn't have asked, and his face grew hot.

Roger seemed unconcerned with the question. "Nothing, really. My dad said maybe there'll be some work at his job, filing and stuff. Boring crap. Can't really go anywhere—I've got PT three days a week."

"PT?"

"Physical therapy." Roger rolled his eyes and made a disgusted face. "They think in a few months I may be able to write with my left hand."

John didn't know how to respond. "I see." Had it been more than six months ago that Roger had been talking about spending the summer at Marlboro, playing violin? John fought the urge to chew on his fingernail.

"Want something to drink?" Roger asked.

"Sure, thanks."

Roger popped up out of the chair he'd been sitting in. The cast was gone, but John noticed that Roger didn't put any weight on his left arm and that the fingers on Roger's left hand seemed unnaturally curled. Roger's new reality hit John in the gut, and he felt suddenly sick. His eyes burned.

Stop it! He couldn't let Roger see him get all teary eyed.

Roger came back in with two glasses of what looked like orange pop. "Here you go." Roger's hand shook slightly as he held one out to John. John took the glass and stared down at it, not wanting Roger to think he'd noticed.

This time Roger didn't return to the chair but sat down on the couch next to John. God! It felt so weird sitting there with him so close. It was as if they'd never been together. He wanted to touch Roger. To hold him. Kiss him. Tell him he was sorry he'd upset him. Tell him the accident was his fault and ask Roger to forgive him for being such a jerk.

"John?"

"Yes?" John was remembering when they'd sat on the floor right in front of the couch, drinking cherry pop. Roger had stuck his unnaturally red tongue out at John, and John had laughed, then stuck his own tongue out at Roger. They'd rolled around on the carpet for ten minutes, laughing until it hurt.

"I'm really sorry." Roger reached out with his good hand and squeezed John's.

"You don't have anything to apologize for."

"It's just that… well, things were kind of crazy and all." John loved the feel of Roger's skin. He fought the urge to lean in to Roger.

"You weren't a jerk."

"I've missed you." It hurt to say it, but John felt compelled to tell the truth.

"I've missed you too." Roger smiled sadly. "I still want to be with you."

John inhaled a stuttered breath. "Me too." Roger still wanted to be with him?

"I'm going to get my shit together. Get this hand working again. Play again." Roger lifted his left hand and studied it. "I want to come back to school."

"That would be so great." John really wanted to believe it would happen. "Um… I was wondering if you'd like to get some pizza or something. Maybe tomorrow?" He hoped he didn't sound desperate, even though he knew he was. Desperate and full of hope.

"I'd really like that. I'll need to let my mom know."

John wanted to shout, he was so happy. "Just give me a call. I'll be home tonight."

The dog barked, then took off for the kitchen. John heard the back door open and close. "Roger?"

Roger released John's hand quickly and looked incredibly uncomfortable.

Miranda. *Time to leave.*

"Roger, I—" Miranda stopped in her tracks when she saw John sitting there.

John stood up and offered her a shy smile. "Hi, Mrs. Nelson."

"I didn't know you were in town." Her tone was brisk but not unpleasant. John was pretty sure she was on her best behavior because Roger was sitting there. Otherwise he figured she'd have tossed him out on his behind in a heartbeat.

"Just for a few days," he said, trying to reassure her he wasn't a threat. "I leave for Traverse City in a week." When she just looked at him without understanding, he added, "I'll be spending the summer at the National Music Camp at Interlochen, in Michigan."

The relief on her face was plain. "How lovely," she said. She wasn't looking at him—her gaze was fixed on Roger, who was staring blankly at one of the plants on the window ledge. For the first time, John noticed the slightly dull look in his eyes.

"I'd better go, Roger," he said as he stood up.

"Okay." Roger slowly shifted his focus to John.

John picked up his half-empty glass, intending to take it to the kitchen, but Miranda said, "I'll take that." She left them alone again, but John knew she'd be back if he stayed much longer.

Roger led John to the door, then opened it. "It was really good seeing you."

John just smiled. "You too. Call you later?"

"Yeah."

John was out the door a moment later, headed down the street as he fought the urge to skip.

CHAPTER *18*

ROGER WATCHED John leave from the small windows in the front door. The glass was beveled, and it made John's body look out of proportion— as if he were seven feet tall and sticklike. He wondered why John thought his visit would bother him. It was good to see him again. He'd missed John. He'd thought about him every single day.

"Why was he here?" Miranda asked as Roger wandered back to the living room, still thinking of John.

"He just wanted to see me. You know, make sure I was all right." *He wanted to know what happens now. Like me.*

His mother frowned. "I don't think you should see him again, Roger. Lord knows his parents wouldn't want him hanging around you."

"He didn't say that." He knew he didn't sound as convinced as he should be. He couldn't blame the Fuchses if they didn't want John to see him. He'd almost killed their son, hadn't he?

"Well, of course he wouldn't say that. He wouldn't want to upset you."

"Yeah." Roger looked down at his hand, then pushed his fingers back toward his wrist like the physical therapist had taught him. It still hurt when he stretched the muscles of his hand. For the first time, he noticed that the calluses on his fingertips from pressing down on the violin strings were gone. He'd had calluses since he'd started playing violin more than fourteen years before, but he'd never really paid attention to them until now, when the skin there was soft and smooth.

"Are you going to see him again?" Miranda asked as she lit a cigarette.

"I... I don't know."

"It's for the best," she said, agreeing with him even though he hadn't said he wouldn't see John.

"I don't know." He couldn't think straight with the pain meds. Everything since the accident was a blur. How many weeks had he dreamed about John after he'd gotten home? He'd thought John was mad at him, and now he knew John wasn't.

"It's better like this," she told him. "He has his career to think of, you know. And you need to move on. Forget about music and focus on what's important. Then, when you start school in the fall, you'll be able to do what you have to do without worrying about the other stuff.

"Dinner will be ready soon," she said as she pressed the half-finished cigarette into the glass ashtray. "Why don't you take a little nap before? You need your rest."

"Okay." He got up and rubbed his face with his good hand. "Wake me up for dinner, please."

"Of course." She smiled at him sympathetically. "I'll do that."

He climbed the stairs and stopped at the bathroom next to his bedroom. He pulled the pain pills out of the cabinet and just stared at the bottle. For six months, he'd counted on the pills to help him forget. Forget John's eyes and how John felt spooned against him. Forget how much he'd loved it when John accompanied him on the piano. Forget the smell of the rosin on his bow and the feel of the violin as it vibrated underneath his chin. Forget that he'd ever played the violin and that he'd ever hoped to have a career as a violinist.

He set the bottle down on the sink and sat down on the cold tile floor. The pills hadn't worked. He hadn't forgotten any of it.

CHAPTER 19

"SORRY I'M late." John offered his mother the most contrite expression he could muster.

"Were you out biking?" she asked with obvious surprise. It had been at least three years since he'd been on his bike.

"Yes. Thought I'd get some fresh air. It's good for you, you know."

Her half smile, half frown told him she didn't believe him, but she didn't press him. He was just glad she hadn't smelled the cigarette on him. Of course he would have told her someone at the park had been smoking. He wouldn't tell her he'd smoked two cigarettes outside the grocery store. He'd gagged on the first one, but the second hadn't been as bad. He could almost see why Roger liked them.

"Dinner will be ready in about fifteen minutes. I want to be sure I don't miss *Upstairs, Downstairs* on *Masterpiece Theatre*."

"No problem. I'll just take a quick shower."

"Are you all right?" she asked as he turned to leave.

"Yes. I'm great. It was a great ride."

"You can join me tonight if you want. TV," she added when he looked at her without understanding.

"Thanks, but I've got some music I need to study."

He headed upstairs and peeled his clothes off before stepping into the hot water of the shower. It felt good on his skin. He wished he could stay there longer, just feeling the water and trying to forget the dull pain that seemed to have taken up permanent residence in his chest. Then again, he figured it would take more than one hot shower to get rid of the sinking feeling in his gut.

Downstairs a few minutes later, he asked, "Did anyone call for me?"

"No. No one called." His mother stirred something on the stove. "Mind setting the table?"

"Sure," he said. He pulled two plates from the cabinet, then opened the drawer with the flatware.

He wouldn't call right away. He might call tomorrow.

"Mom?" he asked as he came back into the kitchen to retrieve two glasses.

"Yes?"

"Can I use the car tomorrow night?"

"Of course. Are you going to meet a friend?"

"I was thinking I'd go for pizza with Roger, if that's okay." He hoped she didn't mind if he skipped dinner with her.

"Of course it's okay. He is your best friend, after all. It must be so difficult for him with the accident and all. He was such a talented boy." She sighed and shook her head. "Such a pity that he'll never play again. And after all that his family went through with his older brother."

"Thanks, Mom." He kissed her on the cheek and she blinked in surprise. "I love you."

"I love you too, sweetheart."

John set the glasses on the table and pulled two cloth napkins from the sidebar. His mother always liked to use cloth napkins, even now that his father had been gone for several years. He wondered if she was lonely. The thought made him think of Roger again.

An hour later he was seated at the upright piano in the basement, going through some of the music he'd be playing at Interlochen, when his mother came downstairs. "Phone call," she said with a smile. "Roger." She turned around and headed up the stairs before he could say anything.

He picked up the extension in the basement, waited until he heard her hang up, then said, "Hello?"

"Hey."

"Roger. I'm really glad you called."

"I've only got a few minutes," Roger said. He sounded a bit less foggy than he had that afternoon. "Miranda's been watching me like a hawk."

"Oh. Okay."

"I just wanted to tell you that I'd like to grab a pizza tomorrow."

John relaxed with these words. "Great. I'll pick you up around six."

"Cool. Oh, and if it's okay," Roger said, "maybe I can meet you in the driveway." He didn't have to say *so Miranda won't see us.*

"Sure. That's okay." John was just as happy not to see Miranda anyhow.

"See you tomorrow."

"Right. I'll see you then." John set down the handset and stared at it for a moment. His heart thudded hard and his hands shook slightly. He went back to the piano and rested his fingers on the keys, but he didn't play. He couldn't think of anything else but tomorrow and seeing Roger.

CHAPTER *20*

THE NEXT morning Roger waited until his mother had left to go grocery shopping before taking his violin out from underneath his bed. He'd taken it out religiously every day, checking to make sure the Dampit was moist, and sliding it back inside the f-hole. The house was dry, and the rubbery snakelike device with the tiny sponge inside kept the wood from cracking. He ran a soft cloth over the surface of the instrument before setting it back in its case.

As always, he picked up each bow, tensioned it, then released the tension. This time, however, he didn't release the tension in the second bow. Instead, he pulled out the cake of rosin and ran the horsehair spanning the bow's wood over the cake until he could see the hair grab the rosin. It looked whiter when he'd finished. He knew exactly how much rosin he liked on his bow—a bit more than his teachers recommended, just enough that he could really dig into the strings and feel the vibrations in his chin.

He glanced at the clock radio by the bed. He figured he had until at least eleven thirty before his mother got back from the store. Enough time that he wouldn't be interrupted. He didn't want her to hear him play—he knew what she would think about it, and he didn't need her to comment about how he sounded. It was bad enough that she kept suggesting he sell his violin.

"It's probably worth at least fifteen thousand," she'd said the last time she brought it up. "You could use that money as a down payment on a house when you graduate."

As if. He could never sell his violin. Ever. His grandfather had bought it for him when he'd been nine years old and nearly big enough for a full-size violin. His grandfather had played viola when he was young, and he'd promised Roger he'd buy him "an old fiddle." Roger wasn't sure what the old man had meant by an old fiddle; he'd figured a fiddle was something people played around a campfire. Roger had asked his teacher about it, and Mrs. Grey had just laughed and said it was the same thing as a violin. "A bit like a nickname, really."

Roger and his grandfather had driven all the way from his grandparents' house in Youngstown to Philadelphia. He still remembered how cold it had been the day they'd gone, and the hotel they'd stayed at downtown, not far from Independence Hall. They'd gone sightseeing the next morning, then eaten lunch at a small restaurant where they stood and devoured huge Philly cheesesteak sandwiches.

They drove over to the violin shop after lunch. The building was old, covered in red brick that reminded Roger of some of the houses in the older neighborhoods near his house. The simple storefront had a sign over the doorway that read "James C. Rester, Fine Violins." He hadn't expected much, but when he and his grandfather walked inside, he was immediately struck by the heady scent of wood and varnish. Even now, the memory of the smell made him smile.

"Would you like to play one?" the salesman, a middle-aged man with wire-rimmed glasses and thinning hair, had asked as he and his grandfather walked around the room that housed all the instruments for sale.

He'd looked up at his grandfather, who nodded and smiled back at him. "Italian. Late eighteenth century, perhaps?" Richard Nelson told the salesman. "Something under ten thousand, ideally."

The salesman smiled. Roger realized later that his grandfather had been talking about the price. Ten thousand dollars was like a million to nine-year-old Roger. "I have a lovely instrument here. Leandro Bisiach. It's been sitting in a collection for the past few decades. Impeccable condition. Needs a bit of playing to mellow it out, but it's quite lovely." The salesman set a violin case on a nearby table and popped open the latches.

Roger had never seen anything so beautiful. The surface of the violin shone as if it had been recently polished, although he knew enough about violins to know that no one ever used polish on a good instrument. The warm brown of the varnish had a slightly reddish tint to it, and the fingerboard was the color of pecans.

He stood and stared, afraid to touch it, even after the salesman handed him a bow.

"Go ahead, Roger. Try playing it."

Roger swallowed and found his throat was suddenly dry. Ever so gently, he picked up the instrument and held it, feeling the weight of it. Inhaling more of the wonderful scent of the wood and varnish. He saw his grandfather smile at him as he tucked the violin under his chin. He drew the bow across the strings to tune it, and the feeling of the wood as it resonated seemed to go straight to the tips of his fingers and toes.

He played nearly half a dozen other instruments that day, but he knew there was no other violin for him. He and his grandfather drove back to Ohio, his grandfather with a smile that didn't seem to fade and Roger with the violin on his lap. When his grandfather died three years later, Roger played for the memorial service, and he'd cried in his room that night, remembering when they'd picked out the violin together. *His* violin.

"Go ahead, Roger. Play it." The words resonated in Roger's mind as he gripped the fiddle under his chin. Normally, he'd finger the notes with his left hand, but now his damaged arm hung limply at his side as he pulled the bow back and forth over the strings. He imagined he was playing the Tchaikovsky again with John at the piano, and how his fingers felt as they flew over the strings as he played one of the more treacherous runs. But that was before he'd ruined everything. When the fingers on his left hand had still moved the way they were supposed to.

Back and forth and back and forth he played the A string until he couldn't stand it anymore. He gritted his teeth and, ignoring the pain in his left arm, lifted his fingers to the fingerboard. It wasn't Tchaikovsky he played but a simple scale. Each time he pressed his fingertips down, the deep, dull ache of pain seemed to vibrate along with the instrument, up his arm to his shoulder. He hadn't taken a pain pill since last night. He wanted to feel the pain—he *needed* to feel it pulse through his body.

It was the first time he'd tried to use his damaged fingers on the violin since the accident.

The simple scale became arpeggios, and the pain shot into his chest this time. It would have been worth every second of the pain if his fingers had cooperated, but they didn't. The spaces between the notes that had been so second nature to him now felt wrong. He winced not only with each movement but with the sour-sounding pitch.

Pathetic.

He gritted his teeth and started over again, slowing down until the intonation was good to his ear. His shoulder stung. His fingers began to stiffen as he tried to pick up the pace.

"Fuck!" He set the violin back in its case and nearly dropped the bow on top of it as his entire hand cramped. He grabbed his left shoulder with his right hand and tried to massage the tension away, but it only hurt worse. "Fuck!" He didn't give a shit if the entire neighborhood heard him now. He kicked the wall and managed to dent the Sheetrock. The pain in his toes was nothing compared to the pain in his hand. He swore again as he massaged his forearm and tried to pry his fingers from his palm.

He thought of the pain pills up in the bathroom. *No. Not this time. Not this fucking time!* He reached for the violin, but his arm felt as though it was on fire, and he couldn't move. It hurt too badly. Badly enough that he had to pant to get through the pain. And all that for a fucking arpeggio that sounded like shit.

Worse than the pain, even, was the realization that he'd failed. He'd thought he'd gotten better, enough that he could try playing again. He *ached* to play again!

"Roger?" The voice came from downstairs.

Shit. His mother was home already? He took a deep breath. "Yes, Mom?"

"Are you all right? I heard a banging noise when I was coming in."

"I'm fine." He quickly brushed the rosin off the violin, loosened the bow, and locked it back in place. Not as easy to do one-handed, but his left hand hurt too much to use it.

He had just slid the violin under the bed when she came in without knocking. He'd told her a million times that she needed to knock, but he'd finally just given up. "I told you I'm fine," he said. His fingers curled tighter and he winced.

"Have you taken your pain medicine today?" she asked as the lines on her forehead deepened.

"I don't need it. It's been six months." He wouldn't tell her how much he wanted it, though. And not for the pain in his hand. He could live with that. But the knot in his gut had just gotten worse since he'd put the violin down, and he longed for something to dull his mind, help him think about something else.

"Fine," she snapped. He knew he'd made her mad, and he felt a twinge of guilt because of it. "Have it your way." She'd been angry with him ever since she'd come home the day before to find John in the living room. She turned to leave, then stopped and said, "Your dad's working late tonight, so we'll have dinner around eight."

"I'm going out."

"Out?" She narrowed her eyes and cocked her head to one side.

"Out to dinner. With John."

He heard her inhale and prepared himself for the tirade. He hurt so much already, he figured it couldn't get any worse. He was surprised when she said only, "Of course you are."

He swallowed hard.

"I'll leave the porch light on for you." She turned and walked out of the room.

Guilt. He wasn't sure that was any better than yelling. Not that he had any say in it. He scrubbed his face with his hand, took a deep breath, and sat down on his bed to do his exercises. The pain would help him stay focused.

CHAPTER 21

"HEY." ROGER climbed into the car and smiled at John. John thought he looked tired.

"Hi." John covered his discomfort by putting the car into reverse and backing out of the driveway. "I'm really glad you could come."

"Me too." He seemed to hesitate for a moment, then added, "Thanks for meeting me outside." Roger played with the seat belt after he'd fastened it, and John guessed Roger felt bad about not inviting him in.

"Look," John said, deciding that he needed to be honest with Roger and hoping Roger would be honest with him, "I know Miranda gives you a hard time about me. It's cool. I'm cool with it." He laughed. "It's not like I really want to talk to her anyhow."

"Thanks."

They stopped at a light and John realized Roger was looking at him with surprise. "What?" John asked.

"Nothing. I guess I just didn't expect you to be that in my face about Miranda's shit."

John shrugged. "We both know she hates me." Roger looked as though he was about to protest, but John continued, "It's okay. I get it." He smiled at Roger. "It's cool."

"Thanks."

A HALF hour later, tucked into a booth at the back of the pizzeria, Roger shoved half a slice of pepperoni pizza into his mouth and grinned back at John.

"You really haven't changed," John said as Roger wiped his mouth with the back of his hand. At least his eating habits hadn't.

"Sorry." Roger grinned again and picked up the napkin, then set it on his lap.

"You're not sorry, are you?" John laughed and picked up another slice.

"Nah. But it's good to hear you laugh."

John smiled. For a moment he'd forgotten how long they'd been apart. The thought made him a little queasy, so he just nibbled at the pizza.

"So you leave next week for Interlochen?"

John nodded. "Saturday," he said after he'd swallowed. "My mom's driving me up."

"That's nice of her."

"Yes." Every time he saw Miranda, he thought about how lucky he was that his mother wasn't like Roger's. "But I'm going to buy a car when I get back. I'll earn just enough this summer for a decent used one. I was thinking maybe a Datsun. They've got this cool turquoise color."

Roger laughed.

"What's so funny?" John set the slice of pizza down and frowned at him.

"Just that you'd buy a car because of the color, that's all."

"And the ones you buy look like crap."

Roger just snorted. "Yeah, but they've got balls, baby."

"Right." It felt good to joke around with Roger again.

"I'm going to buy one too. I finally convinced my parents that if I have a car, I'll visit them more often."

"Visit them?"

"Yeah. I'm getting an apartment near school."

John took a drink of his watery beer. All they'd serve nineteen-year-olds in Ohio was 3.2 percent, but John was glad for the stuff anyhow. It made him relax a little. He was pretty sure Roger was nervous too, since he kept fidgeting in his seat. "Wow. That's great!"

"Yeah. The one advantage of working at my dad's office—I've got enough money that I don't have to live at home while I go to UT."

So Roger really was going to transfer to the University of Toledo. The reality of it sank in like a lead weight, and John's face began to twitch as the smile he'd plastered on faded. He knew he needed to be supportive of Roger—the guy had been through hell—but the realization that Roger wasn't coming back to Michigan was just too overwhelming.

Roger tilted his head to one side, clearly noticing the change, and said, "It doesn't mean we can't see each other, you know."

John's heart raced to hear this. "Really? I mean, with Miranda and all—"

"I don't give a shit what she thinks."

John knew Roger was lying, but "yes" was all he said.

"I started playing again," Roger said after a pause.

"Really?" John noticed Roger didn't seem as excited about this as he sounded.

"Yeah."

"How's it going?"

"Good. Real good." Roger laughed. "Maybe good enough that I'll be able to come back to Michigan next year. My teacher says the scholarship's still good if I make it back."

"That's great."

"Yeah."

John was pretty sure Roger was lying about this too, but he wanted it to be true for so many reasons, not the least of which was that he wanted to be with Roger. His face warmed as he remembered what he'd said to Roger when he'd seen him in the hospital. Guys didn't tell each other "I love you," did they? He wished he wasn't such a dweeb!

"So I was thinking," Roger said when John remained silent. "I know it's kind of weird... I mean, with you being in Michigan and me being here. But it's only an hour by car." Roger fidgeted again and ran his good hand through his hair. "And I was wondering if you still want to... well... you know... be together?"

"Huh?" John wasn't sure he'd heard Roger correctly.

Roger laughed, and it came out a bit higher than usual. "I still want to be with you. I mean, if you're cool with it."

"I... y-yes. Of c-course I w-want to be with y-you."

Roger could have laughed at John's stuttering, but he never did. He'd told John once he knew John was telling the truth if he stuttered, and he kind of liked that. "A built-in lie-detector," Roger had called it. Instead, Roger stilled and looked directly at John, as he if was surprised. "Really?"

John could only nod.

"Hell yeah!" Roger shouted.

Some of the other patrons turned around to stare at them, but Roger ignored them. John was pretty sure his face was pink, and he was glad his back was to the other tables. Then again, he felt better than he had since Roger had left Michigan. Hopeful, for a change.

"You look pretty surprised," Roger said a few moments later.

"I... well... y-yes. I g-guess I am." John took a deep breath, then added, "I guess I figured since you never wrote back all those months—"

"Wrote *back*?" Roger frowned. "You mean you wrote to me?"

"I... y-yes." Shit! Why was he stuttering again? "L-letters. C-cards. Y-you know."

"I never got any letters. No cards either."

Miranda. John swallowed hard, then shrugged.

"Fuck her."

"Roger, maybe they got—"

"No. Don't make excuses for her. You know she intercepted them." Roger was gripping his glass so hard his knuckles were white.

"You don't know that—"

"I know *damn* well it was her." Roger clenched his jaw and pressed his lips together. "I'm going to tell her where she can take her prying."

"P-please d-don't." John spoke in a half whisper.

"The hell I won't!"

John struggled not to stutter this time. "It'll just m-make it worse."

Roger appeared to consider this. He swirled his glass of Coca-Cola around and took a long, slow breath.

John glanced around the restaurant to make sure no one could see, then reached out and put his hand atop Roger's. "You need your parents, Roger."

Roger opened his mouth as if he were going to protest, but closed it again. "Yeah. But if Miranda's just going to keep butting into my life...."

"Let her."

Roger gaped at him. "*What?*"

"Let her pry." John wasn't sure why he was saying this—he'd told himself he wouldn't say anything bad about Roger's mother—but knowing what she'd done made him angry too. "She won't find anything unless you want her to."

Roger stared at him, eyes wide, lips slightly apart. "You...," he began as a smile crept over his face.

John chewed his lower lip and nodded.

"Shit." Roger laughed. "You're a lot sneakier than you let on."

John felt the heat in his cheeks. Was he sneaky? Maybe. It felt kind of good.

"Let's get out of here," Roger said. "If I don't get to kiss you soon, I'm going to lose it."

Now John's face was on fire. He nodded dumbly as Roger set a few bills on the table and stood up.

"SO HOW do we do this?" John asked Roger an hour later as they sat in the car in the empty parking lot of an office building not far from downtown. Roger had asked John to pull over somewhere—neither of them wanted to go home yet. Besides, John's mother was home and Roger's parents would be at his place. They'd spent the last ten minutes kissing, and Roger's lips were swollen and pink. He guessed his looked the same.

"Weekends. At my place." Roger seemed to realize he was taking a lot for granted, because he added quickly, "When you can come, I mean. And I'll help pay for gas if you need."

John thought Roger appeared a little uncomfortable. He took a deep breath and reached out to touch Roger's face with a shaky hand. "It's okay," he said. "Really. We'll be together. That's what matters."

"You sure you're okay with driving?"

John nodded. "I'm sure." He'd drive to Florida if it meant being with Roger. The hour between Toledo and Ann Arbor was a breeze. "What about your parents?"

"They don't need to know. Like you said, we show them what they want to see. Maybe a letter from you saying how much you miss me, asking me to visit?"

"Sure." He could do that.

Roger smiled a sweet, genuine smile that made John shiver. Then he pulled John against him, not an easy feat since John's mother's car was a lot smaller than Roger's old car. The bucket seats didn't help either. But John barely registered the emergency brake as it dug into his hip, or how his arm bumped the steering wheel. All he could think about was how incredibly good it felt to have Roger hold him again.

CHAPTER 22

Winter 1975

ROGER WATCHED the snow fall outside the window of his apartment before glancing over at the clock. It was nearly 9:00 p.m., and John should have arrived an hour before.

"Promise me you won't come if the snow gets too bad. You know how I-23 can get," he'd told John that morning over the phone.

"I'll be fine," John had reassured him. "With the opera rehearsal schedule and Professor Menard's vocal performance class, I'd never get to see you if I waited for perfect weather."

Now, an hour after John was supposed to be here, Roger was pacing the apartment. Worrying. Imagining John's car somewhere in a ditch. Or worse.

He pulled a beer out of the fridge, popped the top, and resumed his pacing. Ten minutes later, the phone rang.

"Hello!" he practically barked into the handset.

"Roger?"

"Oh, hey, Mom." *Fuck.* "How're you doing?"

"Fine." She paused, and Roger tried to think of something to get her off the phone. If John needed to get a hold of him, he didn't want him to get a busy signal. "I'm surprised you're around on a Saturday night. You usually aren't."

"I've got an exam on Monday," he lied. "I can't talk long."

"No, of course. I wouldn't want to keep you from it." She'd been thrilled when he'd told her he planned on finishing school in three years.

He hadn't told her he planned on moving to New York, where John had already been accepted to do his master's in conducting at Juilliard.

"Thanks, Mom." Roger pushed back the curtain on the window in the kitchen with his foot—the long telephone cord didn't go quite that far. From here, he could see the parking lot. A blanket of white covered the stripes on the asphalt. No John.

"… aren't you?"

"Huh?"

"I asked if you were coming over on Monday for dinner." She sounded irritated.

"Oh, yeah. Right. Sure. I'll be there." He had to get her off the phone. "Look, Mom. I gotta get back to studying. I'll see you Monday, okay?"

"Are you sure everything is all right, dear?"

"It's great, Mom. I really need to go."

Her huff was audible through the handset. "Of course."

"Bye."

He hung up the phone before she could say anything more, and opened the drapes a bit farther. There had to be at least six inches of snow outside. He pressed his nose against the cold glass like he had when he'd been a kid, then closed his eyes. A moment later, the buzzer to the apartment sounded.

Thank God!

Roger scrambled over to the door and opened it to find a disheveled John smiling back at him. "Had to ditch the car over by the Woolworth's. Forgot my keys. The ploughs haven't made it this far yet—"

Roger grabbed John and pulled him inside. He was soaking wet, his shoulder-length hair curled at the ends, but Roger didn't care. He drew John against him, wrapped his arms around his shoulders, and just held him.

"You okay?" John's voice sounded muffled against Roger's cheek.

"I am now."

"Can I take this backpack off?" John asked with a soft laugh. "It's a little heavy."

"Oh. Shit. Sorry." Roger grabbed the pack off John's shoulders and kicked the door shut behind them.

"You were worried about me." Not a question, and the way the edges of John's mouth edged upward, Roger could tell he was teasing.

Roger was tempted to lie, but he was so relieved, he just sighed and said, "Yeah."

John stared at him in surprise. "You really *were* worried."

"Fuck, John, I—"

John kissed him. He tasted of snow and Coca-Cola. Roger closed his eyes as their tongues skirted each other in a now-familiar dance. God, he loved John! More than he could get up the nerve to admit.

For two years they'd stolen every moment they could, working around John's busy schedule and Roger's mother. Miranda suspected something. Roger was sure of it. She'd even shown up at the apartment early in the morning on the weekend. John said he was sure she was trying to catch them together. It made things a bit more difficult, but they'd worked it out. John stored his things under the bed, and the bedroom closet was big enough that he could slip inside and hide. They'd left a few pillows behind Roger's clothing, as well as a flashlight and a few books.

"Don't worry about it," John had said the first time he'd hidden there. They both knew Roger needed his parents to pay tuition—at least they hadn't threatened to stop when Roger announced he was getting his own apartment. "It's just for a little while."

Roger came back to himself and realized John was shivering. "Shit, John. You're freezing your ass off." He took John by the hand and led him into the bedroom. In the light, John's cheeks looked pink in contrast to his pale skin. Roger unzipped John's wet jacket and pushed it off his shoulders. "Stay right there," he said before stepping into the bathroom to retrieve a towel.

John smiled as Roger dried his face and hair. "Feels good. I like it when you fuss over me."

Roger's cheeks heated. "Your pants are soaked," he said in an effort to mask his embarrassment. He reached for John's belt, undid the buckle, and unbuttoned the waist of John's pants. The room was silent except for the sound of the zipper and Roger's heart pounding in his ears. His hands shook as he pulled John's pants down—he still hadn't quite moved past the sinking feeling in his gut that had lodged itself there when he'd worried something had happened to John. He could handle a lot, but the thought of losing John terrified him.

"Are you okay?" John was studying him with a strange expression.

"Yeah." *I am now.*

Roger focused on helping John step out of the cold, damp pants. He knew if he met John's gaze, everything he felt would be obvious. It wasn't just that he was embarrassed. What he felt was something he'd only begun to understand: vulnerability. The feeling you get when you realize your entire world would come to a screeching halt if the certain someone in your life were to vanish.

John shivered again.

"Get under the covers. I'll be there in a minute." Roger watched John pull the warm comforter over himself as he got undressed. He joined John underneath and skated his palms over John's cold thighs until they warmed to his touch.

"Feels good."

"You're still cold." Roger wrapped his body around John's and held him. John's skin was slightly damp against his own.

"I'm fine." John tucked his chin into the space between Roger's neck and shoulder. "Really."

Roger just held him tighter.

"Roger?"

"Hmm?"

"You okay?" John pulled away a bit and looked at him with obvious concern.

"Yeah."

"Talk to me, Roger. What's up?"

It was Roger's turn to shiver. "I told you. I was just a little worried."

"About me?" John reached for Roger's face and pulled it gently so that Roger had no choice but to look at him.

"Yeah." He didn't want to talk about this. He just wanted to hold John and reassure himself John was safe. He looked away again.

"Hey." John rolled onto his side so his face was next to Roger's. "You can tell me, you know. I'm not going to laugh or anything."

"I know." Roger hesitated another moment, then said, "It's just that I feel like an idiot."

"Worrying about me doesn't make you an idiot." John leaned in and kissed Roger's nose. "It makes me feel good."

Roger's breath stuttered. "I kept thinking back to that night... the accident. I kept imagining you in a ditch somewhere. Hurt.... Shit." He grabbed John and buried his face in his chest. "I dream about that night sometimes, except in my dreams, you're...." He clenched his jaw and blinked back tears. He'd had a lot of those dreams—nightmares, really— since John had started driving down from Ann Arbor to stay with him. He dreamed he woke up in the hospital and instead of John being all right, the doctor told him they'd done everything they could, and then he was standing in front of a headstone and he knew, he just *knew* whose headstone it was.

"I don't know what I'd do if I lost you," Roger whispered. "I'd lose my mind. I love you so fucking much, I don't know what I'd do." It took him a moment to realize what he'd just said.

John leaned over and kissed him again, this time on the lips. In the semidarkness, Roger saw John's eyes sparkle. The edges of his mouth curved upward in a tentative smile as the kiss broke. "You love me?" he asked.

Roger could only nod.

"Thank God. Because I don't know what *I'd* do if I was the only one who felt like that."

"You love me too." He said the words as though he didn't believe them.

"Always, Roger."

CHAPTER 23

Fall 1977

JOHN RAN a hand through his hair, forgetting he'd tied it back with an elastic. It had gotten so long now that it tended to flop in his face when he was bent over a score, studying it. He absentmindedly pulled the elastic out and resecured the errant strands that had fallen into his eyes, then hummed a few measures of the piece. The sounds of cars honking and people talking outside his third-floor New York walk-up faded from his awareness as he imagined the sound of the french horns and trumpets playing a slow and steady chromatic scale.

The piece was good, atonal modern music for chamber orchestra written by Serena Young, one of his Juilliard classmates. The composition had taken first place in last year's young composer competition. John had been lucky to get the composer to agree for him to conduct it, luckier still that his teacher, Roberto Pirelli, had convinced the faculty to give him some rehearsal time with the school's orchestra. It was one thing to do a good job conducting the classics. It was another to take a modern piece and show his fellow students what he was made of.

He'd been studying the damn thing every night for the past two weeks, and he still hadn't quite figured it out. He'd have to meet with Serena after fall break and ask her some questions about the score. The modern repertoire never came easily to him—he needed far more time to master new music than the more melodic works. Still, he enjoyed the challenge of it, even if he didn't enjoy the music as much.

The apartment's buzzer nearly made him jump. He hadn't been expecting anyone tonight. He wondered vaguely if his former roommate, Brian, had decided he needed a few more T-shirts over at his girlfriend's place and had forgotten his key again. Brian had moved in with Rose at the beginning of the semester, leaving John with the single bedroom and the bed instead of the pull-out couch. John had been so happy to sleep on a mattress after two months on the lumpy sofa bed that he'd nearly kissed Brian when Brian had apologized for bailing on him. But not to worry, Brian reassured him, his parents would continue to pay his half of the rent on the place as long as he and John didn't tell them about Brian's arrangement with Rose.

John walked to the kitchen and buzzed the visitor in. He didn't bother with the intercom—it had never worked, and Brian didn't want to ask the super to fix it. Something about an illegal sublease and not wanting to lose the rent control if the building's owner realized Brian's sister no longer lived in the place. John didn't worry—he doubted anyone would try to break into apartments in their crappy little building in the West Village. All the thieves were uptown where the rich people lived.

John grabbed a cigarette from the table by the front door and stuck it in his mouth, then reached for the lighter just as the doorbell rang. "Just a sec," he said as he set the lighter down and began to work the line of dead bolts and locks on the steel door. He took a drag on his cigarette as he opened the door and, in his surprise to see who was standing there, exhaled smoke in the visitor's face.

"Fucking hell." Roger waved away the smoke. "Is this how you say hello in the big city?"

John was pretty sure he'd forgotten how to speak, since neither his lips nor his tongue seemed capable of movement.

"Surprised?" asked Roger as he flashed John a grin.

"I… ah… y-yes." He was stuttering again. Only Roger could reduce him to a stuttering mess.

Roger's grin grew wider—was that even possible?—as he walked past John and into the apartment.

"R-Roger?" *Brilliant. Four months apart and that's all you can say?*

"Not who you expected?" Roger kissed John, who barely managed to set the cigarette down on an ashtray as Roger pressed him up against the wall.

"I thought you couldn't come until December," John said after he caught his breath.

"Change of plans." Roger bit his lower lip suggestively, then added, "Is that a problem?"

"Hell no!" John closed the door behind Roger and bolted the locks, then grabbed him and snaked his arms around his waist.

"You let your hair grow," Roger said after the kiss broke. He pulled the elastic out and carded his fingers through John's long hair. "I like it. Very New York."

"Thanks." Someone at school had told John long hair was trendy. He didn't really care about trendy—he'd already decided he couldn't afford regular haircuts at New York prices if it meant forgoing tickets to the Philharmonic. His scholarship covered most of his expenses, but the small stipend he received as a graduate assistant barely covered his rent, let alone the cost of food.

For the first time, John got a good look at Roger. Because of John's summer job in Europe accompanying voice students at a program in Graz, Austria, it had been four months since they'd seen each other. Roger hadn't changed much, although his hair was cut shorter than he'd worn it when they were in school together, and he'd traded in his jeans and T-shirt for chinos and a polo. He looked good.

"So how did you manage to come earlier? I thought you were starting at the petrochemical company in January. Not that I'm complaining, but...."

"I called and asked them if I could start sooner." Roger sat down on the couch, and John followed. "One more week at my parents' and I'd have killed my mother."

"That bad?"

"Worse." He ran a hand through his hair and screwed up his face. "I think Miranda found out about us. I found her poking around in the closet where I hid the letters from you."

"She went into your room?" He wasn't all that surprised, but it still pissed him off to hear it. He was sure Miranda had known about them all along, although he'd hoped she'd stay out of their business.

"I knew it was a bad idea to move home after graduation." Roger shook his head. "I should have listened to you and just stayed here until I started work. I just figured it'd be easier for us to move into our own place during your winter break."

"Don't worry about it." John put an arm around Roger's shoulders and offered him his most reassuring smile. "I'm just glad you're here."

Roger exhaled audibly. "I was kind of worried you'd be ticked off with me showing up without calling or anything." He looked a little nervous. John could count on his hand the number of times he'd seen Roger nervous. Fewer still when he'd seen Roger so obviously insecure.

"I'm not ticked off." John leaned in and brushed his lips against Roger's. "I've missed you. I never thought I'd wish I was still driving between Ann Arbor and Toledo." This time he kissed Roger, lingering longer to taste him. As he pulled away, he heard Roger's stomach rumble. "When's the last time you ate?" he asked.

Roger shrugged. "I grabbed something in Pennsylvania last night— some truck stop off the interstate. You got anything to eat?"

Of course he didn't. He'd finished the two-day-old pizza for breakfast. Other than a few beers Brian had put in the fridge at the beginning of the semester, John had nothing. "Are you up for going out?" Going out was the last thing on John's mind, but he figured there'd be plenty of time for sex after dinner. Roger was moving in with him, after all.

"Sure." Roger's stomach rumbled louder this time, and they both laughed. "As long as I can save a little room for you after."

John rolled his eyes and kissed Roger again. "What am I going to do with you?"

Roger answered with a grin.

"YOU SURE I'm dressed okay for this?" Roger asked as they exited the subway at Astor Place and headed down Eighth Street.

"You look great." John meant it too.

"Thanks. So do you."

John's face warmed at the compliment. He'd hoped Roger would notice the new clothes he bought. It didn't matter that he'd found them at a thrift store in the Village—he felt good in the slim black pants and black button-down shirt. Less like geeky John Fuchs and more like a sophisticated graduate student studying in Manhattan at a prestigious school.

"How's Juilliard?"

"Good. I'm conducting the school orchestra next month. A modern piece one of the students composed. Bleep-blop music."

"Bleep-blop?"

"Atonal stuff. All over the place. It's all the rage now. No sign of a melody anywhere." He stuffed his hands in his pants pockets and said with a grin, "I hate it."

Roger laughed. "But you'll conduct it."

"I'll conduct anything. You know me." John met Roger's eyes before looking quickly away.

"You'll do a great job with it."

"Thanks."

"You're welcome."

John pulled out a cigarette and lit it. He needed the nicotine to calm his jittery nerves. Alcohol would help too.

Roger shot him a disapproving look. "Bad habit."

"A habit you share," John pointed out before taking a long drag from the cigarette.

"I quit." Roger grinned.

"You're serious?"

"Yeah." The light changed and they waited for traffic.

"Shit." John laughed. "Knock me over with a feather. I didn't think you could give it up."

Roger snorted. "Just cigarettes," he said with an evil grin.

CHAPTER 24

ROGER WATCHED John laugh and realized with surprise that he'd changed since he'd moved to New York. John looked great. Better than Roger remembered. Not that John hadn't been good-looking before, but his clothes fit him well and the long hair was sexy, more sophisticated. He moved with more confidence, the awkwardness Roger remembered now replaced with something more along the lines of what Roger had seen when John conducted.

Still, there was something about John's new confidence that made Roger uncomfortable, even nervous. For three years they'd been together whenever they could, and it had been great. Maybe not as good as when they were together all the time, but still great. Roger's apartment near school had felt as though it was their place, and he'd been confident that they'd be great together in New York as well.

"Hey," John said, bringing Roger back to himself. "You okay?"

"I'm great." Well, he was, wasn't he? They were together, hundreds of miles away from his mother's judgment—they'd be fine. This was New York, for shit's sake! Two men together wasn't a freak fest here.

"Good." A few strands of hair fell into John's eyes, and Roger reached out to brush them away. Why had he decided eating needed to take precedence over sex again?

"Why are you grinning?" John asked.

Roger hadn't even realized he was. "Thinking about dessert," he said as he licked his lips.

John blushed. Seeing that made Roger feel better. Maybe John hadn't changed as much as he figured.

THE RESTAURANT bar was upscale. Old. As if it had been here forever. Maybe it had. Roger had expected something along the lines of the hole-in-the-wall place where they'd hung out their first year in Ann Arbor, dark and dingy. Allegro was anything but.

A sunken mahogany bar stretched from the front of the building nearly to the back. Bartenders stood at eye level with customers seated on red-leather-covered stools. The array of bottles set against a mirrored wall was impressive, and dense smoke from cigarettes filled the air. Banquettes with leather-covered seats and backs, the leather made dark from use and smoke, made up the seating area to the left of the bar. The high tin ceiling above was painted black, the embossed surface still visible. Copies of Italian impressionist paintings hung on the dark damask walls, and teardrop pendants hung on long cords, barely illuminating the tables. "Cherchez la Femme" by Dr. Buzzard's Original Savannah Band played in the background.

Roger saw nothing but men at the bar. He glanced over at John, and John smiled. "Gay bar," John said.

They'd heard of a gay bar in Toledo, but they'd been too afraid to be seen together to go. Roger felt a sudden sense of elation when he realized nobody knew him here, and even if they did, they probably wouldn't care anyhow. "Cool."

John waved to the two men seated at the end of the bar as he led Roger over. Both men were dressed in black like John. One had a short, spiky haircut dyed red at the ends. The other wore his hair like John's, tied back with an elastic. Roger felt underdressed. Preppy amidst a sea of New York chic. Except the waiters and bartenders: they were all wearing khakis and polo shirts.

"Hot date?" the guy with the spiky hair asked.

"Jim"—John blushed as he spoke—"this is my good friend Roger Nelson. Roger, this is Jim Riker and Cal Venezzi." Roger noticed John ignored the date comment outright.

"Good to meet you, Roger." Jim smiled up at Roger and offered his hand.

"Hey, Rog," Cal added before taking another swig of his beer. Imported beer. Roger wanted to tell the guy his name was Roger, not

"Rog," but he restrained himself. These were John's friends, after all, and he could make nice. At least for now.

"What can I get you gentlemen?" the bartender asked.

"I'll have a Heineken. Roger?"

"Same." Roger settled onto a stool next to John. He hoped he'd like Heineken. He'd really wanted a Bud.

"So, Rog," Cal began, "you're the boyfriend?"

Hearing the nickname again irritated the hell out of Roger, but he let it go once again. Still, he liked the fact that John had told his friends about them, even though he trusted John not to see other men. It felt really good that people knew about them and didn't care that they were both men.

"Yes." Roger liked admitting it too. He did his best not to react to the obvious pleasure on John's face. It wasn't so much that he didn't want John to see his reaction, but he knew he needed to keep a cool head.

"We've been together since high school," John added.

"Really? How cute."

Cute? Roger was going to have to keep himself from strangling Cal. The guy was really pissing him off.

"Roger's a violinist," John offered.

Roger's stomach roiled. "Was a violinist." He hadn't gotten used to saying that.

John appeared immediately remorseful, as if he'd just realized he'd said the wrong thing. "Shit. I'm sorry," he said in a low voice as he reached out to touch Roger's forearm.

Roger smiled reassuringly. "It's okay. The past is the past." *Except when it doesn't leave you alone.* He remembered the last time he'd tried to play, a week before. He'd barely been able to get through his usual warm-ups without his fingers stiffening up. He'd almost left the violin at home when he'd set off for New York. What the hell good was a beautiful fiddle like that when the best he could handle was the simplest scale?

"Cal's a violinist too," Jim put in.

Figures.

"We're going to get a table." John frowned and appeared slightly irritated.

"We'll join you," Cal said. "I'm hungry, anyhow."

"Maybe another time, Cal." John was polite but firm. Another surprise. The shy kid was taking charge? "I think we need a little time alone. We haven't seen each other in forever."

Cal frowned into his beer, but Jim smiled and said, "That's cool, man. Good meeting you, Roger. See you around."

"You too, Jim."

When they were seated at a table a few minutes later, the farthest away from the bar they could find, John smiled uncomfortably and said, "Sorry about Cal. He's an ass. I should have realized taking you here was a mistake. And bringing up the violin... shit, Roger. That was totally insensitive of me."

"Can't escape the truth." Roger ran a hand through his hair and immediately regretted it when his hand came away feeling slightly sticky. He hated the gel shit, but he'd gotten into the habit of using it to tame his multiple cowlicks. His mother had told him it looked better for work.

John said nothing but looked down at his beer.

"So what's up with your folks? You said something about your dad moving to Florida and a girlfriend?" Roger figured changing the topic might help.

"My dad moved in July. He's marrying the girlfriend. She's a year older than I am." John said this in an offhanded way, as if he didn't care, but Roger could tell it bothered him more than he'd admit. "Mom just got a promotion to office manager."

"Good for her. How's she dealing with the whole remarriage thing?"

John shrugged. "We don't talk about it. I wasn't invited to the wedding, so I don't know much more."

"Seriously?" Roger couldn't imagine John's father not inviting his only son to his wedding.

"You know how he had a shit fit when I came out to him last year." John took another long drag of his cigarette. "If he can't talk to me without calling me every epithet in the book, screw him."

"Can't blame you."

"I don't want the bullshit anymore. You know, the stupid questions about when I'm going to settle down. Getting fixed up on dates with women. Maybe it's living here in the city." John shrugged. "I don't know. Nobody at school gives a crap who I date. I figured if my dad couldn't deal with it, then fuck him."

"Wow." Roger flagged down the waiter, who took their orders, then disappeared into the growing sea of people.

"I'm lucky my mom's cool with it. She doesn't talk about it much, but she told me she's proud of me and she loves me. She said she thinks she always knew." He smiled at Roger. "And she likes you."

John crossed his long legs and held his cigarette a bit like a starlet in the movies. He wore a single diamond stud in his left ear—when had he gotten that?—and the way he pushed his long hair from his eyes as he spoke reminded Roger of some of the girls he'd dated. Roger realized he liked this more effeminate John. It seemed right somehow, as if John had tried to be someone he wasn't all those years and had finally figured it out. John seemed less awkward too, more in rhythm with his own body.

"So tell me more about your mom," John asked as he mashed the cigarette into the ashtray. "Why do you think she knows about us?"

Roger hesitated. "She's been acting weird." He laughed, then added, "Weirder than usual. I guess she heard it through the grapevine that you were living in New York. I told her I was moving to New York and that I'd probably stay with you until I got my own place, and she got suspicious. Sometimes I wonder if she figured out you and I were still seeing each other. She started to ask me questions about you."

"What kind of questions?"

"It doesn't matter," Roger said after a moment or two. He tapped his foot against the leg of his chair and tried to think of how to avoid upsetting John. He wouldn't repeat what Miranda had said about him.

"I can handle the truth, you know." John's voice was calm, but Roger noticed how his eyes shifted from his glass, to the table, to the bar, and then back to his glass again.

"She just asked questions about what you were doing.... Why I couldn't stay with someone else." He didn't add that she'd reminded him how appearances were really important when you had a prestigious job, and that accountants were supposed to be "upstanding citizens." The implication that John was something less than upstanding really pissed him off.

"Sounds like she knows about me." John's words were matter-of-fact, but Roger heard the undercurrent of deep resignation.

"It isn't your fault," Roger blurted out. "That I'm—" He nearly said "gay," but he thought better of it. "—with you. I'm with you because I want to be."

"I know she thinks it's my fault. About the accident." John picked up one of the remaining hot wings and studied it intently.

"Stop." Roger hated it when John blamed himself, mostly because he knew the accident had been his own damn stupidity.

"It's okay. I know it's not anyone's fault. I'm sure it was hard for your mother when your brother died. I can understand why she's so protective of you."

"Yeah." Roger wondered vaguely if his parents had talked to John after the accident. He'd wondered a lot of things after the accident, like why John hadn't come to the hospital if he hadn't been angry, and why Miranda had hinted around that John's mother hadn't wanted them to see each other when she'd been cool with John being gay and had suspected it before he'd even told her. Then again, it wasn't as if he'd been with it most of the time after the accident.

The waiter brought another round of drinks. Roger took a long pull of his beer—Heineken wasn't half-bad—and took a long breath. Then, tentatively at first, he reached out and took John's hand across the table. It felt both strange and wonderful that he could do that. Nobody seemed to care.

"I need to use the bathroom."

Roger nearly laughed. "Now?"

"I should have just ordered us takeout." John's face was flushed, and Roger realized John was trying to get him alone.

"I need to go too," Roger said as he repressed a grin.

ROGER HELD the bathroom door open for John, who walked inside without saying a word. Roger turned John around, pushed him up against the door, and pinned him there with a kiss.

"Roger," John gasped as their mouths parted.

Roger bolted the lock.

"Christ, Roger," John said between gasps.

"Want me to stop?"

If he listened to his body, he'd have already unbuttoned Roger's pants. But his mind—God, his mind was telling him to stop. They should go back to the apartment. Use the bed. "I... I... no."

Roger's only response was to press his lips to John's neck as he began to work open the buttons of John's shirt.

Roger licked a line from John's neck down to the exposed skin of his chest to find one of John's nipples. John arched his back to meet Roger's mouth, then hissed his response as Roger took his nipple between his teeth and pulled and sucked until it hardened.

He carded his fingers through Roger's wavy hair, separating the strands. The controlled waves yielded to the familiar tousled curls John had loved when they were kids. They suited Roger. Still suited him.

John slid his hands under Roger's shirt, feeling the coarse hair of his chest and pausing there. Roger was no longer the college kid whose body hinted at manhood. In the past few years, he'd changed. Funny, how they'd been together for more than five years, but he'd never really noticed it until now. John ached to be naked in Roger's arms, to explore Roger's body and take his time doing it. When he'd been commuting from Ann Arbor, their time together had always felt rushed.

John glided his fingertips over Roger's belly and downward until he met the cool metal of the top button of Roger's pants. His hands shook as he undid Roger's fly and pushed the pants over his hips.

There was a loud knock on the door.

"Busy," Roger said as he grinned at John, who had gotten to his knees and was mouthing Roger's erection through the cotton fabric of his underwear.

Another knock. For the first time, John noticed the grimy tile on the floor and the hint of urine on the air. He stood up and reached for Roger's face. "Let's go back to my place." He didn't want their first time in New York to be here. This was supposed to be a new start for them, the end of their long-distance relationship and the beginning of something more stable.

Roger nodded. John pulled Roger's face to his, brushed his thumbs over the slightly rough stubble of Roger's chin and then his lips. "God, I missed you!"

CHAPTER 25

THEY TOOK a taxi back to the apartment, Roger firmly holding John's hand out of sight of the driver. "Roommate?" Roger asked as they climbed the stairs.

"Still living with his girlfriend."

"Good." Roger grinned.

John set the keys on the front table and led Roger back to his bedroom. The light from the streetlamps and buildings was enough for him to see but not so much that it intruded upon the dreamlike quality of the moment. John allowed Roger to undress him, shivering not from cold but from the mixture of embarrassment and pleasure he felt as Roger's gaze raked over his body. John didn't expect Roger to express his pleasure; he didn't need to. He knew Roger well enough to see it in the way his lips parted and in the quickening of his breaths.

Roger pushed John against the end of the bed and eased him down on the comforter. John felt vulnerable, naked when Roger was still fully dressed, but he realized he liked it. He loved the way he stopped thinking and just *felt* when he was with Roger, and how he knew he belonged in Roger's arms.

"You're beautiful, you know." Roger straddled him and kissed his lips, then feathered kisses downward.

"Women are beautiful."

"So are you." Undeterred, Roger nipped and sucked at the base of John's neck. "I like that about you."

John knew he was blushing, though he hoped Roger hadn't noticed. Roger licked a circle around one of his nipples, and John sighed like he imagined a teenage girl might at her first kiss. Roger combed fingers through John's long hair and pulled on it just enough that John moaned. "Roger... God.... Please...."

"Please what?" Roger was clearly enjoying torturing him. Not that John was complaining.

"Shut up and fuck me, Roger. Because if you keep talking about it, I'm going to lose my mind."

Roger laughed.

"Lube's between the mattress and the box spring," John told him. When Roger shot him a quizzical look, John said, "Where else am I supposed to put it? The kitchen? I don't have a nightstand."

Roger reached under the mattress and slid his hand around, holding the lube up triumphantly a moment later.

"And I thought I was the nerd," John said as he looked up at Roger. Roger just grinned, then dropped the lube on the bed and bent over John to take his cock in his mouth. "Not fair."

Roger hummed happily.

"So not fair."

This time Roger swallowed John to the root and cupped his balls. John could only manage a strangled moan. "Roger. Oh fuck. So good."

Roger stopped for a moment, then looked up at him. "I want to make you come," he said as he pulled off his shirt and began to undo his pants. "I want to taste you."

"Yes. Please."

"So fucking polite." Roger laughed as he stepped out of his pants.

John watched and chewed on his lower lip.

"So," Roger drawled, "let's see. Where was I?"

"Making me come with your mouth." John watched as his words achieved their intended effect.

Roger climbed back on top of him and licked his way down his belly to the curls at the base of his slightly flagging erection. "Needs some help," he rumbled before he began to lick his way around John's tip. Then he ran his teeth gently over the same spot. He swallowed John again, and as he sucked, he reached up and rolled John's nipples between his fingers.

"Roger. God, Roger."

Roger trailed a finger down John's chest, then slipped it between John's ass cheeks and rubbed it over his opening. John heard Roger open the top on the lube, and the next thing he felt was Roger's finger pressing inside.

"That's it. Stretch me." John loved telling Roger what to do to him, and he knew Roger loved it even more. "Work me open."

Roger let up the pressure on John's cock while he slipped his finger inside until it was knuckle-deep inside John, and gently worked it around. John caught Roger's eye, then bit his lower lip and nodded.

"Feels great. Better than great." He took a deep breath and fought back the orgasm building at the base of his spine.

"What do you want me to do now?" Roger said as he paused, looked up at John, and licked his lips. "Come on. Tell me."

John groaned and closed his eyes. "Shit. Put another finger in. Open me up."

The burn as Roger slipped his second finger inside was amazing, the sharp tang of it yielding to pleasure. John opened his legs wider and Roger sucked harder while he pushed and pulled with his fingers. "Please," John whimpered. "Give me one more. Because after I come"—he struggled to hold back—"I want you inside of me."

Roger added a third finger to the others, and this time, as he pushed inward, he brushed the place inside that made John lose any coherent thought. "I can't…. Oh, fucking hell!" He arched his hips toward Roger's mouth and came hard, shuddering and falling back onto the bed. Roger just laughed and licked his lips, then rolled onto the bed next to John.

"Good?" Roger asked with an expression that told John he knew it was the best orgasm John had experienced in a long time. John was too far gone to call him on it. "So now what?"

"Now I make *you* beg for it," John said as he climbed onto Roger's thighs and stroked Roger's cock until it was hard. The pathetic sound that escaped Roger's lips as John slicked him up and positioned himself over Roger made John shiver. Knowing he could give Roger something that Roger wanted so badly made him feel good. Wanted. Sexy. He pressed down onto Roger's tip, and Roger's throaty moan echoed through the bedroom.

"John. God. Please…." Without the pretense and the snark, Roger was so beautifully vulnerable. Honest. Like the Roger John had seen when they were kids, just goofing around.

He gritted his teeth as he slowly impaled himself on Roger, never taking his eyes off Roger's face, wanting to know everything he was feeling. He ignored the burn and opened himself to Roger, body and soul.

"John. You feel amazing. Fucking... amazing." Roger looked into John's eyes, as if he'd finally found the courage to reveal the rest of himself. For just a moment, John was sure none of this was a mistake—that there was a future for the two of them, together like this.

Roger ran his hands over John's chest until John leaned over to kiss him. "Come for me, Roger," John said by Roger's ear. "I want to hear you come. I want to see it."

"So... fucking... amazing... John...." Roger's body tensed as he cried out his release and wrapped his arms around John's back so that they were chest-to-chest. "God," Roger whispered against John's ear. "I love you so much."

John closed his eyes, his muscles protesting, his body clenched around Roger's. Hearing Roger speak the words left him more breathless than the orgasm had. He'd missed hearing Roger say it when they'd been apart.

"I love you too." John was half-hard again, but he didn't need more sex. He just needed Roger.

CHAPTER *26*

One week later

"KATHERINE, RICK, Becky, this is my best friend, Roger," John said as they joined a group of people by the window of the SoHo loft.

Roger smiled and held up his drink. "Good to meet you." He was glad he'd downed a gin and tonic as soon as they'd arrived at the party. He felt incredibly uncomfortable meeting John's friends at all, let alone in large groups. Even worse, the party was being held at the apartment of one of John's professors and was far more sophisticated than the frat parties and let's-drink-beer-and-watch-football get-togethers Roger was used to in Toledo. At least he'd had the presence of mind to wear a black T-shirt with his jeans. He wouldn't make the mistake of wearing khakis and a polo again in Manhattan, at least not in any social settings.

Roger's second drink loosened his shoulders and neck a bit, and he began to ease into the conversation. At least this one wasn't about music. Not that New York mayoral politics were even on his radar screen, but it was more comfortable than hearing about who was playing where and with whom.

"So how long have you known John?" Katherine asked as John and the others continued to debate to one side. She smiled at him, and Roger tried to focus on how bright blue her eyes were instead of how her breasts nearly popped out of her corset and how the cameo she wore on a ribbon around her neck emphasized the curve of her shoulders.

"Since high school." He finished his drink in one long swallow and found the courage to smile at her. This wasn't really much different than high school. He'd done okay talking to girls then, hadn't he? Not that the sex had thrilled him—sex before John was just plain vanilla—but he liked looking at women.

"Really?" She laughed and brushed her long hair off one shoulder. Roger caught the scent of patchouli on the air. "What was he like in high school?"

Roger debated how much to tell her. "I don't know... I guess kind of what he's like now, except less cool?"

They talked for a few more minutes. At least she played oboe and not violin. If Roger had to talk music, it was a lot easier if it didn't involve anything having to do with the violin. She asked him about his new job, and he was surprised she didn't seem to care that he wasn't a musician. He relaxed a bit more and realized with some surprise that he was actually enjoying the conversation.

After a few more minutes, she put her hand on his forearm, then leaned in and asked in a conspiratorial whisper, "So are you and John... together?"

He should have expected the question. "I... well... yeah, I guess."

She laughed again and moved closer, her hand still on his arm. "I wondered, you know. I heard one of the violists say John was homosexual, but you just never know."

Roger swallowed hard and wished he had another drink.

Perhaps sensing his discomfort, Katherine said, "It's perfectly fine with me, you know. I mean—" She stepped back and gave him a look of appraisal that took him in from head to toe. "—you're a very attractive man. I can guess what he sees in you. I'm just sorry you play for the other team."

He was just about to tell her he didn't really play for any team, but Cal, whom Roger had been avoiding most of the evening, took the opportunity to join them before Roger could respond. "Katherine, you look lovely tonight," Cal drawled. "I see you've met Rog." Cal gave Roger a knowing look that made Roger feel guilty even though he wasn't exactly sure why.

"My name's not—"

"Roger and John are getting an apartment together," Cal said. "Isn't that wonderful?"

"Yes, of course." Katherine's expression said otherwise. "Look, I'd better say hello to Professor Rothstein. Thank him for the party." She offered Roger a sympathetic smile, and Roger guessed she was trying to get away from Cal but didn't know how to include Roger in her escape plan. She reached into her pocket and pulled out a piece of paper. "I made some cards up. I do some calligraphy to make extra money," she added, as if having a business card was a strange thing. "Give me a call sometime and we can have coffee together or something. I'd be happy to show you around the city."

Roger took the handmade card and shoved it into his back pocket. "Great meeting you," he said as she walked away.

"I really must be going too," Cal said a moment later, to Roger's great relief. "See you around! Cheerio!"

Cheerio? Roger watched Cal leave, then went to snag another drink and find John.

JOHN WATCHED Roger and Katherine talking out of the corner of his eye and tried to ignore the pang of jealousy he felt when she put her hand on Roger's arm. He'd barely been following the discussion about the fall primary elections. He told himself Roger was just being friendly, but there was something about the way Roger looked at Katherine that reminded him of the girls Roger had dated in high school. Or Elizabeth, in college.

Stop it! You know he's not interested. Roger had come to New York early to be with him. They loved each other, and even though Roger's mother was a piece of work, John knew Roger wanted to be with him.

Katherine's musical laughter rose over the din of conversation, and John felt sick to his stomach. He'd get another drink. He didn't need to let his overactive imagination get the best of him. He politely excused himself, then headed over to the drink table.

"Rum and Coke, please," he told the bartender. He made a mental note to thank Professor Rothstein for the party—he'd obviously gone to some expense to have hired someone to tend bar, not to mention to purchase the large selection of alcohol. When Rick had told him the professor's fall party was the highlight of the school year, he'd been right.

"Having a good time?" Cal asked as John waited for his drink.

"Yes. It's a great party."

"Roger seems to be having fun, doesn't he?" Cal looked toward where Roger and Katherine stood. Her face was very close to Roger's. Any closer and she'd be kissing him.

"We both are," John said. He took a long drink and fought the urge to interrupt Roger and Katherine's literal tête-à-tête. "You?"

"I'm having a marvelous time." Cal put his arm around John's shoulders and smiled back at him.

On the other side of the room, Katherine laughed again.

"Excuse me, Cal," John said as he did his best not to storm over and tell Katherine to leave Roger alone.

"Of course. See you later, John."

John glanced once more at Roger and Katherine, then took off down the hallway to find the bathroom.

Back at the apartment a few hours later, John lay in bed, staring at the stars through the nearby buildings. Roger encircled John's waist and pressed his lips to John's back.

"Something bugging you?" Roger asked.

"Me? No, why?"

"I don't know. You just seem a little tense, that's all." Roger kissed John's back again, and John let his body relax a bit.

"I'm fine." Well, he was, wasn't he? Roger was here, with him. He wasn't with Katherine. In fact, when he'd found Roger after spending a few minutes in the bathroom convincing himself he had nothing to be jealous of, Roger had been looking for him. Alone.

"Good." This time Roger nipped at the skin and John sighed. "Because I'm horny as all get-out, and I'm hoping you'll let me fuck you into the sheets."

John laughed. "I can handle that."

"You think you can?" Roger nipped again, causing John to hiss in response. "'Cause I can get a little demanding when I get horny, you know."

"I can take it. Hit me with all you've got."

Roger's response was to dive beneath the sheets and start sucking John.

John moaned and closed his eyes. *You have nothing to be jealous of,* he told himself. *Nothing at all.* And for a brief moment, at least, he believed it.

THE NEXT morning Roger waited until John left for school before he pulled his violin out from the hall closet. It wasn't a secret that he'd brought it with him to New York—Roger wouldn't go anywhere without his fiddle—but he only practiced when John wasn't around. He guessed John knew he played, but if John thought it was strange that Roger didn't play when he was around, he never mentioned it.

Why the hell had he told Cal he still played? No one in their right mind would call what Roger did in the privacy of John's apartment "playing." Scratching, maybe, the sound of claws against metal Roofster made when he wanted to get back inside. This wasn't playing.

Cal had asked Roger to play some duets with him. As if. Roger wasn't sure if Cal was doing it to yank his chain or if he was actually serious about it. Knowing Cal, it was all about watching Roger squirm.

"You seem a little distracted," John had said the night before. "You okay?"

"Fine," he'd said a bit too quickly. "Just tired." He doubted John believed him—it wasn't as if he did anything that would make him tired. He'd taken the train out to Jersey to fill out paperwork for the new job. He'd hoped he could start a little earlier, but they were moving the corporate offices to Newark in December, and the HR lady had told him there weren't any free offices.

He'd just finished warming up when the phone rang. He set his violin in its case and picked up the receiver. John had said he'd call if he finished early at school. Roger was hoping he would—they'd talked about taking the ferry to Liberty Island. Weekdays were less crowded.

"Hello?"

"Roger?"

Shit. He shouldn't have given his mother John's number. "Hi, Mom."

He must have sounded irritated, because she asked, "Am I interrupting something?"

"Nah. Nothing."

"What were you doing?" she pressed. Damn, but she could be a pain in the ass sometimes.

"Just playing a little." Another mistake. He should have just made something up.

"Violin? Why on earth would you do that?"

Something about how she said the word made him cringe inwardly. He wanted to say something about how he was playing with John, but knew it would make things a hundred times worse. "No idea."

"I don't understand why you insist on playing that—"

"Was there something you wanted to talk about?" he asked, not caring if she got angry with him for interrupting her. "Because I'm heading out in a few minutes."

"Oh. I'll try to make it brief, then." Her voice resonated with hurt, and he felt the familiar buzz of guilt resurface. Why was it that the only way he could get past the guilt was to be angry at her?

"Okay. Thanks."

"Your father's going into the hospital for a procedure tomorrow. I just wanted you to know."

"Tomorrow?" There was no way he could get back to Toledo by tomorrow, and she knew it. "Is it an emergency? Is he okay?"

"He's fine, dear. It's nothing serious. A hernia that needs to be repaired. He'll stay overnight, but if everything goes well, he'll be home the next day."

"Oh. That's good."

"I'm sure he'd appreciate your calling to talk to him in the hospital," she said. "Or maybe a card."

"Sure, Mom. I'll call him." He wrote down the main number for the hospital and set the scrap of paper aside.

"Good."

He waited, expecting her to say more, but when she didn't, he said, "It's great talking to you, Mom. Thanks for letting me know about Dad."

Five minutes later, having stuck the phone number on the fridge with a magnet, he picked his violin and bow up once more and played a few more scales. Out of the corner of his eye, he saw the score for the Tchaikovsky Violin Concerto poking out from underneath the stack of music. He tried to ignore it, instead returning to some arpeggios and then working his way up to a simple étude he'd played when he'd first started studying music. At least that wasn't a disaster.

After about an hour, he headed to the kitchen for a glass of water. He'd meant to play a few more simple pieces, but the draw of the Tchaikovsky was just too strong. He took a deep breath and set the music on the rickety folding stand he'd set up by the window.

He wasn't such a dreamer that he thought he could handle the last movement—his favorite movement—a bright, energetic, technically challenging allegro he'd practiced until his fingers had ached. No, he knew that was far beyond anything his fingers could handle. But the first movement… maybe he could handle the beginning with its sweet and haunting melodic line.

He tuned his fiddle again, then studied the notes for a full minute. He didn't need to study them—he knew every one of them, every nuance, every sweet phrase of the music by heart.

Heart. He'd once imagined this piece was a bit of his heart that he'd held out for others to share. And when he'd played it in the practice room, he'd played his love for John. He was pretty sure John had heard it too.

I can do this. He'd repeated the words over the years since the accident. If he could just convince himself he could play, the pain in his hand and shoulder would vanish. But every time he tried, it was the same. Pain, accompanied by the realization that the music in his soul couldn't be heard through his damaged body.

No. This time would be different. He had his whole life ahead of him. He had John. It would take time until his playing would be refined enough for him to audition for a new teacher and a school, but he would do it. He only needed to believe he could.

He imagined John at the piano and began to play….

JOHN WALKED into the apartment a little after seven. The rehearsal had gone far longer than expected, so he'd called Roger to let him know he'd be late. Roger hadn't answered. He figured Roger had gone out. They'd talked about the Metropolitan Museum of Art's new exhibition of Italian painters, and Roger had mentioned he might go.

The apartment door opened onto darkness. John flicked on the light in the hallway and deposited the mail on the front table. Most of it was for

Brian, but there was also a check for some studio work John had done the month before. They'd have dinner at the new Indian restaurant down the street when Roger got back.

He turned on the kitchen light and looked around for a note. There was none. Strange. Roger usually let him know if he was going out so John would know when to expect him back. It wasn't a problem. Classes tomorrow started at eleven, and he didn't need to be back early. They could go out when Roger got back.

He dropped his backpack on the kitchen table and headed through the living room toward the bedroom. He nearly jumped when he noticed Roger seated on the couch, just staring out the window at the firehouse across the street.

"Shit," he said. "I didn't see you there."

Roger's smile was forced, his expression unreadable in the darkness. "Sorry."

John sat down next to Roger. "Something wrong?" he asked.

"Nah. Nothing."

"So nothing has you sitting in the dark staring into space?" He said it half-jokingly, hoping to give Roger an out.

"Yeah."

"Roger," John said, "if something's bothering you, you need to tell me about it. If I've done something—"

"You haven't done anything."

At least they were getting somewhere. "Then what's up?"

"Nothing important. I'm just a little tired, I guess." Roger had been saying that on and off for a while now. "Ready to start working. I guess I've got a little cabin fever."

John put his arm around Roger and pulled him close. "I'll get done sooner tomorrow. Promise."

"It's not about that," Roger said. He pulled away from John as he spoke, then stood up and walked across the room. "It's nothing you need to worry about."

"Roger…."

"Please, John. It's my own shit. I promise it's nothing you've done. I just need to work it out."

"Sometimes talking about stuff helps."

"You know I talk to you," Roger answered. "But this isn't something you can help with."

John didn't know. Other than Roger's mother, Roger rarely talked about anything other than easy, comfortable stuff. At least nothing having to do with himself.

"I really think—"

"I told you," Roger snapped, "it's nothing to do with you. Let it go."

John realized his mouth was hanging open. Roger had never raised his voice to him before, and it stung. He needed to get away from Roger before this turned into a real argument.

"I n-need to w-wash up." Lord knew his parents' fights had never gone well. The last thing John needed was to get into something with Roger, especially since he was beginning to get irritated with Roger. Maybe it was that they'd really never lived together before, or maybe it was just that Roger was getting used to living in New York. Whatever it was, it made John really nervous.

CHAPTER 27

One month later

"MORNING."

John opened his eyes to see Roger grinning down at him. "This is a first. You're up before me."

"Couldn't sleep. Besides, I want to get out. See Vienna."

"I still can't believe you came with me." John wouldn't have admitted it to Roger—he didn't want Roger to worry about him—but John had been really nervous about this conducting gig, and having him here helped. He rolled onto his side and kissed Roger. "Thanks."

"Like I wouldn't have."

The airfare to Austria hadn't been cheap, but Roger had told John his signing bonus was coming when he started his new job in a few months, and he'd saved up enough money to cover it by working summers at his dad's office. Coming with him to Europe was about the most romantic thing John could imagine. And even though it was really a working trip for John—his first European job—John had come to think of it as their first real vacation together. More so because Roger had seemed increasingly restless in New York, and John hoped the change of scenery would do him some good.

"THIS IS amazing," Roger said a few hours later as they rode the Wiener Riesenrad and drank coffee at a table inside the Ferris wheel's large cabin. "I'd never have figured they'd have a restaurant inside of one of these things."

"I thought you'd like it. You should see the fancy cabins. You can do a candlelight dinner. I hear the food's pretty good too."

"Then we'll come back again. When we have more money to blow. I wonder if you can dance in these things." Roger's eyes sparkled, and John couldn't help but fall in love with him more.

"I'd like that." Funny, John thought, that he'd hated it when kids in grade school had called him a princess, but now he felt a little like one and he didn't give a damn.

"So I'm thinking of starting my own business," Roger said. He looked uncomfortable, as if he'd realized how romantic he was being. Roger always said he wasn't a romantic, although John thought the only one Roger was fooling was himself. John didn't push the issue today—he was having far too much fun.

"Really? What kind of business?"

"No idea."

"That's my Roger."

"*Your* Roger?" Roger had that look on his face that John knew meant he was in so deep there was no way to wiggle out.

"Come on," John said, ignoring the jab, "you must have some idea of what kind of a business you want to start?"

"Nope." Roger grinned and ate a bit of his Sachertorte.

"What about something with computers? They say that's where the money is going to be."

"Nah. Not my thing. Too dry. And I get enough numbers in my day job already."

John shook his head. "You can't start a business if you have no idea what you want to do."

"So what do you suggest, Maestro Fuchs?"

"Open a violin studio." John met Roger's gaze and didn't blink.

"Violin?" Roger tapped his fork against his plate and shifted in his seat. "No. I couldn't do that. I mean, who would want me to teach them?"

"More people than you think. You're a good teacher. You helped me with math. What's so different about teaching violin?"

Roger didn't answer but looked out the cabin window and ran a hand through his already tousled hair. John wouldn't push the issue.

"So how was rehearsal this morning?" Roger asked, as if suddenly conscious that he had avoided John's question.

"Good. The players are excellent and the church's acoustics are wonderful." He didn't add that he'd been a nervous wreck anticipating the rehearsal and even more so when he realized he was half the age of some of the musicians.

"So what do we do next?" Roger seemed once again uncomfortable, and John began to wonder if he was avoiding discussing music in general.

"I thought we might take a walk through the gardens at the Schloss Schönbrunn, then have a late dinner."

"The palace? Sure." He pulled out the dog-eared guidebook they'd found at a Manhattan thrift shop and paged through it. "There's a maze and labyrinth that sounds cool. And some fake Roman ruins."

"Fake?"

Roger nodded. "Yep. At least that's what this says. 'Built in 1778 to resemble Roman ruins, the architectural structure was designed by Johann Ferdinand Hetzendorf von Hohenberg and is representative of the Romantic movement,'" Roger read with a really lousy German accent.

John chuckled. "So they built something to look run-down on purpose."

"Yep." Roger grinned. "Of course, it says that the structure is also meant to be incorporated into the gardens themselves."

"Like a distressed pair of jeans."

"Something like that."

BACK AT the hotel that evening, John stroked Roger's hair as they dozed on the bed after sex.

"Why do the bathrooms have to be down the hall?" Roger asked.

"Because it's a cheap hotel." John kissed Roger's head and smiled. "It's only about fifty feet away, you know."

"That's a long way to go when it means getting up and putting on sweats."

"Might have thought of that before, you know." John kissed Roger again.

"You mean before I finished that second bottle of wine?"

"Or before you got naked."

"Can you blame me for getting naked?" Roger looked up at John and batted his eyes.

"After hanging out with me all day, I'm surprised you didn't get naked in the hallway." John chewed his lower lip suggestively and snaked a hand beneath the sheets to find Roger's reawakening cock.

"Fuck. I really need to piss."

John shook his head and chuckled. "Have I ever told you what a romantic you are?"

"No."

"My point exactly. So make up your mind, Nelson. Sex or the WC. What'll it be?"

Roger's answer was a pathetic moan.

CHAPTER 28

THE SMALL church was filled to capacity. Roger had been amazed at the beauty of the place the moment he'd walked inside. The simple exterior, painted in an understated cream, opened onto a riot of brightly colored frescos that seemed to bloom at the apse, right behind where the orchestra was seated. Some of the woodwork that edged the wooden seats in the chancel was gilded, and the gold appeared to shimmer in the early afternoon sunlight from the high stained glass windows.

Roger and John had arrived almost two hours before the performance. Roger had guessed John was nervous and needed time alone to prepare. He hadn't let Roger come to the rehearsals; he hadn't wanted him to hear the music as a work in progress. Roger hadn't minded. He'd understood that his presence in Vienna was a distraction. He was just happy John had wanted him to come anyhow. Even now, as he sat in the back of the church, where John claimed the acoustics were best, Roger didn't mind the long wait. If it meant waiting a day at the back of a church, he'd do it for John. Not just *for* him, either, but to hear John conduct. He'd loved to listen to John conduct in college. He couldn't wait to hear what he could do four years later.

The church was now filled to brimming as the orchestra waited for John to give them the signal for the downbeat of the first movement of Mendelssohn's Symphony No. 4. From where he sat, Roger couldn't see John's face, but he could sense the intensity of John's focus in the way he held himself at the podium. John wore a dark-gray tuxedo, and his long hair fell onto his shoulders like a cascade of silk. Roger had joked that he could never resist a handsome man in a tux, but now that he watched John raise his baton, Roger's chest warmed with the knowledge that John was *his*.

John flicked his baton and the orchestra began to play the unrestrained and brilliant opening movement. Roger imagined John's face lit with joy as the chamber orchestra filled the church to the rafters with the warmth of the music. Roger knew few pieces that brimmed with so much happiness and promise as the Italian Symphony. He closed his eyes and just reveled in the music.

John was amazing. He'd been amazing in college, but he was a hundred times better now. He brought nuances to the piece Roger hadn't even considered. Tiny flourishes of brilliance illuminated places in the score Roger had never quite heard, as though they had hidden behind the more obvious musical expression, waiting for John's baton to coax them out from behind their more gregarious counterparts.

The movement ended and Roger's eyes filled with tears. Since when had he become such an incurable romantic that he couldn't listen to music without tearing up? He brushed the thought aside just as he'd done with the tears. He told himself that it was Vienna, and seeing John again, and all the promise their relationship seemed to hold that left him so emotional. Fragile, even.

Roger sat straighter in his seat, glad that few, if any, people might see him. He'd just managed to refocus on the concert when the orchestra began the more introspective second movement. His resolve, his self-control fled with the onslaught of the music, and Roger began to cry. Only this time, he couldn't stop.

What the hell is wrong with me?

He wiped his tears on his shirtsleeve. And still they fell. He needed to get away and be alone. The last thing he wanted to do was embarrass John or disrupt the concert. He slipped out of his seat, hoping no one would notice, and walked down the hallway to the offices, where he found the men's bathroom. He latched the door behind him, then leaned against it. More tears, this time accompanied by a tightness in his chest that left him nearly breathless, and a single image: the memory of playing the Tchaikovsky Violin Concerto with John.

"I like the way you play that passage. It makes me feel as though I'm a bird looking down at the ocean, ready to dive under the waves. It's like you're opening a door to some other place." John's cheeks pinked as he said it. Roger had never felt so happy. It was as if the music was greater than both of them. As if two stupid college kids had somehow stumbled into the most amazingly beautiful palace, and for just a moment, it belonged to them.

"You say that to all the people you coach," Roger teased, *uncomfortable to let John see how much the words meant.*

"No." John's eyes were full of light. Roger was afraid to call it what it was: love. John's love for him and for his music.

"Stop it." He said the words aloud. Whatever his relationship with John was going to be now, it would never be like that again. And that was fine. It had to be fine, because there wasn't any going back, was there?

Sometimes I think there's something wrong with me, Marc. John and I are finally together all the time, but I still feel like crap. You know, kind of the way I felt after the accident? I know it's stupid. I'm going to be starting a great job in a few months, and John and I are going to rent an apartment together. What the fuck is wrong with me?

Ten minutes passed. He couldn't spend the entire concert locked in here talking to his dead brother, could he? He willed the tears away as surely as he'd willed away his grief after the accident. Shoved it down to where he could deal with it and move on with his life. Five minutes more, and he had it together enough that he was pretty sure he'd make it through the rest of the concert. A little cold water on his face, and he was back before the orchestra had finished playing the last movement.

"What did you think?" a breathless John asked him after he made his way past a crowd of admirers a few minutes later.

"Beautiful." He wanted to kiss John, but he couldn't. He wanted to convey just how beautiful it had been and how much the performance had moved him, but he was afraid if he did, he might… what? Cry again? Scream? "I wish I could have seen your face during the concert," he managed to say. He was glad John hadn't seen his own.

John took his hand and squeezed it. "I thought of you, you know." His cheeks flushed as he said this. "The Mendelssohn reminds me of you. Bright, wild, funny."

Roger swallowed back another wave of emotion and hugged John. He could do this. Just listen to the music. Enjoy it. Appreciate John's talent. So why did it hurt so damn much? Why couldn't he just let it all go?

"Are you all right?" John looked at him strangely.

"I'm fine. The performance was just a bit more… I don't know… intense than I'd expected. Moving. More than that. I—"

"John!" one of the musicians shouted from across the room. "There's someone you need to meet."

John gave Roger an apologetic look.

"It's okay," Roger said. "Don't sweat it. We'll have time to talk later."

"You sure?"

"Sure." This was John's time, not the time to talk about whatever the fuck had come over Roger during the concert. He would deal with that on his own.

"TO JOHN!" Martine Depuy raised her glass and smiled broadly at John. Roger noticed the look of pleasure and embarrassment on John's face as he thanked her and the other guests at the party after the concert.

Martine's apartment was lovely, with its high ceilings and intricately carved moldings. The high windows looked out over one of the parks he and John had walked through on their explorations of the city. Roger imagined what it might be like to live in a city like Vienna. They were scheduled to fly back to New York the next afternoon, and he already regretted having to leave.

"Are you John's friend?" one of the guests asked as she walked over with a glass of champagne.

"Roger Nelson." He offered her a smile and they shook hands.

"I'm Annemarie Bauer," she said. "I'm a friend of Martine's."

"It's good to meet you."

"You're a musician too, then?" She twisted a bit of her long hair around in her free hand, her expression eager, even hungry.

"No." He didn't need to tell her he used to be a musician. "I'm an accountant."

"Oh." She appeared at a loss as to what to say. "That's interesting."

It wasn't the first time someone had assumed he was a musician, but it somehow felt worse this time. He was relieved when, a moment later, someone waved to her and she smiled and moved on.

He found his way over to the balcony through the crowd, avoiding speaking to anyone unless absolutely necessary. He caught a glimpse of John, surrounded by a small crowd of admirers, then slipped outside to escape the party. He leaned against the outer wall of the building, hidden from the guests inside, alone and glad for it.

The park below was still filled with people as the sun set through the trees. A street musician by the entrance played waltzes on a synthesizer for tips. He wasn't half-bad, Roger thought. Blue Danube morphed into a more familiar piece—Rachmaninoff's Vocalise, a beautiful vocal piece he'd played in high school. He closed his eyes, breathed in the sweet scent of the flowers, and imagined how it had felt to play. He could almost smell the sharp tang of rosin from his bow mingling with the falling leaves.

He didn't even try to stop the tears. Something about the city, the beauty of the music, and the warm autumn evening seemed to give him permission to let go of the pain that overflowed from his soul.

Hadn't he proven to himself that he could no longer play? He'd held his violin in his damaged hand, unable to play anything but the simplest of scales. He'd religiously exercised his fingers the way he'd been taught. He'd worked through the pain. Hoping. Praying. And still his vibrato had been wide and cumbersome, like the painful wobble of an aging soprano. The intensity of his musical desire came out as a pathetic warble, like a raspy voice trying to sing a glorious melody. But the beautiful voice—the sound the way *he* heard it in his mind—was still inside him. He longed to let that voice soar even as he knew it would never leave the confines of his thoughts.

The street musician finished playing and began to pack up. Roger was thankful for the silence. He needed to get his shit together before John saw him like this.

I want to tell him, Marc. Explain how much it hurts. Tell him maybe I need to skip some of the performances. But what then? Knowing John, he'd avoid taking gigs just to make me happy. Then we'd both be miserable. I can't do that to him.

There was no answer, only the rustling of the dried leaves that clung stubbornly to some of the trees in the park.

"ARE YOU all right?" John asked that evening after they'd made love. "You seem a little distracted."

"Just wishing we didn't have to go back." Wishing he could take it all back. Change the past.

John kissed Roger's chest. "I know. This—all of it—it's been wonderful." He kissed Roger's lips. "Being here with you. It was great talking to you on the phone and seeing you on weekends, but I like this a lot better."

"I do too."

John yawned and hugged Roger. "I'm beat."

"Go to sleep."

"Mmmm." John rolled onto his side, and Roger spooned him. "I love you, you know."

"I love you too."

CHAPTER 29

THEY STUMBLED into John's apartment around dinnertime the next evening, having stopped for takeout Chinese on their way home from the airport. "These stairs are killing me," Roger grumbled as he dumped his suitcase on the floor in the entryway.

"Maybe we'll find an apartment with an elevator."

Roger smiled. *Their* place. No roommates, no bullshit. "Yeah."

The corner of John's mouth edged upward in the makings of a grin.

Roger grabbed him and kissed him, then hugged him tight. "Do you know how much I fucking love you?"

John laughed. "Show me."

Roger took John's hand and led him back to the bedroom. Roger ignored the violin case poking out from under the bed and turned his attention back to John.

"WELL? WHAT do you think?" Sherri, the real estate broker, looked at them with raised eyebrows.

"We need to talk it over," Roger told her with a quick glance back at John. John nodded. It was the fourth apartment they'd seen that day, but Roger was pretty sure this was the one.

"I'll meet you downstairs." Sherri smiled knowingly. "No rush." The door to the apartment closed, the sound echoing throughout the empty space.

"Well?" Roger grinned.

John just laughed and shook his head. "You know me too well."

"It's perfect, isn't it?"

"Yes."

Roger threaded his arms through John's and kissed him on the neck. It was hard to miss the shiver that ran through John's lean body. Roger loved that he could still do that to him. "Want to do it here?"

"Roger."

"Okay, okay. But when we move in...."

John slipped out of Roger's arms and walked over to the glass doors that led to the balcony. "Did you know that if you stand on the edge of the balcony and look to your left, you can see the Empire State Building?"

"Better not tell anyone, or they'll charge even more for this place." Roger wasn't worried. He'd be making enough money at his job to pay the rent without John's help.

"You sure about this?" John asked. "I mean, commuting to Jersey every day?"

"Easier than commuting the other way. Besides, would you rather live in Hoboken?"

"No. Not really."

"Good. Then I'll write a check—"

"*We'll* write a check," John said with a shake of his head. "Remember, I'm making money too."

"Okay. How about I write the check and you pay me back with lots of great sex?" Roger waggled his eyebrows and John hit him on the ass. Roger had no intention of letting John use the tiny stipend he received from Juilliard to help pay for the place, but he figured he'd fight that battle later.

"Shut up. I'm too expensive for you anyhow." He offered Roger his best pouty face, which of course Roger had to kiss.

"Welcome home, John Fuchs," he whispered in John's ear once their lips parted.

John just sighed.

"NO, MOM," Roger said as he rolled his eyes for John. "I'm not coming home next week."

"I'm going to pick up the paper and get something for breakfast," John mouthed as he slid into a pair of black loafers by the door.

Roger covered the phone. "Nice look. Sweats and leather shoes."

John waved his hand dismissively. "I'm sure the clerk at the corner store will be outraged."

"Probably." Roger uncovered the phone. "Yes, Mom. I understand that you and Dad want to know what I'm up to."

John waved and slipped out the door after grabbing a jacket from the coat-tree.

"Roger," his mother repeated, "you know how important this is to your future. You need to make the right decision."

Roger put his feet up on the coffee table and leaned back into the couch. "I've already made a decision, Mom. I told you three months ago that I accepted the job in Jersey."

"You're with him again, aren't you? Is that what you're not telling me?"

Roger didn't respond. He supposed he'd have to come clean about John at some point, but he'd been hoping to do it later. A *lot* later. Maybe when he and John moved into their new apartment.

"Mom," he lied, "I'm just staying with John while I scout out a place."

"How long does it take to find an apartment? It's been more than a month now."

"I don't know. A while, I guess. Things are expensive here." He closed his eyes and took a deep breath.

"And why haven't you called me? Your father and I were worried."

"You shouldn't worry, Mom. I'm fine. Really."

"How can you expect me not to worry? They told me not to worry about Marc, and look what happened to him." She had that tone of voice that told Roger the guilt trip wasn't too far behind. He braced for it, wishing he hadn't had that second cup of coffee as the sick feeling in the pit of his stomach intensified.

"Mom. Please don't bring Marc into this." Why was it always about Marc? "I'm not Marc. I'm not in the army, and the war's been over for years now."

He wasn't surprised when she ignored him completely. "Roger, we've given you the benefit of the doubt. We let you indulge in your little fantasies about music. We took care of you after the accident. Really, I can't understand why you'd want to put yourself in a situation where you're constantly reminded of your poor choices."

"What?" He hadn't followed that last bit. Maybe he'd been wrong about the coffee—he could usually see her angle even before she started in on him.

"After the accident, we protected you. You were so heartbroken about the violin. And even though we didn't understand why it meant so much to you, we made sure you didn't have to think about it. The music. And you've done so well without that nonsense. Why do you insist on being part of that boy's life when you need to stay away from him?"

"His... *life*?" He was having a hard time wrapping his brain around her words. Had she just lumped John and music together and then blamed them *both* for the accident?

"You need to be focusing on your new life, not his music. Whose fault is it, anyhow, that you can't play anymore? If it hadn't been for him—"

"Stop it." He'd been prepared for the guilt, but he still had to keep himself from shouting into the receiver. "What happened to me wasn't John's fault. And since when can't I enjoy music? I don't have to play to enjoy it. I like listening to him. He's an amazing musician. One of these days you'll be bragging to your friends that you knew him—"

"Come home, Roger. Your dad's been having chest pains. He can't handle all this upheaval. And if he ever figures out what you and that boy are doing together—"

"We're not doing anything, Mom. He's my best friend." A partial truth, at least.

"Then you're dating?"

Shit. He shouldn't have lied to her. *One lie always leads to another.* But maybe it would get her off his case. "Yeah. I'm dating."

"A girl?"

Double shit. "Of course, Mom."

"That's wonderful." Her voice was overly bright now. "Who is she?"

Great. Just great. "Her name's Katherine," he said. She was the only woman in New York he even sort of knew. "She's a Juilliard student."

"Really? What instrument does she play?"

"Oboe."

"How lovely. I'd like to meet her sometime," his mother said.

"Sure." Easily said when your mother was five hundred plus miles away in Ohio. He and Katherine could have a short and very torrid imaginary relationship that would be long over by the time Miranda made it to New York for a visit. He didn't expect what she said next.

"Wonderful. I'm flying in for the weekend, so we'll have some time to get to know each other."

"You… you're what?" He hoped he'd just imagined the last thirty seconds, or that he'd wandered into some weird alternate universe. He thought he'd just heard her say she was coming to town in three days.

"I said I'm flying in for the weekend," she repeated. "You know, Roger, sometimes I wonder if your hearing needs to be checked. Maybe that accident—"

"There's no place for you to stay," he blustered without even thinking. Holy fuck, she couldn't be thinking she'd stay with him and John, could she?

"I have reservations at a hotel in Midtown. It's bad enough *you* are staying with that boy, I'm certainly not going to add insult to injury." She huffed into the phone, a perfect coda to the bile in her words.

Roger closed his eyes and exhaled a long, slow breath. He might be able to handle Miranda, but he wouldn't subject John to her if he could help it. Then he realized what she'd also said: she wanted to meet Katherine. "Look, Mom," he began, "she may not be in town to meet you."

"She's a student, isn't she? Where would she be?"

"I… ah… yes, but—"

"I knew it," Miranda snapped. "You made her up."

"Mom, please." Would someone please shoot him now? Twenty-three years old and he was acting like he was thirteen again. Worse, she was right, at least partially. "Katherine isn't made up. I'll let her know you're coming in and we'll have lunch, okay?"

"All right."

He could tell by her tone of voice that she was unconvinced. "Look, Mom, I gotta go. Why don't you call me tomorrow and we can figure out the schedule for your visit. Tell Dad I said hello. Good-bye." He hung up the phone before she could respond.

Fucking hell. When would she stop with the fucking guilt trips? And yet her words stuck with him more than he cared to admit. After the accident, he hadn't listened to music for nearly six months. He'd thought he'd gotten past that. Then he'd lost it in Vienna. As it was, he'd made up an excuse not to go with John to a concert the weekend before. John hadn't pressed the issue, but Roger knew he'd been disappointed. Now he'd gone and made up a girlfriend for his mother. What the hell was he doing?

"I can do this." He spoke the words as if by speaking them he might believe them. Of course he could do this! His mother would only be in town for a weekend. He could bullshit for a few days. Then he could go back to his life with John.

John wanted him around. John loved him. He loved John. He just needed to keep his mother off his back and take it easy with the music. He could do that. He'd ease back into the music stuff, get his act together. He could work up to going to concerts with John. Maybe he'd avoid any violin recitals, at least for a while.

"You're a good teacher. You helped me with math. What's so different about teaching violin?" What was so different? He wouldn't be playing. That was what was so different. And what would he say when starry-eyed kids told him they wanted to be soloists when they grew up? Would he lie to them and tell them they could have the sun, moon, and stars? Or would he tell them the truth: that even if they were really, really good, they'd probably never do more than teach violin and maybe play an orchestra gig from time to time? That even if they were the best, they might wake up one morning and find they couldn't play anymore? And what then?

"Hey." John was staring at him. How long had he been standing at the entrance to the living room holding a bunch of shopping bags?

"Hey."

"Bad call?"

"Are there any good ones with my mother?" Roger ran a hand through his hair.

"I'm sorry." John focused his gaze firmly on the floor. It reminded Roger of high school, the old insecure John. Roger knew John was acting that way because of his mother, and he felt a pang of guilt.

"Don't be. It's not your fault."

John set the bags down on the table and sat next to him. "What did she say?"

"She's flying in this weekend."

"You're joking." John looked at him as if he really, *really* hoped Roger would admit he was joking.

"Nope. But she's not staying with us."

"Oh, thank God!" John closed his eyes and leaned against the back of the couch.

"She's staying at some hotel. You don't even need to see her."

John threw himself at Roger. "You're the absolute best, you know. I can't even begin to tell you how happy that makes me, because if I saw her, I'd…. Well, I'd probably just be a stuttering, blubbering idiot like I usually am with her. But still…."

Roger had been ready to tell John about Katherine, but he decided against it. John didn't have to know about that. He'd explain the situation to Katherine, they'd have lunch with his mother, and that'd be the end of it. He and Katherine had gone for coffee a few times near school, and she'd be fine with the charade.

"I'm sorry you have to deal with her."

"I'm okay with it." John leaned over and kissed Roger. "Even better because I don't have to see her."

"Works for me."

John kissed him again, then stopped as though he were considering something. "I did want to ask you something," he said, his voice tentative.

"Sure. Shoot."

"I've been worried about you," John said slowly. "I mean, you seem a little preoccupied, and I was worried that maybe something was wrong."

"Me?"

"Yes. You."

Roger hesitated. He wouldn't talk to John about the music thing, at least not yet. It was bad enough that Miranda was waiting to pounce. Still, he knew he needed to say something. "I guess I'm just nervous about starting the new job. It's no big deal."

"You don't have to pretend everything's great for me, you know. Just because we're together doesn't mean I'm not your friend. You know you can talk to me, right?"

"Sure." Roger popped up from the couch and went to inspect the bags. "So what did you bring me to eat?"

CHAPTER 30

"NO. DEFINITELY not." Roger watched as Jim Riker shook his head and pursed his lips. "Mozart will never become pedestrian. Genius survives all the esoteric crap."

Leave it to Cal to dump on Mozart. God, he hated the man! What the hell John saw in him, he just didn't get. He was starting to wish he hadn't suggested John invite some of his friends over so he could get to know them better.

"Everyone's entitled to his opinion." Cal huffed and picked up his wine. "Personally, I think it's time we moved on to something *greater.*"

"Who's to say what's greater?" Shit. Roger hadn't meant to get involved in the discussion. He'd sat there quietly, hoping they'd move on to something other than music, but Cal just pissed him off. Why the hell did they always have to talk shop anyhow?

Cal glared at him and huffed again. Apparently huffing was the only response he was capable of making.

"How about some dessert?" John glanced at Roger, who noticed a muscle in John's cheek twitch.

Finally. Dessert was one step closer to seeing Cal out the door.

"Then *you* tell me, Mr. I-Know-Everything-About-Music," Cal drawled as he pointed his fork at Roger. "Mozart churned out hundreds of pieces of shit just to pay the bills, but we fawn all over them like they're some sort of fucking jewels. You know they're just crap, but because they're Mozart, you—"

"Cal," John warned. "Let it go."

"Why?" Cal waved his fork again. "Roger here hasn't played a note in years. What the hell does he know—?"

Roger stood up and grabbed the fork out of Cal's hand. "Shut the fuck up!"

Cal just blinked back at him, looking a little afraid. *Damn well should be. I could beat the crap out of that little shit in a fast—*

"Roger?" John, who had just returned from depositing some of the dirty dishes in the kitchen, stared at him in shock.

Roger gritted his teeth and took a deep breath. The last thing he wanted was to start a fight in front of John, although it was damn tempting to punch Cal's face in. He dropped the fork on the table, where it landed with a clatter on his plate. Then he turned and headed into the bedroom without saying a word.

Fuck. Even now, he was so angry he wanted to hit something.

"Hey." John put his arm on Roger's shoulder as Roger walked down the hallway. "Are you okay?"

Roger nodded.

"I asked Cal to leave."

"You didn't need to do that." Now Roger felt like a total shit.

"Yes, I did."

"God, John, I'm sorry." What the fuck had come over him? He'd dealt with people like Cal before and he'd never lost his temper.

"Don't be." John turned Roger so Roger had no choice but to look at him. "He was goading you. I should have stopped it sooner."

"I overreacted."

"No, you didn't." John studied him with eyes full of concern. "But there's something you're not telling me. What's wrong, Roger?"

Roger just shook his head. "The guy pisses me off." That was true. Still, hearing Cal say it—that he hadn't played a note in years—hurt more than he was willing to admit.

"I need you to talk to me." John's words were tentative. "I need you to tell me if something's wrong. If I'm doing something wrong—"

"You're not doing anything wrong." The last thing he wanted was for John to think any of this was *his* fault. "The guy's a jealous jerk."

John's cheeks flushed, causing Roger to laugh. "You knew? I mean, we never dated, but...."

"Yeah." Roger smiled and pulled John closer. "I figured that was his problem." He leaned in to nuzzle John's neck as the last of his anger evaporated.

John sighed. "But you would talk to me if I did something, wouldn't you?"

"Of course I would. But you haven't done anything."

"Good." John smiled at him.

CHAPTER 31

"JIM SAID he'll drive his parents' truck into the city and help us move at the end of the month," John said, setting the baskets of laundry they'd just lugged up from the basement on the dining table. They'd been trying to figure out how to move all his stuff to the new apartment without having to pay for movers. He'd meant to tell Roger, but he'd forgotten after the dinner party fiasco the night before.

Roger said nothing.

"Roger?"

"Huh?" Roger glanced up from the pants he had just shaken out. "Did you say something?"

"Are you okay?" For the past week, Roger had been even more obviously distracted. John was beginning to wonder if he was having second thoughts about them moving in together. Roger kept passing it off as something—a conversation with Miranda, getting used to living in New York, even Cal—but John was pretty sure he wasn't telling him the truth.

"Oh. Yeah. Sure. That's great." Roger looked entirely clueless.

Best to change the subject. "So," John began as he folded one of Roger's T-shirts, "how'd you like to go hear a chamber music concert tonight? My friend Mara's trio's playing at school. It's free."

John thought he saw Roger's shoulders tense. "I'm a little beat. Didn't sleep well last night." Roger seemed overly preoccupied with the pair of boxers in his hand.

"Sure. It's okay. We can stay home."

"No. You should go. I'm sure they'll want to see you there." Roger still didn't look at him.

"Roger?"

"Yeah?" Roger's eyes were still focused on the same boxers.

"I know you said it wasn't something I've done, but if you want to get your own place… without me, I'd underst—"

"I'm the one who suggested we move in together," Roger said, dropping the boxers and hugging John with such ferocity that John was momentarily overwhelmed. "I love you. Of course I want to be with you."

John forced a smile. "Sorry. I just wanted to be sure. I don't want you to make a mistake and do something you'll regret."

"Stop worrying." Roger took John's face in his hands and kissed him tenderly, then stroked his thumbs over John's cheeks.

John wished he could.

"JOHN. WAIT up!"

John turned to see Cal walking quickly toward him down the practice room hallway, violin case slung over his shoulder. "Hi, Cal." He honestly wasn't sure he wanted to talk to Cal after what had happened at the dinner party, but he also didn't want to be rude. He'd see what Cal had to say and then decide if he'd ever talk to the guy again.

"Hey. How's it going?"

"Busy." John opened the door to the closest free room and plunked his books and scores on the piano stand.

"Oh, sorry." Cal stood in the doorway, leaning on the doorjamb. "I didn't mean to take you away from anything."

"It's all right, Cal. I can take a few minutes. What's up?"

Cal smiled. John was pretty sure Cal knew he wouldn't kick him out, but at least he'd asked. With Cal, that was something, at least.

"I just wanted to apologize for the other night," Cal said. "At dinner, I mean. I was a total asshole."

John didn't even attempt to disguise his surprise to hear this. He wasn't sure he'd ever heard Cal apologize for something. "Come on in," he said, motioning Cal to the chair by the piano.

"Sure. Thanks. After what I did, I wasn't sure you'd even talk to me again." Cal set his things down on the floor, then sat in the chair and put his legs up on the piano bench.

"You're pretty hard on Roger, you know." A few years ago, John wouldn't have had the guts to say anything about it. But when he arrived in New York, he'd quickly realized part of being a conductor meant taking charge, even when there was no music involved. His newfound self-confidence served him well, even if underneath it all, John was still uncomfortable asserting himself.

"I like you, John," Cal said. "I've never tried to hide that from you. I know you and Roger are together, but that doesn't mean I just stop feeling what I feel. I at least want us to stay friends."

"I know." John forced a smile. "But it's been hard on Roger, moving here. You need to cut him some slack or I don't think we can stay friends." He wouldn't add that he was pretty sure it was hard on Roger being around other violinists like Cal, too.

"I know. I really am sorry. I'm glad he's making some friends in town. You know, getting out a little." Cal scratched the back of his neck and slouched a bit lower into the chair. "I saw him on Saturday, and he looked like he was having a good time."

"Oh? I didn't realize you two had seen each other." Now *that* was a surprise. Cal and Roger had talked to each other and hadn't gotten into a fight?

"Well, I guess you could say I saw *him*. He looked like he was having fun, and I didn't want to interrupt." Cal's expression was neutral, as if he didn't give a crap about it, but John was pretty sure Cal cared a lot about this.

"What didn't you want to interrupt?"

"He and Katherine were having lunch at this little Italian place not far from my apartment. There was an older woman there too. Blonde? Fifty, maybe?"

Miranda. But what was Katherine doing having lunch with Roger's mother? "And?" John asked as he schooled his expression.

"I don't know." Cal shrugged. "They just looked really happy. All of them. And the way Roger had his arm around Katherine—"

"That was Roger's mother with them." He wasn't going to get jealous. He'd as much as told Roger he didn't want to see Miranda. And there was nothing wrong with Katherine coming along either. Roger and Katherine were friends.

"Oh. I didn't know his mother was in town." Cal laughed. "Not that Roger would have told me, of all people." He stood up and gathered his things. "No biggie. I really only wanted to apologize for the other night. That's all. See you later, okay?"

"Sure. Thanks, Cal." John watched Cal walk out of the practice room, then closed the door after him and sat down on the piano bench. He fought the urge to call Roger. No, he'd see Roger at dinner. He could ask him then.

"YOU'RE AWFULLY quiet tonight," John said as he gathered the dishes off the table and brought them over to the sink.

Roger, who had been staring blankly at something on the wall behind John's head for most of the meal, just shrugged. "I got a call from the HR lady at my new job. She said she was sending over a bunch of paperwork for me to fill out."

"Like what?" John set the empty glasses on the counter.

"Nothing, really. Stupid shit. Retirement accounts, tax forms."

John got the definite impression there was more than just stupid shit involved. "Oh. Doesn't sound so bad."

"Nah. But she told me the regional manager wanted to talk to me."

"Really? That sounds serious." John figured it wasn't losing-your-job sort of serious. Why would they have Roger fill out all the forms if they were just going to tell him he was fired?

"I called him." Roger paused and stared at the tablecloth this time.

The entire conversation was making John really nervous. He had meant to talk to Roger about what he'd learned from Cal, but the way Roger was acting, he decided to wait. He was pretty sure he knew what *that* was all about, at least. Not that it made him happy, but—

"They offered me a bonus if I'd transfer to their Chicago offices."

Shit. John felt suddenly queasy.

"Don't worry," Roger said with a nervous laugh, "I'm not interested. I just told him I'd think about it so he wouldn't think I hadn't. Thought about it, I mean."

"Oh." Roger's words weren't exactly reassuring.

Roger said nothing but gathered up the tablecloth and stood next to John at the sink, where John had begun to do the dishes.

"Look, Roger," John began, happy to have something to look at where he didn't need to meet Roger's gaze, "I know you're not very happy here, and—"

"Why do you say that?"

"I don't know." John poured some dish soap onto a sponge and squeezed it a few times.

"What's eating you?" Roger asked. Out of the corner of his eye, John could see him run a hand through his hair. He did that when he was nervous.

"I don't know." John shrugged and started in on one of the pots.

"You just said that. And I think you *do* know."

"It's just that sometimes I wonder about us." John knew he'd made a mistake in saying anything at all.

"Getting a place together? Because we've been through this already. I told you, I want this. I'm the one who asked you."

John turned and looked at Roger this time. "Not getting a place together. Not really, I guess. I mean more like *being* together."

"*What?*" Roger seemed genuinely surprised.

"Just that you don't do a lot of things with me. I mean, we live in New York City, and you and I have never gone to the symphony together. Or even a school concert. Sometimes I think you're embarrassed to be with me." There, he'd said it, for what it was worth. He still didn't feel any better having said it, though.

"I'm not embarrassed to be with you." Roger snaked his arms around John's waist and hugged him.

"Then why did you bring Katherine to lunch with your mother?" He hadn't meant to bring that up like this, but it just seemed to come out.

"You... you saw us?"

"No. But s-someone else d-did." John absentmindedly poked at a bubble on the sponge, popping it.

"Who?"

"It d-doesn't m-matter." Well, it didn't.

"Tell me who," Roger demanded. When John didn't respond, Roger said, "It was Cal, wasn't it? I thought I saw that little shit—"

"Stop it!" John pulled away from him. "It really *doesn't* matter who it was. The point is that you brought her with you."

"And what difference does that make?"

"It makes a difference because it's like before, back at school. Y-you were using her to pretend you're not what y-you are," John said indignantly. He didn't even realize he'd put his hands on his hips until he felt the wet warmth of the soapy water at his waist.

"I'm not—"

"Don't bullshit me, Roger." A little voice in John's head told him to slow down, take a breath and just think, but it was as if he couldn't stop now that he'd started. "You told your mother you and Katherine were going out, didn't you?"

"What diff—"

"Are you going out with her?" John's heart pounded. He knew the answer, but he wanted Roger to say it anyhow, for what it was worth.

"Of course not. You don't think I would cheat on you, do you?"

John tried to swallow, but his throat was so dry he nearly coughed. "No. Of course I don't."

"Then what's the problem?" Roger scowled back at him.

"The p-problem is that w-when you d-do that… when y-you pretend y-you're with someone like th-that… l-like she's y-your girlfriend… I f-feel l-like shit, that's what."

"You don't need to feel like that."

Hearing this really pissed John off. As if Roger didn't know how he'd felt before? As if this hadn't been the thing that had nearly broken them up for good, nearly killed them both? How could he even say something like that?

"Fuck you." The stuttering was gone. It always went away when John got angry. "Fuck you for telling me how I should feel. Since you moved in here, you've been telling me there's nothing wrong, but you act like you're somewhere else half the time. What the hell am I *supposed* to feel? I know what Miranda says to you. I know you believe her bullshit too, even though you don't want to."

"John," Roger protested, "I don't care what she says."

"But you're embarrassed to be with me. Embarrassed that by being with me, by saying you love me, that you're gay. And you can't be gay, can you?"

"I can't tell people I'm gay. I'd lose my job."

"I know." John shook his head in frustration. "I know that. But it's always in the way. It's always between us. And I feel like it's my fault and somehow I made you this way."

"Shit, John, you know that's not true." Roger looked genuinely contrite. "You know that this isn't about you."

"I d-don't know anything." John fought back tears.

Roger took John in his arms and held him tight. John fought the urge to lean his head into Roger's shoulder but gave in when it became too difficult to resist. "I love you, John. I really do."

"Then talk to me. If we're going to do the pretend thing with your mother, let me in on it. I don't want to have to find out about it from someone else."

"Okay." Roger spoke in a low, rough voice. "I promise." He hugged John. "I'm sorry I didn't tell you."

"Thanks." John rubbed his tears away with his palms. He felt a little better. Just a little.

"Want me to finish the dishes?" Roger asked.

"Nah. I can finish them. Why don't you wait for me in bed? I'll be there in a few minutes."

Roger looked at him with obvious concern but finally nodded and left him alone in the kitchen. John looked down at the remaining dishes in the sink and took a deep breath. They'd work this out. Figure it out. Whatever it took, right? So why did he still feel so bad?

CHAPTER 32

THE NEXT afternoon John climbed the stairs faster than usual and arrived at the apartment winded, gasping for air. "I... got... it!" He held up an envelope and waved it around as Roger laughed and took the rest of the mail from him before John dropped it on the ground.

"What is it?"

"Marlboro. They... want... me... to... conduct!"

"That's great news." Roger set the mail down and hugged John. "I remember we used to say we'd both go there. You said you were going to play piano, but this is a million times better."

"I can't believe it." John finally caught his breath. "There's only one spot for a student conductor. I figured there was no way.... Shit! I've got to call Maestro Pirelli and let him know."

"Sure."

Roger smiled as John raced into the living room and grabbed the phone. John would need to call his mother too. He'd been hoping for a break like this ever since he'd started at Juilliard. Finally he'd have a chance to do more than just conduct the school orchestra. And if he did well, there'd be other jobs. How many years had he worried that the entire idea of becoming a conductor was just some stupid kid's dream?

"SOMEONE SAID Marlboro in Vermont is the best for chamber music. You could go as a pianist and maybe we could find a cellist. There's some great piano trio music."

Roger stared up at the ceiling. God, he felt like shit! Here he was, wishing John hadn't gotten the conducting gig when he knew how important it was. He was jealous. Worse, it hurt. They'd dreamed of going together, and now he'd spend a summer alone in New York and John....

I can't do this. Roger shivered beneath the heavy covers. John lay next to him, warm and inviting. All he needed to do to get warm was hold John. All he *wanted* was to hold John.

"It's beautiful, Roger. I know the concerto is all about the fancy stuff, and that's great too. But this—" John's eyes shimmered with emotion. "I've never heard the second movement played as beautifully. It's stunning."

He knew John was right: in that moment suspended in time, he'd known there was nothing else for him but music. No other expression, no other work, no other love for him. With one exception. And here he was, wishing John *failed.* John, who'd worked so hard. Who wanted this so much. Who'd wanted this even before they had met. Who damn well *deserved* this.

It was too close. Too much.

"I'LL BE back after lunch," John said as he kissed Roger and grabbed his satchel. "Maybe we can walk over to that vegetarian place I told you about and grab some dinner."

"I love you." Roger lingered a bit longer, inhaling John's crisp scent. "I really do."

"I know." John smiled and unbolted the locks on the front door. "But you can show me how much after dinner, if you'd like."

John was gone a moment later. Roger just stood and stared at the door for a couple of minutes until a taxi's honk stirred him out of his trance. He took a deep breath and went to retrieve his violin from under the bed.

He'd been playing about an hour—if you could call it playing—when someone buzzed from downstairs. Roger set the violin down on the dining room table and pressed the button to let them in. A few minutes later, he opened the door to find Cal standing there.

"Cal?"

"Hey, Rog."

Roger forced a smile and reminded himself that he needed to be civil even though he was doubly pissed off after what Cal had told John about seeing him with Katherine and his mother. He was pretty sure it *had* been Cal.

"John's not here," Roger said. Cal was still standing outside the apartment door.

"I didn't come here to see John." Cal shifted on his feet and scratched the back of his neck.

Roger liked seeing the guy squirm, although he had no idea why Cal would want to see him of all people. "Why did you come, then?"

"I…. May I come in?" Cal asked.

Roger considered telling him no, then thought better of it. Cal was John's friend, after all, even though he was a little shit. "Sure." He motioned Cal inside.

"I'm really sorry," Cal blurted out before they'd even gotten to the living room. "About being such an asshole at dinner the other night."

"What?" Roger was so surprised, he wondered if he'd heard Cal correctly.

Cal scratched the back of his neck again. "I wanted to apologize for baiting you the other night. I shouldn't have."

"Thanks." What the hell was Cal up to? He was the last guy Roger would have expected to apologize.

"Yeah. I guess I got carried away."

"I know you asked John out." Okay, so he could accept Cal's apology, but it wasn't as if he'd give the guy too much credit, either.

Cal flushed to the tips of his ears. "Yeah… about that…."

"It's cool."

"You… you're okay with it?" Cal frowned and appeared slightly confused to hear this.

"Sure." Only partly true, but Cal didn't have to know that.

"Shit. Thanks, man." Cal reached out to shake Roger's hand, but Roger didn't move to take it. Cal just laughed uncomfortably and withdrew his hand before continuing, "I honestly didn't know he was seeing someone, or I wouldn't have, you know. He didn't mention he had someone until I asked him out. Really."

"I believe you." Roger did believe Cal, but the knowledge that John hadn't mentioned him to anyone niggled at him too. And then there was the "hot date" comment at the bar when he'd first met Cal. "Can I get you something to drink?" Roger asked, if only because he was feeling a little uncomfortable himself and needed a minute to think.

"Sure. Water would be great, thanks."

Roger went to the kitchen and filled a glass with water, then returned a moment later to find Cal seated on the couch.

"Thanks, Rog."

"No problem."

"So, yeah, well, John just seemed a little lonely when I first met him. Kind of lost. And… well… I felt bad for him." Cal took a quick sip of his water. "We had coffee near school. He really wanted to talk about music. I guess that's what music school's for, in a way. Other than the learning and stuff. I think since you weren't living here yet, he just needed someone to bounce things off of."

"Sure." Roger forced a smile. Of course John would need to talk about music with other people. When they first got together, he and John had talked about it a lot. They hadn't discussed music much since the accident except when John filled Roger in about his gigs. But that was just logistical stuff. Roger couldn't remember the last time he'd really talked about the music itself, other than the argument with Cal over dinner.

The thought made his gut ache. Why the hell was it so difficult for him to just let go? He needed to do this for John. If he couldn't be part of the most important thing in John's life—

"Not that he needs a lot of help," Cal was saying when Roger focused once more on the conversation. "He's freaky talented. Even some of the doctoral students are hitting him up to coach them. I guess ever since Christian Lazar got the gig with the Cleveland Orchestra."

"Cleveland?" Roger knew it was one of the best orchestras in the world.

"Yeah. Word has it he asked John to play through some of his audition stuff right after John came to New York. John made some suggestions and Christian coached nearly every day with him until the audition at the end of September. Chris swears it was John who helped him nail it. But I'm sure you heard all about it. John was so excited when he heard."

"John's great like that." Roger wondered why John hadn't mentioned that to him. *Maybe because he knows you don't want to hear it.*

"I bet in a few years, he'll barely have time to breathe with all the gigs. If he doesn't get hired by some symphony." Cal picked up his water again and took a long drink before standing up. "Look, I'd better go. I've got class at two and I still have to analyze the last movement of some atonal mess before then. Don't want Professor Thayer to shoot me."

"Thanks for stopping by," Roger said, relieved to have Cal on his way out. "I appreciate your—"

"That your fiddle?" Cal had discovered Roger's violin and was reaching for it.

"Yep."

"Pretty. Nineteenth century?"

"Late eighteenth," Roger corrected. "Italian."

"May I try it?" Cal asked. "Mine's nowhere near this nice."

"I'd prefer you not." Roger didn't care if he was being rude. In fact, he liked being rude when it came to Cal, apology or no apology. He still hated the guy.

Cal just laughed and set the instrument gently down again. "No problem. I know a lot of folks are that way about their instruments. What'cha working on?"

"Tchaikovsky," Roger lied. *In my dreams.*

"Can't wait to hear you play it. We've got an informal concert we do at school every other month. You and John could—"

"I don't want to keep you." Roger pointed Cal to the door.

"Yeah, I really should go before I'm late." Cal picked up the backpack he'd set down in the hallway and opened the door. "See ya later, Rog."

"Later."

When Roger went to close the door, Cal said, "I'm really glad for you and John, you know."

"Thanks."

Cal waved and headed for the stairs as Roger closed the door. Cal hadn't said it, but Roger could read between the lines: John needed someone who understood and supported him. Someone who shared his music.

He walked back over to the table, picked up the violin and bow, and packed them back into their case. He wouldn't practice anymore. He couldn't. What the fuck had he been doing, trying to convince himself he might play again? He'd never play again.

CHAPTER 33

SOMETIME BETWEEN Cal's visit and dinner, Roger decided to go out for a drink—after he'd made the phone call.

The Irish pub a few blocks from the apartment smelled like cigarettes and beer, but after the second drink, Roger didn't really notice. By the time Katherine met him there—he'd really needed someone to talk to—he was pretty much wasted. And he stayed that way the entire evening. He wanted to stay that way.

He tried to be quiet when he stumbled into the apartment at nearly two in the morning. He didn't really want to wake John, he figured he'd talk to him in the morning. He didn't expect John would fall asleep on the couch, waiting up for him.

"Hey." He grinned at John.

John looked hurt. "I was worried about you. We were supposed to have dinner together, remember?"

"Dinner?" Shit. He'd forgotten.

"Dinner." John sat up and scowled.

"You don't need to worry. I'm fine."

"Drunk isn't fine." No stuttering. That meant John was mad. Maybe this wouldn't be so bad. Mad was better than hurt. Roger could handle mad. The hurt thing, not so much, especially since he knew he was the cause of it.

"Depends on who's drunk." He offered John a smile.

John visibly struggled to control his temper. "Why didn't you leave me a note or something?"

"Sorry. Forgot."

"Cal said he stopped by today," John said after a moment. "He wouldn't tell me why."

"He came to apologize."

"No way."

"Yeah." Roger ran a hand through his hair and scratched his scalp. The cigarette smoke made it itch. "Said he was an asshole at the dinner."

"What else did he say?"

"What do you mean?" Roger knew exactly what John meant, he just didn't want to go there.

"What m-made you g-go out and g-get t-trashed?" John asked.

"Cal had nothing to do with that."

"Bullshit. He also said you were at the bar with Katherine." John had his hands on his hips now and was glaring at him.

"What the fuck?" Oh, Cal had played him like a fucking Stradivarius. Not that it would matter in the end, but still. "That little—"

"So it's true. You were there with her, weren't you?" John's pale skin flushed deep pink with anger.

"Yeah. What difference does it make?"

"What were you doing with her?" John's body shook. "Who were you trying to bullshit today, Roger?"

"Bullshit? Nobody. I just needed someone to talk to." Roger realized too late that this was the worst thing he could say.

John said nothing, but Roger saw the anger on his face turn into a hurt far worse than what he'd seen there before. Shit. He'd really done it now. And when John realized he'd actually talked to HR about the possible transfer, wanting to find out more about it....

"Shit. I'm sorry, John. I didn't mean to imply—"

"That you can't talk to me?" John wiped away angry tears. "I don't think you're implying anything. It's obvious to anyone with half a brain."

"I didn't want to bother you at school."

"Bullshit. That's bullshit," John snapped.

This really pissed Roger off. "You had class. I couldn't just waltz in there and pull you out of it, could I?"

"No. But you wouldn't have to if you'd just fucking talk to me, Roger. Or were you too embarrassed to do that?" The glare on John's face cut Roger almost as deep as his words.

"Of course not."

"You're bullshitting me again. I'm tired of the bullshit. If you can't talk to your fucking best friend, who the hell *can* you talk to? Not to mention that we're living together?" John demanded.

Roger had never heard John so angry. He guessed he deserved it. It had made sense at the time, asking Katherine to join him for drinks. "I... I guess I didn't think about it like that."

"Of course you didn't." John took a deep breath. His face was flushed. When Roger didn't immediately respond, John said, "I'm going back to bed."

Roger watched John leave. John was right. He was a bullshitter. He couldn't admit that he was miserable living in New York to himself, let alone to John. Worse, he was screwing things up for John. Roger hated Cal, even knew he was angling for John, but he couldn't deny the truth of Cal's words: John needed someone to support him, someone he could share his music with.

And then there was the whole gay thing. He told himself he didn't give a crap what his mother thought or said. He didn't care what anyone said. But that was bullshit too.

ROGER DIDN'T hear John leave for school the next morning. He'd slept on the couch, fully dressed, because he felt like a total shit, and John didn't deserve to have to sleep next to a total shit. When he finally awoke around lunchtime, the first thing he did after he took a shower was call the regional manager in Chicago about the transfer. The next thing he did was call the real-estate broker to prepay the first two months' rent on the apartment he and John were supposed to have moved into in a week. He wouldn't saddle John with a place he couldn't afford alone, but he'd leave it up to John whether he wanted to move.

By the time he walked into the kitchen and grabbed a pen and a piece of paper, he was feeling like the world's biggest heel and his chest hurt.

I'm so sorry was all he wrote.

Four hours later, after packing all the clothes he could stuff into a single large suitcase, Roger hopped a cab and boarded a flight to Chicago.

PART 2

September 17, 1978.

EGYPTIAN PRESIDENT Anwar El Sadat and Israeli Prime Minister Menachem Begin signed two framework agreements at the White House, which led to a peace treaty between longtime enemies Israel and Egypt. The peace negotiations, held in secret and lasting thirteen days, were facilitated by President Jimmy Carter and held at Camp David, the presidential retreat outside of Washington, DC.

CHAPTER 34

August 1978

"JOHN. HEY. It's me. Can you call me, please? I know you probably don't want to talk to me, but I really need to talk to you."

John watched the flashing display on the answering machine with a rock in the pit of his stomach. He hadn't spoken to Roger since he'd left New York without an explanation more than a year before. He'd been too angry and too hurt. It had been all he could do not to run after Roger and demand to know why he'd left. But he wouldn't do that. He couldn't do it. He wouldn't beg.

He pressed the button for the next message. This one was from his mother, and the sound of her voice reminded him of the warm summer sunshine outside. Even at twenty-four, he still smiled to hear her voice.

"Welcome home, sweetheart. Thanks for sending me the newspaper clipping from Cologne and translating it for me. I'm so happy for you. Oh… I meant to tell you to send my best wishes to Roger and his mother if you talk to him. I was so sorry to hear about his father."

"Christ."

JOHN STOOD at the front door to Roger's parents' house two days later. It had taken a bit of juggling to arrange his rehearsal schedule so he could fly to Ohio, but his mother had been thrilled to see him and happy to put him up for the visit. He felt strange being back home again, stranger still to be visiting Roger in the home where they'd spent so much time together as kids.

He'd expected to see Roger or his mother, but the woman who answered the door was someone he'd never seen before. Dark-haired, petite, dressed in jeans and a sweater, she smiled at him warmly. "You must be John." She offered him her hand. "I'm Dorothy James."

"Good to meet you, Dorothy."

"Roger's checking on his mother." She gestured him inside. "She's not been sleeping much since the funeral, so the doctor gave her something."

"I'm sorry to hear that." He was relieved that he wouldn't have to see Miranda immediately. His mixed emotions at seeing Roger again were enough to make him slightly sick to his stomach—Miranda would have made things a hundred times worse. He'd come to hate the woman and hate what she did to Roger, not to mention how she'd treated *him* over the years.

He followed Dorothy into the house. Nothing had changed, except the old console TV had been replaced with a newer rear-projection number that dominated the living room. No dog. Roofster had died a few years back. John missed the dog and his barking. The place seemed dead without it.

Dead. John wondered how Roger was handling his father's death. John wasn't sure how he might handle his own father's death. He'd barely spoken to his father since he'd remarried. He supposed he'd feel something.

"Can I get you something to drink, John?"

John had nearly forgotten about Dorothy. "Water would be great. Thank you."

"You're welcome. Please make yourself comfortable. I'm sure Roger will be down in a few minutes."

"Thanks." He watched her head for the kitchen and wondered vaguely why she seemed so comfortable in the house. She was probably a cousin. Roger had some relatives in town.

He'd just sat down on the couch when Roger came down the stairs. "John." John got up and Roger gave him a hug. "I'm so glad you came."

"I'm sorry I didn't get the message sooner."

Roger released him from the embrace before backing away. He seemed both uncomfortable and happy to see John. He probably figured John was still angry about how things had ended between them. Of course, he'd have been right.

Dorothy came into the room with a glass of water. "Here you go, John."

"Thanks."

"I'm going back to my place," she told Roger. "If you need me, just call, okay? It was nice meeting you, John."

"You too."

"Thanks, Dorothy." Roger kissed her on the cheek and she was gone a moment later, leaving them alone. "I don't know what I'd have done if she hadn't been around to help," he said after a long pause.

"She seems really sweet. Is she a relative?"

"She's a friend. We went to grade school together, before she went to private school." Roger pursed his lips and sat in the chair across from the couch.

"Oh. That's nice." John didn't want to ask anything else. He was afraid of what that meant. When Roger was silent for a moment, John said, "So how are you holding up?"

"I'm doing all right. Took a three-week leave of absence from my job in Chicago to help Mom take care of things here."

"How's the job going?" Small talk. Was he really sitting here with Roger making small talk? Was he the same John who'd been Roger's lover for more than four years? John had never felt worse in his life, except for the day he'd come home to find Roger's note and no Roger.

Keep talking. If he didn't, he'd start to cry. Or scream. No. He wouldn't scream. Roger had just lost his father, after all. He'd walk out of the house and never look back.

"It's good. I just bought a little house in Lisle. I got a pretty good bonus last year." Roger draped his arms over the chair and appeared to relax with the familiar territory of the conversation. In spite of this, John saw he was tapping his foot on the floor and not looking him directly in the eyes. "How about you?"

"Good. I'm looking into a conducting job in Connecticut. Good little orchestra. Doesn't pay much, but their season's short enough that I can keep coaching or take guest-conducting gigs. And I can still live in New York." Shit. He'd thought he could do this for Roger—be there for him—but now he was struggling to stay in his seat. He needed to leave. He'd offer Roger his condolences—was that what you called it when you wanted to comfort your best friend but the wall between you got in the way?—and leave before he said something he'd regret. Fuck. When had he become so angry with Roger? He knew the answer: the minute Roger left him without an explanation. "I was really sorry to hear about your dad," he managed to say.

"Thanks." Roger shifted in his seat. "Mom's having a really rough time of it. I hadn't planned on staying more than a week, but my mom told Dorothy she wasn't sure what she'd do on her own after I left. I figured I should stay until she's a bit more stable."

John was tempted to point out that Miranda never seemed to rely much on Roger's father, but he thought better of it. Miranda had done everything in her power to make sure Roger's life was a living hell, but the woman had just lost her husband, after all.

After an extended silence, Roger said, "Look. I need to get this off my chest, because I've been feeling like a total shit since I left New York."

John took a long drink of his water in an attempt to disguise his emotional response. For the past year he'd been telling himself he didn't need to understand why Roger had left. He knew now that had been a lie: he was afraid of what Roger might say. Afraid that he'd done something to push Roger away. He was just as angry and confused now about what had gone so wrong between them as he'd been a year ago.

"Sure."

"This is really hard for me."

"It's okay." John set the glass down on the coffee table. "You really don't need to go there. It was a mistake. We should never have—"

"I couldn't handle it. Being with you. Being… well… you know. And then there was the music."

"The music?" John struggled to understand. He got the gay part. Even now, the fact that Roger couldn't say the word still hurt. But the music?

Roger rubbed a hand across his jaw and mouth, stood up abruptly, and walked across the room. When he turned back to look at John, his eyes sparkled. Was Roger fighting back tears?

"Yes." Roger's voice sounded rough with emotion.

"I don't understand."

"I've always loved to hear you conduct, you know," Roger began. "I remember the first time I heard you conduct that first year at Michigan. Not that I hadn't realized before what an amazing musician you were." He laughed softly. "I realized that when I heard you play piano back in high school.

"I know... I'm not making any sense." Another moment passed. This time Roger rubbed his eyes. "God, John. I'm so fucking sorry for what I did to you."

"It's okay." John had no clue what to say. Of course it wasn't okay. It had nearly killed him when Roger had disappeared from his life without explanation. How many weeks had he gone back and forth about whether to run after Roger, ask him what he'd done, and beg him to come back? How many times had he called Roger's house only to hang up when Miranda answered the phone? He still didn't understand what Roger was going on about.

"No. It's not. Of course it's not."

"Look, Roger," John said, feeling uncomfortable and just wanting the whole conversation to end so they could get back to being friends. "It's done. Over with. I'm good. Really." He'd spent too long trying to put the tiny pieces of his heart back together again—he couldn't keep talking about this. It hurt too much. If he didn't believe Roger needed him now, he'd have stayed in New York and pretended he didn't still hurt.

"It was never you. You were... amazing. Vienna was incredible. I felt so good. Happy. But then I heard you conduct and—God, John, it hurt so *fucking* much I couldn't handle it.

"I told myself I was just moved by the performance. But I was bullshitting myself. Every time I tried to tell myself that, I'd think back to when I played violin. Or played with you. About all the things I'd hoped for and not the fucking mess I'd made of my life. All along I kept telling myself that I'd play the violin again. I practiced every fucking day."

"You practiced?" Why hadn't he even noticed it?

"Yeah." Roger *was* crying now.

John stood up and walked over to him, hoping to offer him some comfort, but Roger just shook his head and backed away. John's gut clenched—he'd never known Roger to pull away from him. John had the definite sense that there was something else he was missing.

"I couldn't do it. I couldn't listen to the music. It hurt to goddamned much. And then when you got the job at Marlboro, I just lost it. We used to talk about going there back in school...."

"Roger. If I'd known—"

"If you'd known, then what? I sure as hell wouldn't want you to give up your music for me. And I sure as hell didn't want you to feel bad because you were doing something you loved."

John reached out a tentative hand and touched Roger's upper arm. This time Roger didn't pull away, but he also didn't move to seek John's embrace.

"I didn't know how to tell you. You were so excited about the job. And then the other stuff... oh, fuck. I'm just sorry. I still feel like shit for leaving. But I'd have fucked up your life like I'd fucked up mine if I'd stayed." Roger wiped his eyes again and appeared to regain his control. "I needed to tell you before it ate away at me."

"It's done." John offered Roger a smile. "We're still friends. I'm here."

Roger's shoulders fell. The knot in the pit of John's stomach seemed to grow exponentially. He'd never seen Roger like this. Even after the accident, he hadn't seemed so miserable. So defeated.

"There's something else, isn't there?" John asked. Better to get it over with now.

Roger's body tensed beneath John's hand. "Yes. You know how I said that Dorothy is a friend?"

I really don't want to hear this. "Yes?"

"She's more than just a friend, John."

CHAPTER 35

June 1979

JOHN WAITED in his hotel room, looking out the only window at the rain coming down outside. It felt like a cell, and the lousy weather that had dogged him since he'd flown in to Toledo hadn't helped at all.

I don't know how to say this, so I'll just go ahead and say it. I've asked Dorothy to marry me. Even now, six months later, he couldn't get Roger's letter out of his mind.

Someone knocked. John looked through the peephole. "It's good to see you, Roger," he said as he opened the door. Roger managed an uncomfortable smile. John didn't hesitate this time—he pulled Roger close and hugged him tight.

"I'm glad you came, man. I know you had to juggle around your rehearsal schedule for me."

"Like I'd miss my best friend's wedding." He'd wanted to be anywhere but here, of course. But he couldn't do that to Roger. He loved him too much. Wanted him to be happy. Wanted him to have a good life, and no matter how much it hurt, he knew Roger loved Dorothy.

"Like I'd get married without you as my best man." John released Roger and they stepped apart.

"You ready to get wasted?" John asked. *He* sure was. In fact, he'd gotten started down at the hotel bar about an hour ago.

"*So* ready. I heard you've got the bar downstairs rented out for the night." Roger clapped his hand on John's back. "You really didn't have to do that."

"What are best men for? I just want to be sure you go out in style." John grabbed the key from off the desk. "Let's go meet the boys."

THE BAR was already half-filled with guests. They cheered when Roger walked in. John hung back, letting Roger greet his friends. John knew a few of them—kids they'd grown up with, including Nate Zimmer, who came up to him and offered him his hand.

"Good to see you, John," Nate said. No longer the fat kid with a face full of zits, Nate looked as though he'd bought into Jack LaLanne's fitness program hook, line, and sinker. His curly dark hair was smartly styled, and he wore a pair of dress pants that hugged his ass enough that it was hard to miss the sculpted glutes, and his casual shirt skimmed the muscled planes of his chest.

"You look amazing, Nate," John said. "What have you been up to?"

"Just finished law school last year. I'm working at a firm in San Diego. General practice stuff." Nate's face lit with obvious pride. "I've seen your name around. Roger said you were appointed music director of some symphony up in Connecticut."

"New Haven. They're a good group of musicians." John didn't mention the review in the *New York Times* that had named him as someone to keep an eye on.

"I always thought Roger would end up as a musician." Nate pressed his lips together and shook his head. "It's hard to see him settled down and working as an accountant." He laughed, then added, "Then again, I don't think I ever saw myself as an attorney either. Funny how reality sneaks up on you."

No joke.

"AW, COME on, John," Paul Stavos shouted over his beer. "Play something for us. You know you want to."

John hadn't planned on any entertainment at the party other than the free booze, so he hesitated. "I don't know. I doubt Roger wants to listen to my piano playing the night before—"

"Damn straight I want to hear it!" Roger pounded on the bar and lifted his glass. "Play something, John. You know you want to."

John raised his eyebrows and laughed. "For you, Roger? Anything."

Some of the men whooped as John walked over to the piano. It was set up on a low platform and looked serviceable. John played a few chords and winced—it had probably last been tuned when Richard Nixon was still president.

"Should I play something for Roger?" he asked the men, who were now gathering around the piano to listen.

"Something romantic," one of the guys said with a snigger and a look in Roger's direction.

Too easy.

"How about 'You Don't Bring Me Flowers' by Barbra Streisand and Neil Diamond?" John asked as he bit back a grin. Roger had always hated that song—hated any song, really, that was over-the-top romantic.

The men standing around the piano groaned and laughed, then pulled Roger up so he stood in the curved indentation of the piano. John forced back the image of Roger standing there with his violin. How many times had they spent their afternoons playing together like that?

"Got it." John played the opening measures of the song, then began to sing. "You don't bring me pizza. You don't bring me vodka. You hardly wash your clothes anymore, so I scrunch up my nose and push you away…." The guests laughed and applauded.

John saw that Roger was smiling. He also looked genuinely surprised. John wasn't sure if that made him happy or sad. Had it been so long since they'd just hung out and had fun that Roger didn't realize John wasn't the uptight, sheltered kid he'd been when they first became friends?

He finished the song and Nate, who John realized was standing nearly behind him, said, "How about 'Lady' by Styx?"

John grinned. He bit his lower lip and winked at Roger. "Roger," he sang, "when you're with me I'm wasted. Give me a-a-all your pot. Your eyes are so bloodshot it's obvious. Inhale, and your troubles all fade… you're my Roger."

More snickers this time and a couple of knowing elbows in Roger's side. Roger just laughed and said, "I don't see anyone offering me any Mary Jane."

Carl Rothstein sidled over to Roger and said in a loud whisper, "Come by my room tonight." Some of Roger's friends laughed, and a few others gave each other questioning looks as they tried to decide if Carl was kidding. Knowing Carl, John guessed he wasn't as he launched into his own twisted version of "Smoke on the Water."

Someone handed John another drink. He'd had at least four beers. Not that anyone noticed that his piano playing had become a bit less precise over the past hour. He was feeling decidedly better. It didn't matter that they were celebrating Roger's last night as a single man. John had missed hanging around with him and their old friends, and for a little while, he forgot the reason they were here.

"This one's for Roger and his future bride," John said as he tried not to slur his words. He could do this, he told himself. He wanted—no, he *needed*—to let Roger know he was all right with things between them. So he began to sing Billy Joel's "Just the Way You Are." And he didn't change the words this time. "I said I love you and that's forever.... I love you just the way you are."

He finished the song, then met Roger's eyes and lifted his beer in toast. "To Roger," he said.

"To Roger!" the guests responded amidst more back claps and shouts.

Roger's eyes seemed to sparkle in the dim light, and John wondered for just a moment if he saw sadness there. Then the crowd shouted and whooped as one of the men brought a woman up to the piano. She was wearing a long raincoat, towering heels, and far too much makeup.

A stripper. Perfect. The one thing John hadn't been willing to do for Roger for the party. *Time to bow out gracefully.*

He slipped out of the bar. In all the excitement of the stripper's arrival, he was pretty sure no one noticed. He walked out onto the patio, set his beer down on a table, and lit a cigarette. The concrete was wet, but the rain had stopped for now. A few stars were visible between the clouds.

For a few minutes, he'd forgotten why he'd come here. He'd just enjoyed himself and enjoyed doing something for Roger. But now it hit him, harder than he thought it could. *Fuck. Fuck, fuck, fuck.*

He picked up the beer bottle and swapped it for the cigarette in his mouth. He drained half the bottle, then set it back down on the table.

"Rough night?"

John started, then turned to see Nate Zimmer standing behind him. "What?" John asked, more because he didn't know how to respond than because he hadn't heard the question.

"You guys were pretty close. This must be difficult for you." Nate smiled affably.

"I'm happy for him."

"You don't look all that happy."

John's jaw tensed. He dropped his cigarette, put it out with his foot, then retrieved his beer. "Look, Nate," he began. "I know you mean well, but—"

"You're in love with him. You've loved him since we were kids. Give yourself a break. It's only normal that this is hard for you."

John wasn't drunk enough. Had they been so obvious, all those years ago? "He's my best friend. Of course I love him."

"That isn't what I said, John. I said that you're *in* love with him."

"I don't know what you mean." He took another pull of his beer.

Nate laughed. "Are you really that dense?" He shook his head, then put his hand on John's shoulder. "Or maybe you are. You never realized what a crush I had on you in high school, did you?"

"Me? But I thought—"

"That I had it bad for Roger? Nah. I liked him. Everyone did. But you were the one I wanted." Nate took a deep breath, then added, "I still do."

John hoped his mouth wasn't hanging open. He'd suspected Nate might be gay, but he'd never realized Nate hadn't wanted Roger all those years ago. "Christ. You're serious, aren't you?"

"Totally serious."

For the second time that night, John realized how attractive Nate had turned out. His eyes were a clear blue—why hadn't he seen that before? "I'm flattered."

"Good. So does this mean you'll come up to my room? It's not like either of us are interested in the naked woman back in the bar."

"I really should go back and—"

Nate kissed him, and John's face grew warm. Not just his face. "Shit."

Nate laughed. "I hope you meant that in a good way."

"I did."

"What about the party?" Nate asked with a grin.

"I don't think they'll miss us."

"Good. I was hoping you'd say that." Nate put his arm around John's shoulders and they walked back inside, headed for the elevators.

Chapter 36

ROGER WATCHED as John and Nate weaved their way across the lobby. A moment later they walked into the elevator. Roger caught a glimpse of John kissing Nate as the doors slid shut.

The Billy Joel song replayed in an endless loop in Roger's mind. *Fucking earworm.* He'd loved John. Hell, he *still* loved John. But he'd fallen in love with Dorothy, and he knew in his gut that he was making the right decision in marrying her. He loved how she made him feel comfortable and how she took care of him. He loved how easy it was to talk to her. How he felt good when she held him. How he didn't feel so goddamned conflicted when he was with her. He was marrying her for all the right reasons. For all the reasons a man marries a woman. Maybe they'd even have a kid or two someday. He'd be a father. The kind of man his mother wanted him to be. The kind of man his father would have been proud of. Someone like Marc.

"Hey, man." Paul's voice brought him back to himself with a start.

"Hey, Paul."

"Guys are looking for you. Something about you getting a free lap dance. That girl is hot."

"How hot?" Just what he needed. A fucking lap dance.

"Really hot." Paul outlined an hourglass shape with his hands and waggled his eyebrows.

"Be there in a minute."

He waited until Paul headed back into the bar, then glanced at the elevator one more time. He ignored the pain in his gut, then spun on his heels and followed Paul.

Roger stood at the entryway to the church, greeting guests. Dorothy smiled at him and touched the back of his hand. He wondered vaguely who all these people were. His mother's friends, Dorothy's family. He glanced at Dorothy in an effort to reassure himself that he'd make it through this. She really was lovely in her long white dress with her hair done up in a twist, the delicate netting of her veil making her dark hair seem to shine more than usual.

John stood at the end of the long reception line, chatting with Nate. He looked handsome in his tuxedo, his hair pulled back into what was now his trademark ponytail with wisps of warm-brown silk that framed his narrow face. With each person who came to greet Roger and Dorothy, John drew closer. It seemed an eternity before Nate came up and congratulated them. A moment later John took Dorothy's hand and kissed her on the cheek as he murmured something in her ear.

"Congratulations," John said as he shook Roger's hand.

"I'll meet you both outside," Dorothy told them with an understanding look.

"Thanks." Roger watched her leave, then sighed audibly.

"She's a good woman," John said. "She knew we'd want a few minutes alone."

"Yeah. I'm lucky." Roger couldn't deny the truth of that. No denying he loved Dorothy, either. He knew he'd known it before, but this was the first time he'd become conscious that he felt safe in that love. The first time, too, he realized he had room in his heart for someone other than John.

"I was hoping to catch you for a few minutes before the reception."

"Thanks again for last night. It was a great party." Great, except for watching John and Nate as they left. *And what about that? You want him to be happy, don't you?*

"You're welcome. I'm glad you had a good time." John pushed an errant strand of hair from his eyes, then said, "There's something I wanted to say to you. Something you need to know."

"Sure." Roger wasn't so sure he wanted to hear it, but he knew he owed it to John.

"Don't look so worried!" John laughed and shook his head. "I just wanted to tell you that I'm here, whenever you need me."

"That's it?"

"That's it. And that I want you to be happy."

"Thanks."

"For what?" John looked genuinely puzzled.

"For being here." *For being my friend, even after everything.*

John smiled. "You don't have to—"

"Roger?" Miranda appeared at the church exit. The frown she wore deepened when she noticed John. "The photographer wants to take a few more pictures before sunset."

"Sure, Mom."

Miranda left without a word to John. Roger wondered if she'd said anything to him at all the entire weekend. She'd been furious when Roger told her John would be his best man, regardless of what she thought about it.

"You'd better go. Wouldn't want to keep Miranda waiting."

"Yeah."

"I'll see you later, at the reception."

"Sounds good." Roger did his best to smile. "Later."

JOHN WATCHED Roger walk out of the church, then pulled a cigarette out of the pocket of his tux and stuck it in his mouth.

"Need a drink?"

John turned to see Nate standing in the doorway to the sanctuary. "Definitely." He lit the cigarette and watched the smoke swirl around in tendrils.

"She looks worried about you."

"She hates me. Always has." John shrugged. "Nothing new there."

"You okay?"

"I'm fine. Really." He was too. He'd made his peace with the new reality. He'd made his peace because he'd seen the love in Roger's eyes when he looked at Dorothy. Sure, it wasn't what he'd hoped for, but then things with Roger had never gone the way he hoped. They were better this way. Friends.

"He still loves you, you know."

"Probably." John didn't doubt it. He still loved Roger. He always would.

"Vodka tonic?" Nate asked as he slipped his arm around John's waist and led him out the church door.

"Sounds great."

PART 3

April 23, 1984.

HEALTH AND Human Services Secretary Margaret Heckler announced today that researchers at the National Cancer Institute have isolated the virus that causes AIDS. Secretary Heckler said a test to detect the virus with near 100 percent certainty would be available within a few months. She also predicted that an AIDS vaccine would be ready for testing in about two years.

CHAPTER 37

Spring 1984

"DON'T TELL me you're thinking of leaving?" John wobbled as he held on to the bar and walked over to the group of men pulling their coats from off the rack. "I thought this was my birthday party."

"Thirty isn't such a big deal," Joe Riley said as he pulled on his jacket. "When you turn forty, we'll do breakfast."

"Gotta work in the morning," Ralph Samson said as he wrapped his scarf around his neck. He looked down at his watch. "Shit. It's already morning."

"Time to go, John. They're closing up for the night." Joe put his arm around John's bare shoulders. "Where's your shirt?"

"Don't know. I want to dance again." John turned and began to walk over to the dance floor. The lights seemed too bright.

"Don't you have a class to teach?"

"Shit." He'd forgotten about that.

"I'll call a cab." Ralph tossed John his shirt. John reached for it, but it fell on the floor. Someone put it over his shoulders and led him outside onto the sidewalk. The sun had already started to rise between the buildings.

"MAESTRO FUCHS?"

John lifted his head from the desk and looked up to see one of the students from his music history class. Office hours usually meant a two-hour nap. No such luck today. *Figures.* Still, the assistant professor position at Rutgers meant he could afford a better apartment. His nap could wait.

"You're Miss Figueroa, right?"

She beamed. "Yes."

"How can I help you?" He ran a hand through his hair and hoped he didn't look like death warmed over.

She giggled. "You were sleeping, weren't you?"

"Is that what you wanted to ask me?"

More giggles. "No. I wanted to give you this." She handed him a folder. When he didn't immediately respond, she said, "It's my paper. I thought I'd turn it in early."

"Great. Thank you." He set the folder down on the desk.

Her cheeks pinked. "I... I just wanted to tell you how much I enjoy hearing you conduct," she said. "I've got an extra ticket to the New York Phil tomorrow night. I was wondering if maybe you'd like to come with me."

"I'm sorry, Miss Figueroa. I don't date students." *And you're the wrong sex anyhow.*

"Oh." Her face was now bright red. "I'm really sorry, I—"

The phone rang. *Thank God for the phone!* "I need to take this," he told her.

The student giggled again and backed out of the office. John smiled at her and waved, then sank back into his chair.

"John Fuchs."

"Happy birthday, Maestro."

"Roger?" John sat up straighter and smiled.

"Sorry I'm a day late. Things at work have been insane, and Dorothy's mom's having surgery in a few weeks. I lost track of time."

"It's not like I've been any better about calling." How long had it been since they last talked? Four months? Five? Hearing from Roger always reminded John how much he missed talking to him. "What's up with her mom?"

"Female stuff." Roger laughed, the sound of his voice warm even through the crackly receiver. "Dorothy won't tell me. Vera doesn't want her to. Not sure I really want all the details. So what's going on with you?"

"Not much."

"You can tell me what you've been up to, John. I can handle it."

"Am I that transparent?" John shook his head and chuckled.

"Yep. Pretty much. So tell me about your career. Any interesting gigs?"

"I'm guest conducting in Dallas and San Francisco next month. I'll be in Europe most of the summer in a few different places. I'm conducting my first *Aida* in the fall." John picked up a pencil and began to doodle on a piece of paper.

"Opera? I didn't know you liked opera."

"You never asked."

Roger laughed again. "What about in the next few weeks?" he asked after a slight pause.

"Next few weeks? Nothing except grading papers and final exams. Why do you ask?" John drew a series of circles that grew larger and larger. Then he began to fill in some of the places where they overlapped.

"With Dorothy helping her mom out, I've got a little free time. I was thinking maybe I'd head up to New York." Roger seemed to hesitate before continuing, "If you're up for company, that is."

"Are you kidding? I'd love for you to come. A friend of mine has a place at the Jersey Shore. We could hang out or drive down to Atlantic City." John smiled. "Or both."

"So how about I look into airfares and see what I can find? I'll give you a call on the weekend, okay?"

"Sounds good."

"Talk to you later."

"Later." John set the handset down. He was ready for this. Ready to spend time with Roger and just enjoy his company. Or at least he hoped he was.

"FARTHER!" ROGER shouted as John backed away from him toward the surf.

"What difference does it make?" John shook his head as his feet sank into the wet sand. "I can't catch worth a damn." He jumped to catch the Frisbee as it flew toward him, missed it, and landed awkwardly on his ass in the water.

Great.

Roger ran over, snagged the Frisbee from where it floated in the surf, then offered John a hand up. John took Roger's hand and ignored the familiar jolt of heat at the touch. Roger's sun-kissed skin, the strong line of his shoulders, and his bare chest made it that much more difficult to ignore. Once back on his feet, John let go of Roger's hand a bit too quickly and began to brush the wet sand off his skin.

"You really have no athletic ability, do you?"

John pursed his lips and fought the urge to kick water at Roger. "And *you're* ready for the NHL?"

"NFL," Roger corrected. "NHL is hockey."

"So? Maybe I meant NHL." John waved a hand around and began to walk down the beach to their rental.

"Right."

"I can run faster than you." His legs *were* longer than Roger's.

"Right."

"Fuck you." John turned and began to run. He kicked up sand in his wake and heard Roger splutter as some of it landed on Roger's face. *Serves him right.*

"You're going to regret that!" Roger shouted as he began to follow.

John looked back a moment later to see Roger catching up with him. John gritted his teeth and ran faster still, aiming for the beach house and ignoring the stitch in his side that threatened to become painful.

They reached the stairs underneath the house at the same time, both of them panting and covered in sand and sweat. John stepped on the first step and turned around to face Roger, hands on his hips, still gasping for air. "I win."

"Cheater."

"As if you wouldn't have cheated if you'd thought of it first."

Roger bent over with his hands on his thighs, taking in huge gulps of air. "Maybe I thought of it and just let you win."

John huffed, flicked his hair with his right hand, and grasped the railing with his left. "You're just a sore loser."

Roger laughed and followed him up the stairs.

"THIS IS really good." Roger looked up from his plate and smiled at John.

"Thanks. I took a cooking class last summer when I was in Italy." John took a sip of his wine. On the deck, the sound of the surf mingled with cricket song. John couldn't help but think how romantic the setting was. He pushed the thought away and let his mind settle on how nice this was, spending time with Roger.

"I envy you." Roger's smile faded. "Dorothy and I talked about spending a few weeks in Europe, but we never seem to be able to swing it. Between my work and her parents' health, we ended up putting it off."

"I'm sorry."

"Don't be. Not your fault, is it?" Roger poured them more wine, then continued, "But I hope I get back there someday."

John knew Roger was thinking of their trip to Vienna. "I'm sure you will."

"So where are you headed this year?" Roger leaned back in his seat and sipped his wine.

"Back to Germany in two weeks. Then I fly to France for a Baroque series in Lyon. I'm back in the States early August."

"Another gig?"

John nodded. "LA. Nate invited me to stay a few weeks. He's in San Diego, but he's thinking of moving back to the East Coast. I figured I'd catch him while he's still there. He's got a cottage on the beach not far from town."

Roger shifted in his seat and ran a hand through his hair. "That's great."

John noticed how a muscle in Roger's cheek seemed to jump as he said that.

"So how about you and Dorothy?" John asked a few minutes later as they leaned on the railing and looked out over the water.

"We're good."

From the tone of Roger's voice, John got the definite impression that things were not as good as Roger claimed. "Kids in your future?"

"Maybe. I don't know. We… we haven't had much luck with it. Dorothy had a miscarriage about six months ago." Roger's expression didn't change, but John saw the tension in his shoulders as he spoke.

"I'm sorry."

For a minute or two, Roger was silent. Then he took a deep breath and said, "Did you know I always wanted kids?" John shook his head.

"Yeah. I figured I'd be a better father to them than my father was." He paused, then added, "I know he tried. But I imagined what I might do with my own son. You know… the stuff I wished I'd done with my father. Someone to toss around a football. Someone to cheer on in Little League."

John put his arm around Roger's shoulder. "You'd make a great father. I'm sure of it."

"Thanks." Roger's eyes sparkled with tears.

Without really thinking, John pulled Roger into his arms and held him. Neither of them moved to break the physical contact. John wondered vaguely how long it had been since he'd held Roger like this—really held him, without one of them pulling away. John stroked Roger's hair and just listened to him breathe.

"I miss you, you know," Roger said in a soft voice.

"I miss you too." John wasn't going to lie.

Roger pulled away after a long moment. "Is this as difficult for you as it is for me?" He looked embarrassed to have said it.

"If you mean do I want more than this?"

"Yes."

"Of course." John smiled as he looked out at the waves. "But I'm happy to be here with you."

"Thanks for putting up with me." Roger leaned against the railing and brushed the hair from his eyes. "Sometimes I wonder why you do."

"You shouldn't. It's not putting up with anything." John had wondered the same thing himself at one time. He didn't wonder anymore. He'd long since realized he loved being with Roger. Loved listening to him and his wild dreams for the future. Loved the way Roger understood him even when he wasn't sure he understood himself. Loved that Roger knew who he was underneath his professional persona.

CHAPTER 38

Summer 1985

JOHN FINISHED his bows and headed stage right. The gig with the Manhattan Modern Music Ensemble had been a last-minute substitution, and he'd spent nearly every waking hour of the past three days studying the piece.

"Maestro Fuchs?" A tall dark-haired woman met him in the wings. "I'm Veronica Simmons."

"So good to meet you," John said as he shook her hand. "I appreciate the opportunity to fill in tonight."

She clasped his hand in both of hers and looked him directly in the eyes. "I'm impressed. To find someone to conduct an entirely new work on such short notice and do it as well as you... I consider it our good fortune."

"Thank you."

"Our board of trustees has been looking for a full-time conductor," she told him. "It isn't much, a dozen performances a year, and we'd be happy to work around your current schedule."

"I'm definitely interested. Thank you." He'd been hoping to quit his teaching job for a few years now, and this was just the opportunity he'd been looking for.

She handed him her card and said, "Have your agent contact me and we can discuss a contract."

"Thank you." He took the card and smiled. He didn't have an agent—he'd been putting it off—although he'd had several agents express interest in working with him. He'd have to call them in the morning.

She left a moment later, and he headed back to his dressing room. He grinned when he saw the dark-haired man leaning against the wall. Waiting for him. "Nate?" Nate looked incredible in his well-cut suit, and his smile was a breath of fresh air.

"I thought I'd come in for the performance and surprise you."

John took Nate's hand and led him inside. A dozen red roses greeted him on the mirrored table. "From you?" he asked.

"I thought you might like them."

"They're lovely. But you shouldn't have." He was glad Nate had sent them, though. He leaned in to meet Nate's lips.

"You look exhausted," Nate said as the kiss broke.

"I'm beat. The composer is in LA, and I spent the last two nights on the phone with him, trying to figure the piece out."

"And days rehearsing?" Nate offered him a sympathetic smile.

John nodded.

"How about I make you dinner at your place? Tomorrow's Sunday. You can sleep in and I can take care of you."

"I'm liking that idea." John covered his mouth with his hand and yawned.

JOHN STUMBLED out of bed at 11:00 a.m., and only because the light from outside was just too bright to block out and the smell of something from the kitchen was too good to ignore.

"Morning." Nate grinned at him from the stove as he padded into the kitchen.

"You're fucking amazing, you know. Dinner last night and now pancakes? I love pancakes."

"And I was thinking it was the sex."

John smiled. "I love that almost as much as I love pancakes."

"Almost?"

"Okay. Better. But right now I'm so hungry, I'll go for pancakes." John sat down at the table, and Nate set a cup of espresso in front of him. "Christ. If you were a woman, I'd marry you in a heartbeat."

Nate laughed and went back to the stove to flip a pancake, then set it on a plate and brought it over to John. "Marriage isn't the only option, you know."

"You spoil me." John knew he was grinning, but he couldn't stop himself.

THE SUN was just beginning to set over the Hudson River as John walked Nate over to Grand Central Station. "You really didn't need to come with me," Nate said.

"I wanted to. Besides, it's a beautiful day and it was a great weekend." John grinned. He couldn't remember the last time he'd felt so good.

"I wasn't totally joking about marriage, you know."

Nate's hand brushed his, and John clasped it. He didn't give a shit what anyone thought, not that anyone seemed to care to see two men holding hands. He loved that about the city.

"The firm's talking about opening an office in Manhattan, and they're looking for one of the partners to manage it," Nate continued. "I've told them I might be interested."

"Might be?" John liked the direction the conversation was headed.

Nate stopped and set his duffel on the sidewalk. "I've been thinking about it a while. Us."

"And what do you think?"

"I'm thinking I'd like us to live together. If you think you're ready." Nate squeezed his hand, and John knew he would have kissed him if they hadn't been standing on Forty-Second Street and Third Avenue with people walking by them.

"Why wouldn't I be ready?" John knew what Nate was getting at, but he understood they couldn't avoid this conversation forever.

"Because of him. Roger." The smile on Nate's face faded, and his lips parted in obvious anticipation.

Moment of truth, Fuchs. It was time to let go. Time to move on. "I'm ready." It struck him as incredibly surreal, saying this on a crowded street—like one of those time-lapse films where one person stands still as everyone else zooms by.

"I need the truth, John." The deep blue of Nate's eyes seemed to flicker in the fading light. "Do you still love him?"

For a long moment, John said nothing. Then, with a sigh, he said, "Yes."

"Good."

John stared at Nate, speechless. He'd just said he still loved Roger and Nate was good with it?

Nate just smiled. "I needed the truth. I needed to hear you say it." He squeezed John's hand again. "So let me ask again now that that's out of the way. Will you live with me?"

CHAPTER 39

Fall 1986

"HONEY? IT'S past three. I thought you were going to play golf with Bill." Dorothy looked at him with motherly concern. Roger hated that, even though he knew she meant well.

"I'm passing this weekend." He honestly didn't feel like golf. He hated golf, but he played because the other men at work did. "Gonna relax a bit downstairs. Let me know when you want me to set the table."

Her smile was forced, but she wouldn't press him on it. He knew that six years of marriage had taught her when he needed time alone. He leaned over and gave her a peck on the cheek, then headed down to the basement. Once there, he pulled out his violin case from the battered armoire in the corner.

Over the past few years, he'd walled off a good section of the basement and laid carpet. He'd even hung ceiling tile in an effort to dampen the sound. Not that Dorothy minded the violin—in fact, she often asked him to play for her (he always refused)—but Roger didn't want anyone to hear him.

He set the case on the coffee table and opened the latches. They'd grown stiff over the years, and in spite of his best efforts to oil them, he was wistful knowing he'd have to replace the old case someday soon. *Getting old, just like me.* He knew it was stupid to even think like that. Since when was thirty-two old? *It's old when your life is the same day in and day out.*

He pulled his bow out of the case to tighten it and inhaled the warm pine scent of the rosin as he unwrapped it from its fabric cover. He closed his eyes as he rubbed the dark-green cake against the horsehair that spanned the wood.

Dear Roger,

I was sorry to hear about Dorothy's mother. I know how close they were. It must be very difficult for her.

Congratulations on the promotion. I know you deserved it. I hope that doesn't mean you're working a lot more hours. All work and no play has never been good for Roger.

I've been busy traveling. I took a leave of absence from teaching. It was getting too difficult to juggle my schedule at school and the conducting gigs. I already told you about the recording. We're scheduled for a week in the studio starting the first of May. I'm meeting with the composer next week to discuss a few issues we've had in rehearsals. She's easy to work with, so I don't anticipate any problems.

The big news is that Nate and I bought a brownstone in the West Village, not far from West Fourth Street. He got the job as managing partner at the satellite office off Wall Street, and they gave him a hefty bonus to move from Connecticut. With my advance on the recording, we figured we could afford to fix the place up. The construction crew should be finished in a few months, so I hope you'll consider visiting us when you have a chance. Dorothy's welcome too, of course. (I promise I'll behave around her!) But really, Nate's a good influence on me. He likes to be in bed by eleven. God help me, he goes for a run at five every morning!

Give me a call when you have time. I miss your voice.

John

Roger went through the motions of tuning the fiddle—it didn't take much thought—then held the violin between his chin and shoulder and played through a few Kreutzer études. The music was simple, meant more to develop flexibility in fingers and bow arm, but it would do. He needed to play something that would keep him focused on something else—he couldn't get John's last letter out of his mind. Funny how he couldn't stop thinking about the letter but it hadn't really sunk in.

John and Nate Zimmer. Living together. He'd expected it would happen eventually, and he knew he could hardly complain. He wanted John to be happy. At least part of him did—the part that wasn't wishing *he* was the one buying an apartment with John.

Nate's a good man.

He flexed the fingers of his left hand. Stiff, as always. But he'd stuck with it instead of just feeling sorry for himself. Sometime between the trip to Vienna with John and his wedding, he'd realized he could stop feeling sorry for himself long enough to enjoy the music. Not that he ever played for Dorothy.

He drummed the pads of his fingers over the strings and smiled—he'd finally begun to build up the calluses there again after two months of playing daily. The bones in his hand ached as they always did, but he ignored them. There was something appealing about the pain. He'd asked the doctor why it seemed to hurt more now than it had years before. She'd just sighed and told him he was more likely to develop arthritis in his injured joints. He'd come to believe it was something like penance to the music gods for having made such a mess of things.

Damn. He was feeling sorry for himself again. *Fuck your pathetic guilt.* He wouldn't give in to the voice in the back of his mind. He'd made his choices, hadn't he? He wouldn't feel guilty about them. He'd move forward.

He played through a series of scales and arpeggios to loosen up the muscles in his hand, his thoughts straying once more to John. They'd made it this long, their friendship stronger even than it had been after he and Dorothy had married. He'd known John and Nate were dating. But this? This was something more permanent.

There was a time when he'd wondered if he could love someone other than John. Then he'd met Dorothy and he'd understood he could. Why shouldn't John find someone he was happy with? Or was that it? He knew this thing between John and Nate was more than just dating. John was in love with Nate. And Nate was in love with the man Roger had spent his entire life loving.

Flexing his hand, he focused once more on the Kreutzer with its repetitive phrases. He'd hated these pieces years ago. They'd seemed so simple, and he'd lived for the challenge of mastering the long and complex runs that punctuated the flashier concertos he preferred. They'd been like obstacle courses for him, those virtuosic passages, and he'd only stepped back to settle into the broader musical expression when his violin teacher or John reminded him that often the true beauty of the music hid in the simplest of phrases. Now, robbed of the agility in his fingers, he'd learned to take pleasure in the simple beauty of Bach or Telemann. Strange, how life had become more of an appreciation of that simplicity. A quiet evening spent on the front porch with a good book, or a friendly game of Scrabble with Dorothy. A telephone conversation with John. A card or a letter. Well, *most* letters.

Roger finished a third Kreutzer étude and set the violin down in its case, then walked over to the metal desk set against the brick foundation. For a moment he stared out the small window near the ceiling. It was just big enough to let the light in, but set too high to see outside. A single plant snaked around the wooden frame, as if it had miscalculated and grown away from the sun, then changed course. He followed the plant's stem around the window. Bent in the middle, it now shot upward toward the light, its bloom beginning to open at last, after all the other flowers had already spent.

Roger smiled and pulled a piece of paper from one of the desk drawers, tried several pens until he found one that still had ink, then put pen to paper as the light from outside began to soften.

> *Dear John,*
>
> *Congratulations on the apartment. I hope you and Nate will enjoy it. Dorothy and I would love to come for a visit once you're settled in. She's been wanting to see* Cats *on Broadway for a few years now, and I'm sure she'd enjoy it.*
>
> *I heard your name mentioned on the radio a few weeks ago. I'm waiting for the recording so I can play it on my new stereo system. Dorothy laughs at me, but she indulges my need for toys.*
>
> *Be well and send my regards to Nate. Tell him if he ever needs someone to complain to about you, I'm always here.*
>
> *Take care of yourself,*
>
> *Roger*

He addressed the envelope and sealed the letter, then set it by the stairs so he wouldn't forget to mail it in the morning. A few minutes later, he was playing once again, doing his best to concentrate on the music.

CHAPTER 40

Winter 1987

"HEY."

John looked up from the piano and smiled at Nate, who had just walked into the living room. "Feeling better?"

"A little. I think the antibiotics finally kicked in." Nate coughed a few times, his pale cheeks pinking with the effort. He looked terrible. Not just pale. Pasty. And that cough....

John closed the cover on the keyboard, stood up, and walked over to give Nate a hug. "I need to start force-feeding you, you know," he said as he wrapped his arms around Nate's increasingly narrow waist. "You hungry?"

"A little. I had a protein shake a few hours ago."

Nate shivered and John held him tighter. "Maybe you should go back to the doctor. Maybe you need something stronger than penicillin. You don't want bronchitis turning into pneumonia."

"I'm fine. Really. Once I start working out again, I'll feel better."

John kissed Nate's cheek. It felt warm. John touched his palm to Nate's forehead. "You still have a fever. Why don't you go lie down and let me bring you some more of that hot-and-sour soup. Maybe a few steamed dumplings and rice."

"Really, I'm good. I can get myself something." Nate pulled away and started for the kitchen, walked a few feet, then stopped and leaned against the wall. "Shit." His breaths came out in wheezing gasps.

"I'll get you back into bed and call the doctor." More than a week of this, and the antibiotics were doing nothing. John was getting really worried. One of his former Juilliard classmates—a gay man—had died of pneumonia a year before, and seeing Nate like this scared the hell out of him.

Stop it. He's fine.

John laid a wet washcloth over Nate's eyes.

"Thanks."

"I'll be back with soup in a few minutes. Stay put, okay?"

Nate coughed a few times before offering John a tired smile. John leaned down and kissed Nate on the forehead, hoping he didn't look as worried as he felt. He pulled the covers over Nate and, for the first time, noticed a rash on Nate's right arm.

John swallowed hard and forced a smile as his heart leapt into his throat. Just the week before, he'd heard about another of his Juilliard friends who'd died. Wasted away. Hadn't he had a rash when he was first diagnosed? No, he told himself, Nate was healthy as a horse. Still, the rash scared him. He'd heard of rashes with scarlet fever. You could cure scarlet fever. He wouldn't even consider the alternative.

Two days later

"HELLO?" ROGER said into the receiver as he rubbed his eyes and glanced at the bedside clock. It was two o'clock in the morning.

"It's me. S-sorry. I know I must have w-woken y-you up."

"John." Roger's heart beat hard as he glanced over at Dorothy, who looked back at him with concern. "Are you all right?"

"I'm fine. I just n-need to t-talk. I'm r-really sorry to w-wake you up."

Roger mouthed for Dorothy to go back to sleep, then got out of bed and headed downstairs with the phone in his hand. "Don't apologize. It's me, remember? What's wrong?" John hadn't stuttered in years.

"I...." John sighed through the speaker. "Nate.... F-fuck, I c-can't even...."

Roger sat on the couch in the living room and tucked one leg beneath him. "Take your time. I'm not going anywhere. What's up with Nate?"

"H-he's in the h-hospital."

"What?"

"He's in the hospital. They admitted him a few days ago." John sounded on the verge of tears.

"The guy's in better shape than Arnold Schwarzenegger. What the hell is he doing in the hospital?" Roger ran a hand through his hair and sat up straighter.

"I... h-he.... He had this cold. Flu maybe... I don't know." John stumbled over the words, sometimes stuttering, sometimes coming to a complete stop. "The doctor gave him some antibiotics, but he didn't get better."

"God, John. How is he now?" Something in John's voice made him think this was far more than just a flu.

"He's okay. I think. At least that's what they told me before they kicked me out of the hospital." No stuttering this time. John never stuttered when he was pissed off.

"Kicked you out? Why?"

"He's in intensive care. They're only letting family in."

"Family? Hell, you're his fucking partner!" Roger popped up from the couch and began to pace the living room.

"It doesn't work like that. They don't care if we live together. They don't care if we own an apartment together. We're two men. Queers. They don't give a shit."

"Damn. I'm so sorry." Roger stopped and looked out at the street. The rain had left a shimmery fog behind, the light from a neighbor's porch casting an eerie white glow like a cloud.

"Not your fault. I called one of his friends from the law firm. He knows about me and Nate. He's going to try talking to the hospital... see what he can do. It's not like he has any family anyhow. His dad died when he was a kid, and his mom died a few years back."

"So what's wrong with him? I mean, they must have figured it out by now, right?"

"Pneumonia. Some weird new strain. Pneumocystis something. Doesn't respond to the usual drugs. They're running more tests. He's not even awake, and they're poking him, taking his blood...." Roger heard John blow his nose. "Sorry. It's just that I get so... I don't even know what. Angry, I guess. And it gets worse. A lot worse."

"What's worse?"

"I heard the nurses talking." John paused as if trying to collect his thoughts. "They were saying they didn't want to take care of him. One of them was going to ask her supervisor to assign someone else to him. She called him—" Roger could hear John's deep breath. "She called him a 'fucking faggot.'"

"Bitch."

John laughed, a bitter, pained sound.

"So she didn't want to take care of him because he's gay?"

"Yes." John spoke so quietly now that Roger had to press the phone against his ear to hear clearly. "But more than that."

"What more?"

"People have been dying here, Roger. Young men. Gay men. People I know. People are talking about it in the clubs. Checking themselves. Freaking out when they catch a cold."

Roger said nothing. What was he supposed to say?

"Nate has it." John inhaled sharply, then released a shuddered sigh. "God. Roger. He has AIDS."

CHAPTER 41

Winter 1988

ROGER OPENED the door to the waiting room and peered inside. He hoped he wasn't too late. From what John had told him the night before, he wasn't sure he'd make it in time. "Hey."

John looked up from the bench and offered Roger a wan smile. "Roger. Thanks for coming."

As if he wouldn't have come! But the widening chasm between him and Dorothy had made it easier to leave. The few attempts he'd made to talk to her about it hadn't done much—she'd just insisted things between them were fine and that she was happy. He'd taken to spending most of his free time in the basement with his violin. He hadn't wanted to burden John with his marital shit when John was barely keeping it together, and even though he knew he wouldn't talk about that now, he was just happy to spend time with John.

The antiseptic smell of the hospital made Roger sick to his stomach. Nearly fifteen years since the accident, and still the memory of it lingered at the periphery of his thoughts. Roger realized he was flexing the fingers of his left hand as he often did when those memories resurfaced.

Roger sat next to John. "What do they say?"

John shook his head. "He's dying. They say they're doing what they can, but you can see it in their eyes."

"Shit." Roger wrapped an arm around John's shoulders. "God. I'm so sorry."

"I'm glad you're here."

"I'd have come sooner, but my flight was delayed. Have you been in to see him?"

John shook his head. "They won't let me. Only family."

"Shit." Roger stood up. "I'll be back in a few minutes, okay? Don't worry. It's going to be all right."

"Where are you going?"

"Nowhere important. I'll be back in a couple." He offered John what he hoped was a reassuring smile.

"Okay."

Roger walked out of the waiting room and down the hallway to the nurse's station. One of the nurses looked up at him. "Can I help you, sir?" she asked.

"Yes," Roger said. "I think you can."

ROGER TOOK the keys from John's shaking hand. "I can get it." It took him a minute or two to find the right keys, then another minute to figure out which way the keys turned. John said nothing, and even after Roger had finally opened the door to the loft, he didn't move. Roger slipped his arm around John's shoulders and led him inside.

"Why don't you sit down? I'll get you something to drink."

John nodded but said nothing. He'd been like this since Nate had died. Silent. Stoic. Lost.

Christ, but Roger wished he could say something that would help. Do something. Take away the pain. Nate. Geeky, wonderful Nate from Marysville. Nate the beautiful man. Nate who made John happier than Roger had seen in years.

Roger fought back tears and gritted his teeth. *So not fair. So fucking unfair.* He took a deep breath and watched the steam rise from the kettle, then poured the hot water over a tea bag. He needed to call Dorothy and tell her he'd be staying with John until he was sure John would be all right. He'd take some vacation days—he had more than enough that he could take a few weeks if he needed to.

"Here you go," he said as he handed John the cup of tea and settled down on the couch next to him. The room was dark but for the light from the front hallway.

"Thanks." John forced a smile.

"How are you doing?" *Stupid question. Of course he's feeling like shit.*

"I'm okay." John set the mug down without even sipping the tea. "I guess." His shoulders slumped a bit more.

Roger swallowed. Or tried to. His mouth was dry, his face hot. He closed his eyes and tears ran down his cheeks. How fucked was that? He was the one crying and it was John who'd just lost the man he loved.

John turned and looked at him with an expression of stunned surprise. He said nothing but reached out and embraced Roger. "Thanks." John's voice cracked. Roger heard his sharp intake of breath, then felt the shudder run through his body.

"For what?"

"I know you got them to let me in to see him."

Roger swallowed hard and held John tighter. He'd spent nearly an hour arguing with the nurse, telling her Nate had no one but John. He'd seen the look of disgust on her face, heard it in her words and in the tone of her voice. If the attending physician hadn't walked by while he'd been speaking to her, he doubted he'd have gotten anywhere. In the end, the doctor had personally escorted John into Nate's room. The first and only time Roger had sensed sympathy from the hospital staff.

"I don't even think he knew I was there."

Roger blinked back tears. "He knew." Right now he needed to believe that Nate really did. It was the only thing that made this entire horrible mess bearable, that Nate knew John was there when he died.

"I got tested a few months ago. I thought I might have it too." John's voice was a monotone. The lack of emotion scared the shit out of Roger. He had no idea what to say. What could you say when you were absolutely sure the next thing you heard would tear you into tiny little pieces? He ended up holding his breath and nodding instead.

"I'm negative."

Oh God. Oh thank God! He held John tighter, the words not enough to reassure him that John wasn't going to leave him.

"It should have been me. Why the hell wasn't it me?" John's body shook and he began to sob against Roger's shoulder. "I'm the one who was out there fucking the world. I'm the one who didn't give a shit about what I did or who I was with…."

"Don't. Please don't. You know it doesn't work like that, and you know no one deserves this."

"No." John pulled away from Roger, knocking the tea from the coffee table as he stood up. He ignored the spill and stalked across the room. Roger followed, wrapping his arms around John even as John tried to pull away. "It should have been me."

"Don't you dare say that!" Roger hadn't meant the words to come out quite so harshly. "Because fuck it—if it had been you, I don't know what I would have done."

John stared at him.

"Fuck." Roger's heart jumped into his throat. He hadn't meant for it to come out like it did, and he immediately regretted it. "I shouldn't have said that. I mean, of course I didn't want it to happen to Nate. I don't want it to happen to anybody, but I—"

"Thanks." John smiled through his tears.

"For what?"

"For being you. For being here."

"I'm an idiot."

"You're not. But you really don't need to stay. I'm sure Dorothy needs you." From the way John still clung to him, Roger was just as sure he needed him more.

"I'm staying. I want to stay." *I need to stay. I need to know you're going to be okay.*

CHAPTER 42

Spring 1990

"TELL ME what you're thinking about?" Roger brushed a hand over Dorothy's hair. He loved the sound of the waves lapping at the beach from the open balcony doors. They'd flown to Antigua for an impromptu second honeymoon two days before, trading rainy March weather for the sunshine. But in spite of the warm weather and the soft, puffy clouds scattered across the bright blue of the sky, Roger felt anything but relaxed. He'd hoped the time away from home would help them rekindle their relationship, but it only seemed to amplify the distance between them.

"Hmm?"

"Just that you seem so far away," he said as he bent down to peck her cheek.

Her smile seemed forced. "I was just thinking how nice the weather is here."

"It is beautiful." He looked out at the water and repressed a sigh. A couple held hands as they walked along the shore in their bare feet. He couldn't remember the last time they'd held hands. After the last miscarriage, she'd been less affectionate. And the sex... he couldn't remember the last time they'd had sex. He knew that wasn't entirely her fault. He certainly hadn't gone out of his way to change the status quo.

"You up for a swim?" he asked, deciding that he needed to take charge, if only to get them out of their room. They hadn't even explored all of the resort yet; they'd just gone swimming at the pool and eaten at two of the restaurants.

Her expression brightened at his words. "Sure. Just let me slip into my bathing suit. I'll be just a minute." She pulled her bathing suit out of her suitcase and went into the bathroom to change. More than ten years of marriage and she still wouldn't undress in front of him.

They walked down the beach a few minutes later. She didn't move to take his hand, and when he reached for hers, she ran into the surf. As she did, water splashed around her legs, and she laughed.

She was beautiful like this. At thirty-six, her body was still trim, her brown hair pulled off her face in a high ponytail, and her long legs looked good in the high-cut floral bathing suit. A few strands of chestnut hair fell onto her cheeks in wisps. He forgot sometimes how young she was. It was easy to do that. Their suburban lives had become mundane, a string of repetitive motions: getting up, going to work, coming home, eating dinner in front of the TV, going to sleep. Roger sometimes wondered if she was as restless as he.

"I'm glad we came," he told her as he ran after her into the surf. He was just a few feet away from her when he landed on his left foot and his leg just seemed to give out on him. He fell into the surf, landing on his ass in water up to his shoulders.

"Are you all right?" Dorothy asked.

Roger laughed as he wiped the water from his face and smoothed his now-wet hair out of his eyes. "I must have tripped on something."

She offered him her hand and they both laughed as he shook the sand from his bathing suit.

"This reminds me of when I was a kid and my family used to spend summers on Lake Erie. My dad had a little sailboat and my brother and I would stay with my grandparents during the week. My mom took care of us. Dad would join us on the weekends."

"I spent a summer at a camp in Pennsylvania. The lake was the best part." He smiled, then added, "Well, maybe the marshmallow fights we had were better."

"Marshmallow fights?"

"We'd work them with our fingers until they were all sticky, then chase each other around the cabin." He smiled at the memory. "The counselors made us wash up in the lake. It was freezing, but I think that was the best part of it."

They shared a comfortable and familiar silence as they walked, she with her feet in the water, he on the shore, just out of reach of the surf. They'd had so much to talk about at one time, or at least he'd thought they had. His job. Her fifth-grade students getting into trouble or bringing her flowers from their backyards. What they'd name their children. How many they'd have.

The ache of another memory intruded into the silence, but he pushed it away, not wanting to feel the emotions that always came in tandem with thoughts of John.

ROGER LAY next to Dorothy in the darkness of their room. He'd hoped to make love to her, but she'd told him she was tired. She had long since fallen asleep, but at 2:00 a.m., he was wide-awake. He'd resisted the urge to jerk off in the shower; he felt guilty when he did. Roger didn't feel bad about the act of jerking off itself. But lately, when he soaped himself up and stroked himself under the water, he saw John's face. He imagined how John's hands had felt on his body and how John's body had felt beneath him. He'd never been unfaithful to Dorothy, but it felt as though he was cheating when he thought of John. He wondered vaguely where John was. Last they'd spoken, he was headed to Japan for two months to conduct. He traveled more and more now.

"I sold the condo," John had told him a few weeks before. "Too many memories. It's time to move on."

"You need to date a little, not just move on," Roger said.

John laughed. "I date plenty."

"I don't mean fucking, I mean dating. There's a difference. Besides," he admitted, figuring he had nothing to lose, "I worry about you. I know it's been hard for you, but—"

"I don't have a death wish. I'm careful." John's voice softened a bit as he spoke those words. "I wouldn't do that to you. Really, I wouldn't."

The lump in Roger's throat made it difficult to speak.

He slipped out of bed an hour later, pulled on a pair of shorts and a T-shirt, and headed to the bar for a drink. He'd call John when he and Dorothy got home. It'd be good to hear his voice. Maybe he'd even fly out to New York and spend a weekend.

PART

December 21, 1993.

IN A compromise likely to anger both sides of the debate over gays serving openly in the military, President Clinton introduced a policy of "Don't Ask, Don't Tell, Don't Pursue," which mandated that military officials may not ask about or require service members to reveal their sexual orientation. Under the new policy, members of the armed forces could be discharged if they claimed to be homosexual or bisexual.

CHAPTER *43*

January 1994

JOHN DRAGGED his bags into the dark apartment and left them by the front door—he was too damn tired to put them in the bedroom. He flicked on the light and sighed. God, it was good to be home! It didn't matter that he had no food in the fridge (he hoped he'd remembered to toss the milk before he'd left more than two months before). It didn't even matter that the only food in the apartment was a can of tomato soup, some pasta, and a box of oatmeal.

He'd been in six different cities, three different countries, and two different time zones, and he was just happy to be back in New York with nothing on his agenda but studying a new piece of music he'd be conducting in February. He'd take advantage of the time off and touch base with a few friends after he caught up on some sleep, then plan an evening out at one of the dance clubs.

He smiled when he thought about what might happen after the club. He'd barely had time to sleep on his Asian tour, let alone find someone to sleep *with*. With the exception of the twentysomething he'd met in Osaka. Gorgeous kid with skin like silk. Good sushi, good sake, amazing sex.

The pile of mail on the front table was already separated into bills and letters. He'd paid a graduate student to water the plants and empty the small mailbox down in the lobby. He ignored the bills. He'd deal with those the next day. He picked up the letters and sifted through them: a postcard from his mother, who was vacationing in Rome with her cousin; a letter from one of his former students, now living in Dallas; and a letter with familiar handwriting. A letter from Roger. He smiled and opened the envelope.

> *Dear John,*
>
> *I know you said you'd be traveling most of the winter, but I figured I'd catch you up on life in Chicago. Not that it's all that exciting. We got about a foot of snow last Monday and the streets are still a mess.*
>
> *If you have a minute when you're around, give me a call. I've missed hearing your voice.*
>
> *Take care,*
>
> *Roger*

He knew Roger well enough to know that the letter wasn't meant to catch him up on snowfall in Chicago. It was Roger's way of saying, "Call me, I really need to talk."

John tossed his jacket onto the couch, and the photograph of him and Nate caught his eye. It had been taken on one of their last trips—this one to a B and B in Vermont the fall before Nate died. Had it been six years already? He'd lost count, mostly because he'd wanted to lose count.

He'd spent the first anniversary of Nate's death at the apartment feeling sorry for himself and working his way through an expensive bottle of wine. If he was going to mope, he figured he'd do it in style. He'd gotten about halfway through the bottle when the phone rang.

"What are you up to?" Roger's voice sounded warm, even through the phone.

"Nothing. Drinking."

"Anything good?"

"Damn straight. You know I don't drink cheap stuff."

Roger laughed. "Can't fault your taste in booze. Or men."

"No." John fingered the photograph he'd set on his lap and smiled.

"You doing okay?"

"Yes." John picked up his third glass of wine and brought it to his lips.

"Good. I worry about you sometimes, you know."

It felt good hearing that. "I know. Thanks."

"I miss him too."

"I know."

He'd cried and Roger had stayed on the phone with him for more than an hour, talking to him, telling him stories about Nate in junior high. Making him smile through the tears. Even now, Roger still called him on February 3, just to make sure he was okay. And he was okay, more or less. He didn't cry anymore, but the hole in his heart was still there. More grief, less guilt. Fading memories.

He picked up the phone and pressed the speed dial.

"Hello?"

"It's me."

"Hey, John. Thanks for calling."

THREE DAYS later, he sat on the floor of Roger and Dorothy's house, going through Roger's collection of LPs and putting them into boxes. Outside, the snowdrifts reached the bottom of the windows, although inside was warm.

"Another beer?" Roger said from the doorway to the kitchen.

"Sure." He didn't mention that he knew Roger had bought the imported stuff for him; he didn't want to embarrass Roger. Still, it made him smile.

"Barry Manilow?" he asked as Roger came back with a beer in each hand.

"Dorothy's."

John raised an eyebrow.

"Swear to God!" Roger laughed and took the LP from him before setting it on the "Dorothy" pile.

"I like Barry Manilow," John admitted. Roger just shook his head. "How you holding up?"

"I'm fine. I'm the one leaving, remember?" Roger carded his fingers through his hair. There were a few more grays than John remembered.

"Doesn't matter. You still care about her."

"Yeah." Roger sat down next to him and pulled a boxed set of Bach from the pile. He brushed the dust off the top with his fingers.

"You going to tell me what happened?" They'd been dancing around it for the past six hours, ever since Roger had met him at the airport.

For a long moment, Roger said nothing. He put the Bach into the box and picked up another record. "I wasn't making her happy," he said.

"Sounds like a reason for her to divorce you. Not the other way around."

Roger shrugged and pulled another record out of the box. "Cool. Led Zeppelin. I used to play this all the time in high school. Practically wore the thing out."

John huffed softly.

"Okay, okay. I know. I'm in avoidance mode." Roger picked up his beer and took a long pull.

"You could say that." John waited for Roger to come clean.

"I came out to Dorothy."

John was sure his mouth was hanging open. "You… what?"

Roger scowled and took another drink. "You heard me. I told her I was gay."

"Shit. Roger. Where the hell did that come from?"

"You need an explanation?" Roger laughed.

He shook his head. "I… I guess I always figured you were bi." He'd never even asked; he'd been afraid to.

"That's what I told myself. Made it easier. Thing is, I like women." He paused and blew a breath from between his lips. "I loved her. Dammit. I still do. And I feel like such a shit."

"How's she doing?"

Roger offered John a tight smile. "She called *me* the other day. Just wanted to see how I was. Can you believe it?"

Of course John could. God only knew he'd had enough reasons to boot Roger out of his life. But there was just something about Roger that made it difficult to stay angry with him. His sense of humor. The warmth John had sensed in Roger's music that had only grown throughout their years as friends. The way Roger had held his hand when he didn't think he could go on without Nate.

"I believe it." He moved over so he was behind Roger, then began to massage his shoulders.

"Thanks." Roger set the LPs down on the carpet and dry scrubbed his face. John knew he did that when he didn't want to show his emotions.

"So what are you going to do now?" John asked after a few minutes had passed in silence.

"I'm not sure. Look for an apartment or maybe a fixer-upper house. I can't stay at the hotel forever."

"I'll be back here in two months," John said.

"Oh?"

"Guest-conducting gig with the CSO."

"The Chicago Symphony? No shit."

John laughed and bit his lower lip. "Leave it to you to make something holy sound crass."

"Not crass. Energetic."

"Right."

"So you've hit the big time now." Roger looked at him while John continued to rub his shoulders. "Damn. Not that I doubted it, but still...."

"It's just a guest-conducting gig. Vittorio Caldi is retiring soon, so they're having some guest conductors come work with the orchestra. I'm small potatoes compared to most of them."

"You know I'll be in the audience."

"You don't have to come," John said quickly. "I know that it's not exactly your thing." Maybe he shouldn't have brought up the gig. He'd really only wanted to reassure Roger that he'd be back again.

"I can handle it. I enjoy listening to music." Roger hesitated for a moment, then added, "I've been playing violin again."

"Really?"

"Yeah. Really. Not that I'm any great shakes, but I'm okay. I hooked up with a few other musicians, and we play through a little chamber music once a month. I'm also teaching a few students on the weekend."

John hugged Roger. "You don't know how happy it makes me to hear that. I told you that you'd make a great teacher."

"Eh. It's nothing." Roger shrugged again, but John was pretty sure it wasn't "nothing."

"I'd love to hear you play again sometime. Maybe we can play together."

Roger tensed beneath John's hands, and John worried he'd pushed him too far. "Maybe" was all Roger said. "Maybe sometime."

CHAPTER 44

December 1994

ROGER STOOD at the door to his mother's Ft. Lauderdale apartment, hesitating. If he hadn't been so goddamn nervous, he might have laughed—he'd been hesitating with her his entire life. He'd been tempted to do this over the phone, but he'd realized he needed to be man enough to talk to her in person. He was tired of cop-outs. Tired of feeling guilty. Forty years old. Too old to lie to himself.

"God, Dorothy, I'm so sorry," he'd said when he moved out. He'd loved her. He really had. But he couldn't run from himself anymore; he'd been doing that for too long now, and she deserved better.

"I feel like a total shit," he'd told John as they sat on the balcony of the Holiday Inn a few miles from the house he and Dorothy had shared for nearly ten years.

"I'm sorry. I can't even imagine."

"I'm giving her the house. I offered to pay her alimony—more than my lawyer suggested—but she refuses to take it. She says she makes enough money from her job with the school system." He knew paying Dorothy alimony would have made him feel only slightly better about how things had turned out. As it was, he felt incredibly guilty.

"Thanks for helping me pack." Roger knew John had flown into town for more than packing. That John had flown out the morning after a conducting gig had made all the difference.

"Anytime."

With John's help, he'd put his stuff in storage while he figured out where he was going to live. When John left two days later, Roger had made up his mind to fly to Florida. He needed to do this if he was going to move on, get his shit together.

He pressed the buzzer and waited, absentmindedly rubbing his right hand, which had pins and needles. He figured he was even more nervous than he'd realized.

"Roger?" His mother looked shocked to see him. "What on earth are you doing in Florida?"

He offered her what he hoped was a reassuring smile and said, "Good to see you, Mom." He leaned in to peck her on the cheek before following her inside.

The apartment was small, but it had a view of the ocean from the living-room window. The place looked like a miniature version of their old house in Toledo. Same furniture, same pictures on the walls. Just a bit more cluttered because of the lack of space. Neat, as always. The slightly stale smell of the place reminded him of when he used to visit his grandparents years ago. There was a hint of baby powder on the air, mixed with the smell of cigarettes.

He'd just now realized his mother was the same age his grandparents were back then. She was getting old. What would she be now? Sixty-three? He'd gotten older too. When he was in college, forty had seemed really old. Now it just felt normal. Maybe even good sometimes.

"Let me get you some pop," his mother said as she gestured for him to sit on the couch. Her formal manner belied her obvious concern. He was surprised how cool she was, given the fact that he never showed up here unannounced. He guessed it was an act—Miranda Nelson never let her inner thoughts show if she could help it.

He tried to protest, but she returned a few minutes later with a glass filled with what looked like cola. He smiled and thanked her, then took a sip. It was cloyingly sweet—regular Coke, he guessed—but he forced himself to drink it even though it made his teeth hurt.

"So," she said after she'd settled onto the Queen Anne chair next to the sofa, "to what do I owe the honor of a visit?"

The temptation to bullshit and tell her there was nothing special about the visit, that he just wanted to see her, was strong. He took a deep breath and reminded himself why he was here. *Time to come clean.*

"Dorothy and I are getting divorced." He'd meant to ease into the conversation a bit more smoothly, but his nerves got the better of him. "I figured it'd be better to tell you in person."

For a moment she didn't move. If he hadn't seen the rise and fall of her shoulders, he'd have wondered if she was just sort of frozen there like in some sci-fi movie when time just came to a screeching halt. Or maybe that was a *Twilight Zone* episode?

Focus. He needed to do this and do it right. Why the hell was he thinking about something so inane at a time like this?

"Mom?" he said when the silence became uncomfortable.

"I heard you." She had that look on her face, the one she made when he'd done something to test her patience. He took a deep breath and tried not to let it rattle him.

"Oh. Okay." Now what the hell was he supposed to say?

"Why." It wasn't really a question; it felt far more like a judgment.

"Well...." Shit. He was hesitating again. *You have to do this. Get it over with.* He couldn't contain the urge to pace. He set down his nearly empty glass, stood up, and walked over to the window. Outside, the surf pounded the sand. Snowbirds and vacationers who'd fled the cold winter to enjoy the warm weather crammed the beach. A few surfers skimmed the waves, and he saw some fishing boats farther out on the horizon.

He turned and faced her. He took another deep breath in an effort to ease the rising tension in his body. *Say it. Just say it and get it over with!*

"She and I... I just couldn't make her happy. I wanted to, but I just couldn't." He ran a hand through his hair. He needed a haircut, he'd just been too preoccupied to get one.

"That's not a reason," she said. Her voice was brittle, raspy. He knew the cigarettes weren't entirely to blame either. She was coiled like a cobra ready to strike.

"No," he admitted. "It's not." He sat back down again, this time on the edge of the couch, leaned in toward her, and said, "I'm gay, Mom."

The silence stretched longer this time, punctuated only by the ticking sound of the clock from the kitchen and someone down the hall from his mother's place shutting the door to their apartment.

"Say something, Mom," he said when he couldn't stand it anymore.

"What do you want me to say?" She wore a hard, almost angry expression. "Do you just want me to say that it's okay and tell you it doesn't matter to me?"

"I... I don't know. I mean, that would be great, but—"

"I told you that—" She paused as if she were trying to decide the best way to say it. "—*boy* was bad for you."

"Boy?" The realization that she was talking about John jarred him back to his senses. "You mean John?"

"Whatever you want to call him."

"John's not a boy, Mom. And he has nothing to do with thi—"

"The hell he doesn't!" He'd never heard her swear before, and he'd rarely heard her raise her voice. "That… that *man* is the cause of this. I told you years ago he was bad for you, that he'd make your life miserable. And now this?" She laughed, an edgy, bitter laugh that made him feel cold inside.

"I'm not gay because John made me that way."

"Oh, and are you implying somehow that your father and I *made* you that way?"

"No, but—"

"But nothing. If it weren't for him, you'd still be married. Don't tell me you aren't doing this for him. I know you want to be with him again."

Roger realized this was partly true. But only in part. Regardless of whether John wanted him for more than just friendship, he wasn't going to change his mind about this. Hell, it wasn't something he could change his mind about if he'd wanted to. Sure, it had taken him more than fifteen years to realize it, but he'd always been like this.

"Please leave John out of this," he finally said as he struggled to contain his growing anger at her reaction. "This is me. It's who I am. I just wanted to be honest with you for once. Be honest with myself."

"It's like the music. It's something you'll get over. You'll move on."

"Get over?" He swallowed back a wave of powerful anger and hurt as he spoke the words through a clenched jaw. "Do you really think I've gotten over that?"

"You've been doing fine as an accountant. Far better than you would have been playing the violin. I told your grandfather it was a mistake to encourage you. Unrealistic. Seriously, how many musicians can afford to feed themselves?"

"I haven't been doing fine." His gut ached at the admission. "I've been miserable."

"You haven't—"

"How do you know anything about what I've been feeling?" He hadn't meant to shout at her. "You wouldn't. You never could understand."

"I understand that—"

"Shut up, Mom, and listen for once." He ignored her icy glare. "You've never listened to me. You've just told me what I'm supposed to think and feel." He clenched his jaw and shot up from the couch. "You never understood how much it hurt, really *hurt* when I couldn't play the violin anymore."

"You've moved on from that." Her words sounded like a challenge.

"No. Never." The familiar ache in his arm returned as he said this. Like a phantom limb, a reminder of what it had felt like to play as he'd played before the accident. "I'll never move on from that." His eyes burned as he spoke the words, but the anger kept his tears at bay. He wouldn't show her how incredibly vulnerable he still was about this.

"I know you may never understand it, but I do. Finally. I get it. How I lied to myself and everyone else about moving on." He shook his head and clenched his damaged hand. "It's like a hole. Right here." He tapped his chest over his heart. "Like someone took a shotgun and blew away my heart. It never went away. It's stayed there." He didn't add that he felt as though the hole had only gotten bigger with time.

"I tried to lie about it. I tried to forget about it. But it's still there." How had he managed to live with it for so long? Maybe he'd never really *lived* with it. Sometimes he felt as though the last fifteen years he'd just skated through life, never digging down deep enough because he knew what he'd find there. "It's time to get on with my life. Time I'm honest with myself and with you."

"You're still a child," she said after he finished. "Selfish. Self-absorbed." When he didn't respond, she added, "Fine. Be that way. See if I care."

He swallowed hard but didn't look away from her. No. This wasn't about being selfish. He'd already *been* selfish, with both John and Dorothy. He'd hurt them both because he'd been unable to move forward and face the truth of his loss. He'd made his decision. From this point forward, he'd be honest with everyone, and he'd start with himself.

"I love you, Mom," he said. "But I can't be what you want me to be. I'm really sorry."

She said nothing, but looked away and crossed her arms over her chest. He waited a few more minutes, but when it was clear she had nothing more to say, he simply walked over to her, kissed her on the cheek, and headed out of the apartment.

Once safely ensconced in the elevator, he leaned against the wall of the car and took a few deep breaths to calm his racing heart. He wasn't sure when he'd ever felt so at peace.

CHAPTER 45

Summer 1995

"MAESTRO FUCHS?"

John opened his eyes, then promptly shut them again. He had a vague recollection of a party at a SoHo loft, a lot of expensive whiskey, and a cute graduate student.

"Maestro Fuchs, there's someone on the phone for you."

John forced his eyes open again. If he had to look at something in the morning while nursing a beast of a hangover, he figured the kid with the green eyes and dark-brown hair fit the bill. What was his name? Paul? Pierre? Peter?

"You answered my phone?"

Preston—John finally remembered the name—looked back at him sheepishly. *Who names their kid Preston?*

"I… well… they called about five times." When John didn't respond, Preston continued, "I saw the caller ID. I thought maybe it was something urgent."

"Coffee?" John looked hopefully at Preston lying next to him in the bed.

Preston blinked, then nodded. He slipped out of bed and gave John a good look at his bare ass. A very fine ass, John decided. Even drunk, he had good taste. *Strike one up for me.*

The phone was still where Preston had left it, sitting on top of the covers near John's knees. He picked it up and, ignoring the lancing pain in his eye sockets, cradled it between his cheek and shoulder. He fixed his pillow and settled back down onto it. He felt like warmed-over shit.

"This is John Fuchs."

"Maestro?"

"Yes. That's me." Not an auspicious start to the conversation.

"This is Doris." When he didn't respond, she continued, "Doris Pinchley-Bates." Another pause, then: "I'm with the symphony association."

"Symphony?"

"The Chicago Symphony."

Holy crap. "Of course. Doris. So good to hear from you." His hand shook. He'd been sure he'd never hear from the CSO again. Not that he hadn't done well when he'd guest conducted for them two months before, but he'd been one of the lesser-known men and women vying for the music director position. And one of the youngest. Maybe they were just calling to let him down gently.

"You sound a bit under the weather." He heard concern in her voice.

"Late night," he said without even thinking. "Party after the concert."

"I see. I'm calling too early, then." She sounded as though she were disappointed not to have been invited.

"It's really not a problem." If she didn't say her piece, his head would explode right then and there. Where was the coffee?

"I'm glad. I'd hate to have disturbed you."

"So what can I do for you, Doris?" he asked as Preston came back in the room with a cup of steaming coffee that smelled divine. If he ended up staying in Manhattan, he'd have to look the kid up again.

"The symphony association would like to offer you the music director position. If you're still interested, that is."

He put one hand over the microphone and said to Preston, "Pinch me. I need to know I'm not dreaming."

Preston pinched something all right, and it was all John could do not to spill the coffee he held in his left hand. Life was good when you got good news and the makings of a celebration were already at your disposal.

"Of course I'm interested, Doris. I'm honored."

"Lovely! Then I'll send the contract over to your agent as soon as possible. Mind you, we can only offer you a two-year contract to begin with, but if things go well, I can assure you the next one will be far longer."

"Thank you. I'll be in touch next week, once I've had a chance to review the contract with my attorney."

"I can't tell you how much I look forward to seeing you in Chicago," she said with breathless excitement. "I have a feeling you'll fit in perfectly around here. Maybe even inject a bit of new life into the symphony."

"Thanks again. Take care, Doris. I look forward to speaking with you again soon." John set the phone down and took a long drink from the cup. It was all he could do not to scream.

"Good news, Maestro?" Preston batted long eyelashes at him and slipped between the sheets.

"The best." John knew he was grinning like a fool. "You're looking at the new music director of the Chicago Symphony."

He needed to let Roger know.

"Really?" Those pretty eyes sparkled. "Congratulations, Maestro. Is a little celebration in order?" Preston's broad smile turned into a tease of a smirk as he dove under the sheets and started to work his way down John's chest with his tongue.

He'd celebrate first and call Roger later.

CHAPTER 46

Spring 1996

"REMIND ME why I'm spending my first free weekend in six months helping you paint?" John wiped a splatter from his cheek and glanced over at Roger.

"Because hunter green's your color?"

Roger looked good in his torn jeans and paint-covered T-shirt. John couldn't deny that it was nice to be spending time with him rather than just talking over the phone. Not that seeing Roger in the flesh didn't present its own problems, but John resolved not to let those dog him. *If* he could get his mind off Roger's body. It had been so much easier to overlook that part of Roger when he was still married to Dorothy.

"Thanks." John set the brush he'd been using down on the paint can and picked up his beer. At least Roger had gotten the good stuff. If he had to drink the Bud Light he knew Roger preferred, he wouldn't have been as happy about being covered in paint.

"So how's the new job?" Roger asked as he put the finishing touches on one of the shutters that lay across a couple of sawhorses in the garage of Roger's new house in Oak Park. He'd moved to the Chicago suburb about the same time John had been appointed music director of the CSO, a coincidence neither of them had spoken much about.

John took another pull of his beer, then set it down by the paint can and retrieved the brush. "It's good. Busy. Just the programming takes half my time—coordinating with the booking agent, trying to snag some of the bigger names before their schedules fill."

"And the musicians?"

"More of a challenge." John sighed. The CSO's instrumentalists were among the most talented players in the world, but they hadn't exactly warmed up to him. "It's going to take time until they get what I'm doing."

"I thought the symphony association hired you because they were looking to shake things up a bit."

"They did. But I've got to get the musicians to buy into my way of doing things. Vittorio Caldi was there a long time. They're used to him." John knew it wasn't just that. The CSO's musicians weren't thrilled that their new conductor was younger than most of them, and John guessed his open lifestyle hadn't endeared him to them either.

"What are you going to do about it?" Roger carried the shutter over to the side of the garage and leaned it against the wall to dry.

"Nothing. I'm not going to change my way of doing things at this point. They'll come around eventually."

"Yeah." Roger appeared to be gazing at the shutter, but his eyes weren't focused on it at all.

"How about you? How's the new job with that downtown accounting firm?"

"Oh. That. With the divorce final and all, I've been thinking things through."

John stopped painting and turned to look at Roger. "What haven't you told me?"

"It's not like that," Roger said as he held up his hands and shook his head. "Really. It's just that I wanted to tell you in person."

"Tell me what?" John waited for the other shoe to drop. Or fly out the window and hit a passing car. Roger's big revelations weren't exactly John's favorite thing to hear about, since they usually meant John would be on the receiving end of any major fallout.

"What's your problem?" Roger scowled at him and massaged a muscle in his upper arm. "You're supposed to be my friend. I'm supposed to tell you things."

"The last thing you told me was that you'd filed for divorce." John missed the corner of the shutter he'd been working on and managed to slop green paint all over his sweatpants. *Great.* "The time before that, you told me you were getting married. And the time before that—"

"Okay, okay. But this one's a good thing." He looked up at John with his bright-green eyes, and John knew he'd deal with it, whatever "it" was. Things were always like that with Roger.

"All right. Shoot." John waited.

"You know how I told you I started teaching a few kids when Dorothy and I moved here a few years back?"

"Yes. You said you had some good students."

"I do."

"So?" John hated the buildup. *Just cut to the chase.*

"I'm quitting my job. I've decided you were right all those years ago when you said I shouldn't give up my music." Roger grinned.

John just stared at him for a moment, at a loss for words. "Did I say that?" he asked. He remembered the conversation, but he needed time to process Roger's pronouncement.

"Yes. And I ignored you."

"You do that often." That much was true.

"Sometimes," Roger said as he gesticulated with his paintbrush, "I get your point. It might take a while, but I get it."

"Are you going to tell me what you've gone and done now, or am I going to have to dump this can of paint over your stubborn block of a head?" John all but stomped his foot.

"Maybe." Roger was enjoying this too much. Way too much.

John picked up the can of paint and walked over, trying to look as threatening as he could while laughing.

"Okay, okay!"

John waited.

"The rooms in the back I told you I've been working on?"

"Yes?"

"My violin studio."

John set the paint can down. "Y-you... y-you're finally going to teach?" *Fuck. Stuttering again?*

"My last day of work was yesterday. So as soon as you help me move the piano"—Roger offered John a sheepish grin—"I'll be good to go. I've got five students now."

John clenched his jaw. He'd be damned if he let Roger see the tears that threatened. "It's about time." He hesitated, then, against his better judgment, hugged Roger. "It's about fucking time."

Roger tightened his arms around him. Why did Roger still feel so good? *Because you're still in love with him.* John tried to pull away. He didn't need to screw up their relationship; he needed Roger's friendship. Somewhere along the way, it had become like breathing to him.

"John." Roger brushed a paint-covered thumb over John's cheek and held him tight.

John forced himself to breathe through the jolt of heat that surged from his chest to his groin. They both leaned in at the same time, and their noses touched. Normally, John would have found that funny, but Roger's expression was so hungry. So needy. John knew he probably looked just the same. Their lips brushed, and John forgot any thoughts other than kissing Roger and Roger kissing him back.

Roger slipped the elastic from John's hair, and it fell free. A moment later Roger combed and pulled at it. John almost laughed to think of the green paint in his hair—why was he thinking about something so inane at a time like this?

"Come upstairs with me?" Roger's voice was rough, but John sensed a hint of something else there as well.

Roger's words finally reached the place in John's brain where his body wasn't in control. *What the hell are you doing?* Christ! What *was* he doing? "I… I don't think I should." *More like you know you can't handle another broken heart!*

"What?" Roger's eyes widened in shocked surprise.

"I… I've got a rehearsal this afternoon downtown." Complete and utter bullshit.

"It's Sunday, John. Even I know there aren't rehearsals on Sunday. Why are you leaving?"

Why was he leaving? He didn't want to go. He wanted to stay here with Roger. He wanted Roger. God, he'd wanted Roger so long! But if he did this…. "I need to go."

"Why?" Roger didn't look angry, just puzzled. "Please, John. Don't bullshit me."

John inhaled a quiet, slow breath. Roger was right—he needed to be honest about this. "Because I don't want to lose you."

"You won't lose me. If you stay, you can have me." Roger's grin seemed forced. "I mean, we can be together and—"

"I can't do that again. I like this. Us. Best friends."

"Stay. Please. I'm the world's biggest asshole. I know I am. I've been a shit. But I thought you'd forgiven me."

John sat down on a plastic chair and looked up at him. "I forgave you years ago. I know why you left New York."

"Then why are you leaving?"

John turned around. "I'm leaving because it won't work between us. Not like this. It never has."

"God, John. I can never get things right with you, can I?"

"It's n-not a wrong or r-right kind of thing." Another slow breath. "I d-don't know how t-to explain it. I d-don't w-want to l-lose you."

"I… God, I want to understand." Roger looked so stunned it was all John could do not to reach out and comfort him. "I want to show you that I'd be good for you. Show you that things between us can be more than just friends. Show you that I've changed. That I've gotten my life together. Tell you I love you."

John tried to swallow, but his heart was stuck at the back of his throat and he could barely breathe. "You could have had the wildest fantasies about how your life would turn out, and I wouldn't have cared. It was never about that. I loved that about you. The way you just *knew* life would turn itself around and that things would be better. How you lived your life believing that the best part of it was just ahead."

"I really don't get it. So what did I do wrong?"

"N-nothing. N-not this t-time. You've done everything right." John hoped his face conveyed how much he cared for him. "But I can't do this again. I can't take the chance. I'm not sure I could survive it if you broke my heart again."

"I won't break your heart. I promise." Roger sat down next to John but didn't touch him.

"You don't mean to." John shook his head and sighed. "You never meant to. I know that. But you don't tell me things, and they sneak up on me and I'm left wondering what the hell happened."

"I tell you things," Roger protested.

"You didn't tell me about how your parents pressured you after the accident. You didn't talk to me about what you were going through with the music stuff. I never wanted to make things so difficult for you."

"You didn't make things difficult. I'm the one who did that." Roger's words surprised John. "I'm the one who wouldn't talk to you."

"But that's just it," John said. "We talk about everything when we're *not* together like that. When we're friends. We're great like this. But the minute we get together, all the shit gets in the way." He blew air from between his pursed lips before continuing, "And I can't let that happen again. No matter how much I want to sleep with you. Besides, it's not like being in a gay relationship is easy." He didn't add that he knew he'd been avoiding relationships since Nate died, although he was pretty sure Roger knew this.

"It was never about the gay part of it," Roger protested, standing up and pacing the length of the garage in obvious frustration. He ran a hand through his paint-splattered hair, then rubbed his shoulder.

"You tell yourself that, Roger, but it's just not true. I'm not saying the music wasn't an issue—I can't even imagine how hard it was for you after the accident. God, I'd have given anything to make that different for you!" He rubbed a hand over his face and leaned back in the chair, which responded with a low scrape against the garage floor. "But it's more than just that. All along you've hesitated. You pretended you were dating girls. I could tell you didn't know what you wanted. I knew your parents found out about us in college. I knew they were making your life miserable."

"That wasn't the problem in New York." Roger's eyes betrayed him; John knew he wasn't telling the truth now.

"Can you honestly say it wasn't at least part of it? Can you really say that you were ready to deal with what it meant to move in together?"

Roger was silent.

"I can't do this." John rubbed his eyes, then stood up.

"You know I've always loved you. You had to have known that." Already John could see the resignation in Roger's expression. He felt guilty, knowing he'd put it there.

John stopped, then turned around and smiled at Roger through his tears. "Of course I knew it. I've always known it. Because I love you too." John walked over to Roger and hugged him tight, then walked out of the garage and got into his car, not caring that he would get paint all over the seats. He didn't give a shit about the car—his only thought as he drove away was that he'd already lost Roger by pushing him away.

CHAPTER 47

New Year's Eve 1996

"DO YOU think someone will wonder what happened to us?"

"Do you care?" John laughed and worked open the buckle on—what was his name? Luke?—Len's belt. He had Len pushed up against the inside of the bathroom door.

"No. But aren't you supposed to be playing something with the other musicians? Doris said you always play something at her New Year's—"

"Don't worry. She can wait. Besides, we've still got an hour and a half before midnight. She won't come looking for me until at least eleven." John pushed Len's pants down and chewed his lower lip. *Nice.* It wasn't just his shoulders that were broad. John had his mouth on Len's cock a moment later.

"Christ!"

John stopped sucking and shook his head. "But if you keep shouting like that, Doris might find us sooner."

"Sorry." Len looked mortified. John didn't care. He was pretty sure Doris knew *exactly* what he was doing. She'd seen them leave together and she knew him only too well. John had begun to think she was living vicariously through him, or maybe that she thought it might be fun to watch. Doris always made him laugh.

John laughed and got back to business.

"HAVING A good time?" Doris asked as he waited the requisite minute or two after Len made his way back to the party, then followed.

"I always have a good time at your parties, my dear." He leaned over and kissed her cheek.

She gave him a knowing look, then snagged two champagne flutes from one of the passing servers and handed one to him. "Charles asked after you the other day," she said blithely. "He said you haven't called him again."

"You must send him my regards." John sipped his champagne and met her eyes without blinking.

"I thought you two would hit it off." She flicked her long platinum-blonde hair with her left hand, and the large diamond on her ring finger glittered as it caught the light from one of the chandeliers overhead.

"When did I ever give you the impression we didn't hit it off?" he parried as he caught her wrist and turned her hand over to admire the ring.

"Like it?" she asked.

"It's lovely. A new acquisition?" He'd heard one of the violinists talking about Doris's new love interest, a wealthy French entrepreneur. He figured it would last a few months, until she got tired of him. They were a lot alike: drawn to sparkly things and easily bored.

"Mais oui."

"You do have excellent taste." He nodded and pursed his lips before he released her hand.

"As do you, Maestro." She took another sip of her champagne, then waved him away. "Now run along and make some music. All play and no work isn't good for symphony coffers, you know."

He bowed with a flourish, then headed for the piano in the middle of the room. He'd accompany some of the symphony musicians and maybe play a solo piece or two. Then he'd invite Len back to his place after the party. What better way to ring in the year than with a handsome man?

IT WAS nearly one in the afternoon when John stumbled out of bed. Len had left a few hours earlier. He told John he always had brunch at his parents' house on New Year's Day. John wasn't sure why, but he believed the guy. Maybe it was the good-bye kiss he gave John, or maybe it was the card he'd pressed into his hand as he told John to call him again soon. John doubted he would. He wasn't interested in getting involved, and he was pretty sure Len was looking for more than just another night of sex.

Lake Michigan appeared almost turquoise in the early-afternoon sun. The color of the water reminded John of the only time he'd ever been to Central America, before Nate got sick. One of the partners at the law firm had a house in Costa Rica, and they'd spent a blissful week together, lounging on the beach and splashing around in the water. He and Nate had half-jokingly talked about buying a place there when they retired.

John smiled. He'd do it someday. Other than buying the condo in town, he'd been careful with his earnings. He'd invested the money from the master classes he taught several times a year at University of Michigan and New England Conservatory.

As he walked down the hallway toward the kitchen, he saw the light on his answering machine flashing. One message. He rubbed the sleep out of his eyes before pressing the button to listen.

"Happy New Year."

John took a deep breath and closed his eyes. Why did hearing Roger's voice hurt so damn much?

"I miss you. I know you're probably not ready to talk to me yet, and that's cool. I'll be here waiting. I hope 1996's a great year for you."

John's eyes burned as he listened to the message.

I miss you too.

CHAPTER 48

Winter 1997

"HEY, MOM." John smiled down at his mother. She looked so small and frail in the hospital bed. He'd tried to visit her at least once a month, but he'd missed the last two because he'd been in Europe conducting. He'd called her, but most of the time she hadn't remembered who he was, and he'd ended up talking to the nurse instead.

"John."

He smiled more broadly this time. She remembered him.

"I missed you, Mom." He brushed a strand of gray hair from her eyes. "I'm sorry I couldn't come sooner."

"You did your best, sweetheart. That's what matters."

For the first time, John noticed the music playing softly in the background. Brahms's Symphony No. 2. *His* recording. He'd sent the CD to the nursing home before he'd left New York. "You like the music?" he asked.

"Rhonda said it was you conducting," she said, frowning. "But it can't be you. You're too young."

"Not so young, Mom."

She patted his hand. "When you graduate college, you'll make a fine conductor."

John repressed a sigh. She recognized him, but she thought he was still a kid. He didn't mind. He was just happy she recognized him at all.

"How's Roger?" she asked a few minutes later.

"Roger?" He forced a smile.

"He's a good boy," she said. "He makes you happy."

Made me happy, once. "Yes, Mom."

"I know his parents don't like that you're together," she continued, undaunted, "but I'm glad for you both. You know that, don't you?"

John blinked back tears. He found it difficult to forget what it had felt like when they'd lived for weekends spent together at Roger's apartment. "Thanks," he said, hoping she didn't catch the quavering of his voice.

That night, he sat alone in his mother's house. He'd known all along he'd have to sell it, that she'd never be coming back. Still, he'd been avoiding it. Selling the house made everything seem so final, as if the last vestiges of his childhood that still resided there would vanish when it was gone. He'd pulled out his Marysville yearbook, knowing it was maudlin to leaf through the photos and give in to his grief. He wasn't even sure what he was grieving. His mother? Roger? Nate?

He traced his fingertips over Nate's photo, then abruptly closed the book. He'd never have Nate back. But Roger?

Five months later

JOHN STOOD in front of Roger's Oak Park house. Had it been a year?

"Stay. Please. I'm the world's biggest asshole."

He reached into the breast pocket of his jacket and pulled out the pack of cigarettes he'd bought at the airport the night before. The last time he'd smoked was just about a year ago. No big surprise there.

"You know I've always loved you. You had to have known that." John could still picture Roger's face in his mind's eye. Defeated. Desperate.

His hand shook slightly as he lit the cigarette and took a long drag of it. Of course he'd known Roger always loved him. But what had it gotten them? Pain. Hope. Loss. And yet he knew this last time wasn't Roger's fault. *He'd* pushed Roger away. Regret mingled with fear. *What are you afraid of? That you might be happy for a change?*

"He's a good boy. He makes you happy." His mother died a week after she'd spoken those words, but their truth still resonated in him. But he hadn't called Roger after her death, he'd gone on avoiding Roger, waiting for something inside of him to change. Waiting for the fear to abate. It hadn't. He was still as terrified now of seeing Roger as he'd been before. If Roger hadn't called him, asked him to come hear one of his students....

He finished the cigarette and waited a minute or two longer before ringing the doorbell. Roger wouldn't be up yet, and the kid—what was his name? Alex Bishop?—wasn't supposed to come until ten. Arriving too early was one habit he'd never been able to kick.

He waited a few more minutes before he heard the dead bolt slide and Roger looked out at him, hair a rumpled mess, jaw covered in salt-and-pepper shadow. He wore a pair of striped boxers and a cotton robe that hung open so his chest was visible. He hadn't changed much. A bit grayer around the temples, a few more wrinkles lined his face. The muscles of his chest were still taut. John guessed Roger still worked out. He fought the urge to run his hand over Roger's skin. Shit. He needed to focus.

John half expected Roger would grumble and say something about his arriving early, but he didn't. Instead, he hesitated a second or two, then grabbed John and hugged him. Roger's body felt so damn good against his own that John nearly moaned. One year was too long, too short, too overwhelming. He realized they'd been holding each other for several minutes when Roger shivered, his robe too flimsy for the cool spring morning.

"Damn," Roger said. "It's so good to see you."

"You owe me." John hadn't meant to joke, but jokes were easier and they helped rouse him from the semitrance he was in at the feel of Roger's body against his own. Once he'd thought he'd gotten over Roger. But he'd never get over him. He knew that now. He wanted Roger just as badly now as when he was a geeky seventeen-year-old. Why had he agreed to come today? He'd made it an entire year ignoring Roger's messages.

"Trust me on this one. The kid's worth the trip."

"And if I disagree?" John was pretty sure he wouldn't disagree. He trusted Roger's musical intuition. Besides, he'd heard the kid play himself, years before on the "L" platform. He'd been impressed then.

"My treat for dinner."

"You already promised me dinner," John reminded him.

"I'm sure you'll figure out what to do with me." Roger grinned and ran a hand through his wickedly disheveled hair. "But for now, I need a shower. So unless you're going to join me...."

"Not happening." John wished it would, in an alternate universe sort of way.

"Your loss." Roger waved and began to ascend the stairs.

John headed for the kitchen. He'd make some strong coffee. He'd need it.

"SO HOW'S Boston?" Roger asked a few minutes later. He was dressed in jeans and a polo shirt. His hair was still wet.

"Colder than here, believe it or not." John relaxed and sipped his coffee.

"Sorry to make you come back from Boston earlier than you'd planned. Alex's audition tape's overdue as it is. I knew he wouldn't let me pay for it, and I figured you could probably put in a good word for him with Mike Samuels." Roger poured himself a cup and joined John at the kitchen table.

"It's fine. Doris is having a party tomorrow at Symphony Hall. Some donor thing to raise money to redo the green room or something."

In truth, he'd normally have stayed at his Boston condo a few days longer and made some excuse to avoid the party. For the past year, he'd spent as little time in Chicago as he could. Living in Boston made it easier for John to avoid Roger. His jet setting hadn't pleased the symphony association—Doris had made it clear that the only reason they tolerated him living out of town during the symphony's season was that they were afraid to lose him to some other orchestra. Doris needn't have worried. John would never leave Chicago—and Roger—behind completely.

"So how've you been?"

"I'm fine." Since when had they started exchanging pleasantries? "Not much new."

"Good. Or I guess it is."

"It's good," John said. It had been a while since he'd landed on the front page of a gossip rag. He figured that was good.

Roger tapped one foot against the floor and rubbed the back of his neck. "Seeing anyone?" He asked the question with casual nonchalance, but John knew it was anything but.

"No." He hadn't been celibate the past year, but he hadn't dated either. He told himself he was too busy, although he knew that was only part of the equation.

"I see." Roger looked relieved.

"You?" Turnabout was fair play, after all.

"No."

John did his best to pretend he didn't care, but he *did*. He hadn't even thought about it until that moment, but the thought of someone else with Roger made his gut clench. Was he jealous? No. Of course not. He was the one who'd pushed Roger away a year before. It might even be easier if Roger *was* dating someone. Then John wouldn't have to think about the possibilities. And dammit, he was thinking about them, in spite of himself.

An awkward silence settled between them.

"When's the kid coming?" John asked when it became unbearable.

"Soon. We should probably finish up and head to the studio." Roger made it sound as though the studio was in the next county when it was at the back of the house. John was just glad they had something to do.

THEY SETTLED onto the couch in the studio a few minutes after ten. Like everything else, it was warm and a little messy. Just like Roger.

"I heard the Beethoven last month. It was beautiful. More mature." Roger smiled. "It suits you."

Roger had come to hear the symphony? John supposed he shouldn't be surprised. "Thank you." He leaned into the cushions and crossed his legs. "Why didn't you come back afterward?"

"I figured you'd rather I not." Roger smiled, but John saw the sadness in his eyes.

"You were wrong." John shifted once again on the sofa. Roger's expression brightened a bit at his words. Strange, that whatever had happened before in their lives, this was the first time John ever felt there was a wall between them. A gap neither of them seemed able to bridge. John's chest tightened painfully. Whose fault was that wall? Not Roger's.

"So tell me about Alex," he said, hoping to lighten the mood.

Roger seemed pleased to change the subject. "Great kid. Amazing talent. He's gotten better since you heard him two years ago."

"His living situation any better?"

"No more group homes—he's got his own place the state pays for. His grades have gone up. He's got an after-school job at a bookstore, and he still plays on the 'L' platform on weekends. Probably makes more money playing for tips than at the bookstore." Roger laughed and glanced at his watch. "And he's late. Probably overslept."

As if on cue, the door to the waiting room opened.

"That'll be him." Roger walked out of the studio, and a moment later, John heard him say, "You really need to get some sleep, Alex. One of these days you're going to sleep right through a performance."

John shook his head. "It's all right, Roger," he said loudly enough that he was sure he'd be heard. "Give the kid a break."

"You still awake, old man?" Roger said as he followed a tall redheaded kid into the studio.

"I may be looking at retiring in a few years—" John coughed and waved his hand dismissively. "—but I'm not dead."

"Right." Roger frowned as he handed John a bottle of water. "You've been smoking again, haven't you?"

"Without your sunny disposition to brighten my days, I need at least one vice to keep me going."

Roger's expression darkened, but John was just pleased they were back to avoidance through snarky banter. He didn't want any more maudlin looks back. He had moved on from Roger, he reminded himself.

"So this is your student, then?" He hoped Roger would realize they'd never been properly introduced. He'd never been good with formalities.

"Alex Bishop, meet John Fuchs."

Alex's eyes grew wide as saucers. Damn, hadn't Roger told him who he was playing for? Leave it to Roger to scare the kid half to death. Alex reached out to shake John's hand. "It's an honor, Maestro. I apologize for being so late, I—"

"Don't sweat it, son." John offered Alex a warm smile and the kid seemed to relax a bit. A very little bit. "I'm guessing Roger made you wait on at least a few occasions. He's certainly kept me waiting a few times."

Roger coughed.

Serves him right. John made a mental note to give Roger a piece of his mind later.

"So I'm told you're interested in NEC." John gestured for Alex to sit down next to him, then motioned for Roger to bring Alex a bottle of water.

"I've always dreamed about going to New England Conservatory. I'm just not sure I can afford—"

"If you've got the talent, there are scholarships available." John knew NEC would be thrilled to find a kid like Alex. They'd make sure he could attend.

He watched as Alex accepted a bottle of water from Roger and guzzled half of it without a breath. John was reminded of when he first met Roger in high school and how nervous he felt.

Alex finished the water and set the empty bottle in the plastic bin by the door, then glanced at John and quickly looked away. He looked scared to death. "I… I'm not sure I'm that good."

"That's not what I've heard." John winked at Roger. "Your teacher seems to think I'm not wasting my time."

"Maestro Nelson is very kind." The look of admiration in Alex's eyes as he gazed at Roger made John smile.

You've matured too, John, he thought wistfully. Funny how he hadn't seen it before.

"He's been teaching me for nearly seven years," Alex was saying when John came back to himself. "He's never charged me for lessons."

"True." Roger looked entirely embarrassed by Alex's praise. Another surprise. The old Roger would have entirely missed Alex's hero worship. Now he downplayed it, as any good teacher would do. "But you've paid your bill by helping me teach the younger students." Roger turned and winked at John. "Alex here's quite the charmer. The female students especially enjoy his work."

"So what are you going to play for me today, Alex?" John asked, noting the slightly pink flush on Alex's cheeks.

"The first movement of the Wieniawski concerto." Alex offered John a tentative smile. The kid was a charmer, both humble and outgoing. If he was anything like this when he played—and John guessed he was based on what he'd seen two years before—he'd make a natural soloist.

Roger took a seat at the upright piano and pulled a ragged piece of music from the substantial pile on the piano's stand. The piano bench creaked as he sat down. For the first time, John noticed a stain on the ceiling of the studio and the cracking paint of the window frame. He wondered vaguely how many students Roger taught whom he didn't charge, but he said only "Excellent!" before taking a swig of his water and sitting up a bit straighter. "Although I suppose I'll also have to put up with Roger's less-than-stellar piano playing, won't I?"

Roger shot John a scathing look as Alex retrieved his violin from its case. "Dear, dear," Roger tutted with a quick glance at John. "We really must do something about getting you a new instrument, Alex."

"This one's fine, Maestro." Alex tightened his bow and tucked the violin under his chin.

"No. I really don't think so. The sound has only deteriorated over the years. It's really not suitable for someone the likes of Maestro Fuchs."

What the hell was Roger up to? He'd just gone on about how the kid had no money, and now he was making a fuss about the damned violin? Sure, it wasn't in very good shape, but he didn't need to hear the kid play a Guarneri to know if he was as good as Roger had said.

"But Maestro, I... I...," Alex stammered as he blushed to the roots of his auburn hair.

John shook his head. Maybe Roger hadn't changed so much, after all. "Really, Roger, do you have to be so cruel?"

"Put the instrument away, Alex," Roger said, ignoring John and watching as Alex's shoulders fell and the kid looked as if he might sink into the floorboards.

"I'm very sorry, Maestro Fuchs. I hope that when I get a better instrument, you'll still be willing to hear me play."

"Roger...." John inhaled a long breath to keep from losing his temper completely.

"Oh... all right," snapped Roger. "But I couldn't help it, could I?"

John scowled and shook his head again. What the hell was he up to?

Roger shrugged, then got up from the piano and walked over to the ancient wooden armoire on the opposite side of the room and withdrew a violin case from one of the shelves inside. A brand-new violin case.

"There's no need to postpone the audition, Alex." Roger held the case behind him as he approached Alex.

"What? Why not? But you said—"

"You have a far more suitable violin to play." Roger offered the case to Alex.

Alex stared at the case, then back up at Roger, uncomprehending.

"Well? Don't you want to see what's inside?" John thought he saw the beginning of a grin forming on Roger's face.

"S-sure." Alex set the case on the table by the doorway and popped open the latches. The case was lined in green crushed velvet, and inside was a beautiful violin. A very familiar violin.

Roger's violin.

"My gift to you, Alex Bishop." Roger glanced over to John, the wrinkles around his eyes more pronounced with his broad smile. John blinked back tears. That violin had been everything to Roger. The promise of a brilliant career unfulfilled. The physical incarnation of his soul. The last time he'd heard Roger play that instrument was the day he'd won the concerto competition. The day everything had changed.

John took in a long, slow breath, then, with a finger, wiped away the tears that managed to escape his control.

"But really, I can't—" Alex was saying.

"Yes," Roger interrupted. "You *can* and you will. But you must promise me one thing first."

"Yes. Of course." Alex gazed up at Roger with a look of unabashed happiness. "Anything."

"Promise me that you'll send me tickets to your Boston Symphony debut," Roger said, deadpan.

"My…?" Alex blushed once again. "Sure. You got it."

"Perhaps I'll be fortunate enough to conduct." John was pretty sure he'd make that happen. He didn't need to hear Alex play again to know that everything Roger had said about him was true.

JOHN SAT back on the couch as Roger showed Alex out of the studio nearly two hours later. Alex had ended up playing the entire concerto and, as expected, his playing had floored John.

"What did you think?" Roger asked as he stepped back inside the studio a few minutes later.

"He's amazing. I can't believe the progress he's made since the last time I heard him. And to play an audition like that on a new violin—by the last movement, I wouldn't even have guessed he'd never played it before. It sounded like it was made for him." John swallowed hard, then stood up abruptly and walked over to the piano, his back to Roger. "But what you did today…." He closed his eyes, and this time he couldn't stop the tears.

"John?"

John turned around and glared at Roger. "Do you always have to make me cry? Damn you!"

Roger looked at him as if he'd lost his mind. "I… I didn't mean… I don't want—"

"Damn you! Damn you for making me love you when all I want to do is hate you and never see your face again. Damn you for making me want you when all I want is to live my life without you." John wiped his face with his hand, for all the good it did.

Roger picked up a box of tissues and held it out to John. "You love me?"

After all these years, you don't know? John took a few of the tissues and blew his nose. "I need to get going."

"But I thought we would get some lunch, maybe spend some time to—"

"I'm going home." He couldn't stay here. Not now, when he'd gone and made a complete fool of himself. One year of resolve, and where the hell was he now? It surprised him to realize he was scared. Angry too. *About what? About something that happened when we were both kids?*

"Home? You mean back to Boston?" Roger looked genuinely upset now.

"No. Back to my apartment downtown. That's home." *Even if I convinced myself otherwise.*

Roger brightened. "Can I call you?"

"I… I d-don't know." John said it without even thinking. Why didn't he say no? He caught the hint of a smile that flickered over Roger's face as he pulled out a cigarette and stuck it between his lips. He headed out of the studio, through the waiting area, and outside into a bright, sunny day. Roger followed him and waited in the doorway. John just pulled the lighter from his pocket, lit the cigarette, then turned on his heels and walked to his car.

CHAPTER 49

April 13, 1997

ROGER WALKED the four blocks from the "L" platform to John's condo on Randolph Street. While he rode the train from Oak Park, it had started to rain. By the time he arrived, having forgotten to bring an umbrella, he was soaked to the skin.

"Sir?" The doorman offered him a sympathetic smile.

"John Fuchs. Apartment 14-H."

"Whom may I say is calling?"

Call? Did anyone say that anymore? It sounded like something out of a 1940s movie. Roger bit his cheek to avoid laughing. "Franz Schubert," he said after a moment's thought. At least it'd get John's attention.

"Thank you, Mr. Schubert. I'll let him know you're here."

He'd been so sure he wouldn't make it past the doorman that he was surprised to find himself standing outside John's door five minutes later. At least he wasn't dripping onto the carpet anymore—the doorman had loaned him a towel. Apparently that was what they did in fancy apartments. For once, he was glad for it.

"You're soaked." John wore his mother-hen expression as he opened the door. A good sign, Roger figured. He both made it upstairs and John wasn't pissed to see him. Now if he could figure out his next move, he'd be doing great. As usual, he hadn't thought that far ahead.

"Sorry?"

"Right." John laughed and gestured him inside. Roger had made it past the third hurdle: he'd gotten inside the front door. "Wait here."

Roger raised his eyebrows, but John just turned and walked down the hallway toward the bedrooms. He returned a moment later with gray sweatpants and a matching sweatshirt. Before Roger could say anything, John said, "Yes. They're mine. And no, they're not Fendi, they're Fruit of the Loom."

"How appropriate."

John ignored him and pointed to the hallway. "Get dressed." Roger hadn't gotten halfway there when John added, "Guest bedroom."

Roger just smiled. Baby steps. And if baby steps didn't get him what he wanted, he figured groveling would do nicely.

HE FOUND John seated at the grand piano in the living room a few minutes later. Roger grinned when he realized what John was playing: the top two hands of Schubert's Fantasy in F Minor. Roger remembered the piece well—he'd played it years ago in the band room at Marysville High with John. He smiled to know that John remembered it too.

John stopped playing and glanced up from the piano. "Well, Mr. Schubert, are you going to sit there watching me play half the piece, or are you going to join me?"

"I thought you said my piano playing was deficient," Roger said as he sat to John's left on the bench.

"You could convince me otherwise." John's eyes sparkled in obvious challenge.

Roger laughed and shook his head. "I doubt it. When you make up your mind about something, you can be a royal pain in the ass."

John glared at him over his reading glasses. "Only when it's well deserved."

Roger just grinned back at him, then focused his attention on the score on the piano stand and inhaled slowly before beginning to play the opening measures of the piece. He stumbled over a few of the passages— he'd gotten rusty just playing the piano reductions of the orchestral accompaniments for his students.

John raised a critical eyebrow and shook his head.

"Oh, please. At least my playing hasn't totally gone to hell in a handbag," Roger told him.

"That's debatable."

"What do you want me to do about it?"

"Start again, perhaps?"

Roger was sure John was doing his best to repress a smile. He'd gotten better at hiding his emotions over the years.

"For you, Maestro," Roger said, "anything."

"I'm honored." Now John really *was* smiling.

They played for nearly a half an hour, and this time John didn't complain about Roger's frequent mistakes. Roger was pretty sure John had picked the piece because he knew it wouldn't overly tax his left hand, although he hoped the choice of Schubert signified something more profound.

For a minute, maybe more, after they finished, neither spoke. Years before, they had communicated so well through their music—at least until Roger gave up playing. Despite its flaws, Roger sensed that his performance connected with John. Musicianship, he knew, had little to do with technique. It was something Roger had realized when he'd begun to teach. You could have the best technique, but without an innate sense of music, you would never be a great performer. Like the difference between Shakespeare and a tenth-grade term paper.

Roger stared at the keys, noting the reflection of the ivory in the highly polished wood of the piano case. He wasn't sure he could look at John. Too much had changed. He needed John. Really *needed* him. He was afraid he'd break the spell and that John would kick him out of his life again. He wasn't sure he could handle that. Finally he said, "I'm sorry."

Roger worried he'd upset John once again when John's jaw tightened, but John turned to him and said, "Don't apologize. I already knew you were a crappy pianist." He smiled and their eyes met. Roger knew neither of them were talking about his piano playing.

Roger stood up. "Thanks for the sweats. I'll bring them back to you."

He waited for John to object, but instead John asked, "Got what you came for?" His expression was kind. Open. Loving, even?

"Yeah." Roger smiled.

CHAPTER 50

Two weeks later

JOHN GLANCED over at the fourteen-year-old kid who'd just played one of the most magnificent renditions of the Saint-Saëns Cello Concerto No. 1 he'd ever heard. *Fourteen going on forty.* The kid's mother was another story—it had been all he could do to keep her from hovering in the wings. He'd considered asking security to escort her to her seat, but the boy already looked mortified, and he didn't want to make him suffer any more than he was.

"Beautifully played." John offered Cary Redding a smile he hoped would convey how pleased he was.

"Thanks." Cary handed his cello to one of the stage crew, then looked back at John and chewed his lower lip.

"Ready?"

Cary nodded, and they walked back out to take the first of several bows. John wondered where the joy in Cary's face went after he finished playing. He held himself like a far more adult performer, but John got the distinct impression that Cary enjoyed none of the crowd's praise. Unfortunate, really, since he'd earned it and then some. The kid looked genuinely uncomfortable.

He'd hoped to speak to Cary in the green room alone after the concert, but by the time he'd said his good nights to some of the musicians backstage, admirers filled the room, all waiting to congratulate him and Cary. Worse, Cary's mother waited, poised to intercept John before he'd even had a chance to speak to the kid.

"Maestro Fuchs," Janet Redding said as she offered him her hand. "That was a lovely concert. I hope Cary didn't give you any trouble."

"Trouble? Of course not." He silently hoped Cary gave his mother trouble; he'd seen nothing but professionalism from the boy.

"Does that mean you'll hire him again?"

Pushy, pushy. He wouldn't hold her breach of etiquette against Cary. "Most definitely. My booking agent will be in touch with you in the next few weeks."

Cary, who had walked over during this last exchange, looked genuinely embarrassed. John put his arm on the kid's shoulder and squeezed. "I look forward to having you back next season. Maybe Boccherini next time?"

"I'd really like that, sir." In spite of Cary's formal response, his eyes sparkled with obvious excitement.

"I'm so glad," Cary's mother began. "I was concerned that—"

"Please excuse me," John interrupted as he noticed a familiar face at the edge of the crowd. "There's someone I need to speak with." He turned back to Cary and added, "If you ever need help with your career, you can always call me."

"Thank you, Maestro Fuchs." Cary appeared genuinely pleased by the offer.

"Mrs. Redding." John nodded, then slipped away as quickly as he could.

Roger smiled and offered John his hand. John shook it. When was the last time he'd shaken John's hand? At his wedding?

The memory made his gut clench. *Let it go.* He took a deep breath and said, "I'm glad you came back this time."

"I figured I'd take you at your word." Roger looked too good in his suit. He had tamed his unruly hair with a bit of gel, and his face was smooth. His green eyes seemed to glow with the green silk of his tie. John decided he liked the gray in Roger's hair.

"Good." John couldn't think of a snappy comeback. Roger looked too good.

"I was hoping you might join me for drinks when you finish up here. Or would that be pressing my luck?" In spite of Roger's casual manner, John could sense that he was nervous.

John considered the question. He could lie and say he'd been invited to a party following the concert, or he could just say no. But why lie when the truth was that he wanted this? "All right."

Roger blinked in surprise. "I... ah... great. How's Racine's? Or we could go to the lobby bar in the Palmer House."

John grinned to see the smile spread over Roger's face. "Racine's is fine. Why don't you head over and I'll meet you."

"Sounds good." Roger nearly bounced on the balls of his feet.

JOHN FOUND Roger at a small table near the back of the bar about an hour later. "Sorry. Took a bit longer than I thought. That kid's mother wouldn't let me go."

"The cellist's mother?"

John nodded and flagged down the waitress. "Scotch neat." He settled back into his seat and said, "The woman's a pain in the ass."

"And the kid's entirely worth it."

"Probably why everyone tolerates her," John agreed. "If she doesn't drive him insane, we'll be hearing a lot more from him. So you enjoyed the concert?"

"I always enjoy hearing you conduct."

"Thank you." John's cheeks warmed at the compliment. Three years as music director of the CSO and Roger could still make him blush with his praise. *Go figure.*

"You enjoying the work?"

"Yes. Although I have this fantasy of moving somewhere tropical and just conducting when I feel like it. No symphony board to deal with. No booking agents to argue over fees. That sort of thing I could do without." He reached into his jacket pocket for a cigarette, then realized with frustration that he didn't have any. Of course he didn't—he'd quit again.

"Sounds nice." Roger sipped his drink. Gin and tonic by the looks of it—Roger's favorite.

The waitress left John's drink at the table, then disappeared again. John took a sip and felt the warmth of the scotch at the back of his throat. He wasn't nervous, but he felt a strange sense of excitement. The feeling reminded him of a first date. Was that what this was? A date?

"How's Dorothy?" John asked. "You still in touch with her?"

Roger nodded. "She's getting remarried in June." He glanced at his drink, then chuckled. "Weird... I was the one who wanted out of the marriage, and there's this little part of me that's sad to hear she's moved on."

"Not so weird. You loved her."

"Yeah." Roger didn't meet John's eyes.

"I'm okay with that, you know. I always was. She's a good woman." He took a deep breath, then said, "I really wanted things to work out for you two."

"Thanks."

Seeing the look of guilt in Roger's eyes, John figured it was best to change the topic. "I put a call in to New England Conservatory."

Roger's expression brightened noticeably. "And?"

"And they're putting together a financial aid package for Alex. He should get a letter by the end of the week. Full ride as long as he maintains at least a B average."

"Thank you." Roger sighed. "I can't thank you enough."

"You love that kid, don't you?" John could see it on Roger's face, although he wanted to hear it for himself.

"I always wanted kids. But after the last miscarriage, Dorothy and I decided it just wasn't in the cards. We'd talked about adoption at one point, but by that time I think she saw the writing on the wall." Roger paused and ran a single finger over the rim of his glass. "I would have adopted Alex if I could have, but I was such a mess when he came to me."

"You have nothing to feel guilty about, you know."

"He needed a family, and I couldn't give him one." John noticed a muscle in Roger's cheek jump as he spoke.

John reached across the table and took Roger's hand. "You've given him a lot. Does he know that was your violin?"

Roger shrugged. "No. But it doesn't matter. I still have an instrument to play when I feel like it."

"Not an instrument like that one."

"I don't need it anymore." Roger met John's eyes, and John knew he was telling the truth.

"You know I didn't need to hear him play. If you'd just asked, I'd have gotten him a place at NEC. Your recommendation would have been enough."

The smile that lit Roger's face reminded John of when they were kids and Roger had just managed an A on a test when he hadn't studied at all. "Yeah. I knew that." He took a sip of his drink, then said, "But I wanted to see you."

"And?"

"And nothing. I just wanted to see you. I figured if things worked out, maybe I'd be seeing more of you. And if they didn't, at least I'd see you again." Roger waited a moment, then continued, "So what now, Maestro? Is there going to be an encore, or is the gig over?" He sounded entirely confident, but John knew him well enough to sense the tension underlying the words.

"I don't know." John put his hands together and touched his forefingers to his chin. "When you left me… in New York? I was sure it was something I'd done. But when Nate died and you were there for me… it all sort of fell into place. It wasn't just your mother. I finally realized we lived in two different worlds."

"I don't understand."

"Just that my world—New York, music even—was far more accepting of what we are. And I understood. I really did." He inhaled slowly and shook his head. "I know you love me. I know you always have."

"I wasn't ready." Roger ran his finger over the rim of his glass again. John noticed Roger was still on his first drink—not at all typical for him. "But I figure it's time I laid it all on the line. Tell you the truth. The *whole* truth this time."

John said nothing.

"I've spent my entire life trying to be something I'm not. And when Marc died, I got this stupid idea in my head that I had to be a substitute for my parents. Someone to take his place. Being gay wasn't part of that. And you—" He shook his head. "—you were everything I'd wanted to be. Successful. Talented. Focused. Okay with who he was. I wanted to be with you, but every time I was, it was like I could see all the things I'd fucked up and lost."

"Music?"

"Yeah." Roger's laugh had a bitter edge to it. "When I think how many years I pretended I'd be able to play again… I wasted so much fucking time. I could have been teaching." His face seemed to light up as he said this. "I love it, you know. Teaching. I can't imagine doing anything else."

"What changed?" John asked.

"A bunch of things. Mostly I realized it wasn't fair to Dorothy to pretend I was straight anymore."

"I know how hard it must have been to tell her."

Roger nodded. "It wasn't the only reason our marriage tanked, though. I realize that now. Things really went south when we stopped talking. Not that I was ever very good at talking. Maybe if I'd talked to you years ago, things might have ended up differently." Roger fixed his gaze on his hands before continuing, "I really did try this time. I didn't want to screw things up like I had with you. But she and I were a lot alike that way. At least maybe now she'll be happy. She deserves it."

"*You* deserve to be happy," John said without hesitation. He picked up his half-empty glass and finished his drink in one long swallow. "I'm just sorry I was such an ass to you when you said you wanted to get back together."

"John, I—"

"No. Please let me get this off my chest, because it's been eating at me for too long."

"Okay." Roger offered him a sympathetic smile.

"I'd gotten used to being alone. Having things my way." John exhaled slowly. "I shouldn't have shut you out of my life. I was a shitty friend. I'm sorry."

"You were scared. I get that."

Christ. John hadn't expected that depth of understanding from Roger. He really *had* changed. "Yes."

"So what happens now?" Roger asked.

"No idea. We spend time together. We go on being friends."

"And what about more?" John knew Roger was trying hard not to push him.

John touched Roger's hand once more and met his eyes. "I honestly don't know. I'll think about it."

"I… that's… well… thank you." Roger's eyes filled with tears. "I promise I won't rush you."

"Thanks."

CHAPTER

Ten days later

JOHN OPENED the apartment door. Roger was ten minutes early. Roger was *never* early. He stood there, smiling and holding a bouquet of flowers, dressed in a pair of jeans and a formfitting sweater. Green, to match his eyes. He looked good. Really good. *Shit. Three dates and you're ready to give up the ghost.*

John hadn't been with anyone since he'd heard Alex play at Roger's. Still, he'd told himself he was going to take his time, make sure he wasn't making a mistake. He wanted to get to know Roger again before he gave in to his physical attraction for Roger.

"For you." Roger handed him the flowers and their fingers brushed.

"They're lovely. Thank you." John admired the bouquet. It was easier than looking at Roger. Why hadn't he noticed how Roger's hair curled at the ends now that he'd let it grow longer?

"Alex got the offer from NEC. Thanks again."

John motioned Roger inside and closed the door behind him. "Happy to do it."

"You'll probably be seeing more of Alex than I will."

"I doubt it." John set the flowers down, then walked over to the side bar and pulled out a few glasses. "I've told them I won't be teaching next year."

"You… what?"

John ignored Roger's obvious surprise. "Cognac or scotch?"

"Scotch. And don't pretend you didn't hear me."

John opened the bottle. "On the rocks?"

"John...."

"Just what I said." John plopped three ice cubes into a glass without waiting for Roger's answer. He already knew how Roger liked his scotch. "I've found someone to take my place. One of my master class students at U of M. David Somers?"

"Never heard of him."

"Outstanding young conductor. Lives in the Boston area now." John handed Roger his glass and smiled. "And just to be clear," he said, "this has nothing to do with you. I just decided it was time for me to focus more on my conducting." He poured himself a cognac and sat in a chair across from Roger. He knew Roger wouldn't buy a word of it—he hardly believed it himself, although he'd told himself that was why he was quitting.

Roger stared at his drink for a moment, then, clearly collecting himself, said, "I'm glad. Regardless of the reason."

John sipped his cognac but said nothing.

"So where would you like to have dinner tonight?" Roger asked.

"I thought I'd cook."

Roger blinked. "You're going to make dinner for me?"

"For us," John corrected. "Yes."

"I... uh... okay."

"Is that a problem?" He'd thought he was ready, that maybe he'd take a chance and ask Roger to spend the night, but he suddenly felt nervous. Antsy.

"No. Not at all." Roger wore an expression between a smile and a frown, as if he was both confused and pleased with John's apparent change of heart.

"Good." John stood up. "Then I'll get to it. Try not to finish all the scotch while I'm gone."

"I'll do my best." Roger settled back in to the pillows on the couch and offered him a lopsided grin—a particularly charming grin that had John forgetting he'd told himself to take things slowly and wanting to kiss Roger then and there.

John walked a bit faster to the kitchen than he'd intended, nearly knocking a bowl off one of the side tables. Once in the kitchen, he leaned heavily against the counter and took a deep breath. What the hell was wrong with him? Since when was he so uncomfortable around Roger?

Since you started thinking this might actually work. He glanced down at the cognac in his hand and, without hesitation, drank it all in one swallow.

ROGER SET the scotch down untouched. He watched John nearly knock over one of his fancy knickknacks. John was clearly scared to death. It didn't take much for Roger to guess why. The strange greeting. Dinner at home. John knew how this evening might end.

Baby steps, remember? That was what he'd told himself. He didn't want John to rush into this; he wanted John to take his time and choose to be with him. He wanted this to last. Still, the knowledge that John's resolve was crumbling—had crumbled?—pulled powerfully at him. He knew John too well. If he went to John now, kissed him, even, John wouldn't be able to resist. Roger knew it hadn't just been him wanting John. John wanted him too.

If you rush him, he'll just convince himself you're the same and he'll pull away. He couldn't risk it. He couldn't go back to the silence between them and the years apart.

He walked into the kitchen a few minutes later. "Need some help?"

John started at the sound of his voice, and the knife in his hand clattered onto the counter. "Shit." John stared down at his hand as a thin red line blossomed where the knife had cut him.

"Sorry. I didn't mean to surprise you like that." Roger pulled a paper towel off the roll, took John's hand, and pressed the paper against the cut.

"No. My fault." John sighed. "I'm just a little… scattered, I guess." He offered Roger a tight smile, then said, "No. That's a lie. I'm nervous."

Roger met his gaze. "I know. I am too."

With these words, Roger saw the tension in John's body ease. "Mind getting me a Band-Aid? First drawer by the fridge."

"No problem." Roger pulled out the box, ripped a medium bandage open, then wrapped it around John's finger. "All better?"

John laughed. "If only it was that simple."

"It's not all that complicated, you know."

Roger let go of John's hand, but John caught Roger's fingers with his own. "Some things are simple." John glanced away from Roger, then back again. "Like how much I want to kiss you."

"What's stopping you?" Roger wouldn't make the first move. It had to be John. Whatever happened, it had to be John's choice. Roger had already made his.

"Me." John pursed his lips.

"No problem. I get it. Really. I just don't want to lose you again."

"You won't. I promise." John's eyes sparkled, but he made no move to kiss Roger.

"Why don't I give you a call tomorrow?" Roger said. He was sure now. John wasn't ready for this. "We can just talk. And if you want to get together for dinner, we'll figure it out."

"Thank you." John was clearly relieved, and Roger knew he'd done the right thing to back off.

Roger smiled. "Any time. I'll take a rain check on dinner."

"You're not staying?"

"Nah. It's better this way. No rush. I'll call you in the morning."

John's lips parted in obvious surprise. But Roger saw something else in his expression that told him he'd made the right call: relief. "Thank you. I...." John paused, then added quickly, "Just... thank you."

FOUR HOURS later Roger lay on the couch in his living room in the dark, listening to music. John's latest recording. The Shostakovich Fifth Symphony. Even now, he could hear high school John saying, *"Shostakovich wrote the symphony when things were pretty rough for him.... The dissonances are all about that. Suffering."*

He'd taken the train back from the city, gotten into the shower, and microwaved dinner. He was still wearing his bathrobe. He hadn't been ready to sleep; he'd been too overwhelmed with what had happened with John to think about sleep.

God, he wished he had someone to talk to! The one person he could talk to about something like this was the one person he couldn't call. Sure, he had a few friends from his old job he played golf with once in a while, but none of them knew he was gay. And now that he'd quit, he couldn't just call them up and say, "Hey, it's Roger. I'm scared shitless because I love my best friend and I think I'm going to lose him for good.... And oh, by the way, my best friend just happens to be a man."

No wonder this whole thing scared the crap out of John—it scared Roger just as much. For a year he'd tried to pretend he was fine without John in his life. He'd thought he'd done the right thing by giving John his space, but what if John wouldn't take his calls? What if John decided never to call him again?

He rubbed his arm absentmindedly and watched a set of headlights dance on the ceiling. It reminded him of when he was a kid and he shared a room with his brother. He and Marc used to play "guess the car" from the sound of the engines as they drove by the house. They'd whispered to each other—they didn't want to get in trouble for talking after lights-out. The memory made him smile.

He didn't think much about Marc anymore, but when he did, it was usually the good stuff. Tossing a baseball around in the backyard, chasing Roofster until they were both out of breath, then letting themselves get licked all over their faces.

Hey, Marc. Am I doing the right thing? Roger could almost imagine his brother sitting on the threadbare recliner, shaking his head at him for being such an insecure idiot. *Yeah. I know. Of all the people in this fucked-up universe, John's the one I know best.* He closed his eyes and tried to relax.

The music ended a few minutes later. Roger got up from the couch and picked up the remains of his dinner: two hot dogs and a handful of carrots. John's dinner would have been much better. Another car drove past the house as Roger put the dishes in the sink. He'd wash them in the morning—it was after midnight, and he didn't have any students until after lunch the next day. He turned the kitchen light off and headed for the stairs. The last thing he expected was the knock at the front door.

Roger quickly retied his bathrobe and ran a hand through his disheveled hair before he opened the door. "John?"

"Sorry." John's hair looked almost silver in the light from the front porch. The ends of his white shirt hung over his jeans, and instead of his contacts, he wore glasses. Roger couldn't remember the last time he'd seen John with glasses. Even in high school, he'd hated to be seen with them. "I know it's late."

"Come in." When John hesitated, Roger said, "Please."

"Thanks."

John walked inside and Roger locked the door behind him. "So what's this all ab—"

John's lips silenced Roger. Stunned, Roger allowed John to kiss him but didn't immediately reciprocate. He worried that if he responded, he might frighten John away again, and he wasn't sure he could handle that.

Roger hesitated for a long moment, then kissed John back. The kiss was tentative. A first step. But John once again took charge with an intensity that surprised Roger. John wrapped his arms around Roger and drew their bodies together. Roger felt the desperation in his embrace.

"Wow." Roger struggled to catch his breath. "What was that for?"

Unlike the kiss, John's smile was tentative. "No idea. I just knew I needed to do that."

"Is that why you came?"

"I have no idea why I came, other than wanting to be with you and realizing I shouldn't have let you leave earlier." John's lips were slightly pink from the kiss, his cheeks flushed.

"I'm not complaining," Roger said. "Just surprised, that's all. In a good way."

"I want to spend the night with you."

For more than a year, Roger had wanted to hear those words, or something like them. Now, though, he wasn't sure how he felt. He'd read the gossip columns, and he wondered how many men had shared John's bed in the year they hadn't seen each other. He didn't want to be one of them.

"If I say yes, does that mean you leave in the morning? Because if all you think I'm looking for is sex…. Shit, John. I can't handle not seeing you, but I want more than just one night."

"I know. I'll be here in the morning." John didn't hesitate.

"Are you sure that's what you want?"

John brushed his fingers over Roger's mouth, causing Roger to gasp. "I'm sure."

"God. I've missed you so damn much." *Like a fucking hole in my heart. My life.*

"I missed you too. I think I just needed a little time away from you to realize I couldn't handle not having you in my life." John offered him a wistful smile.

This time Roger kissed John, a long, desperate kiss he hoped would communicate how much it meant that he was here and giving them a chance.

"Come upstairs?"

John nodded. As they climbed the stairs, neither spoke. John stopped at the door to Roger's bedroom and pulled Roger close. "I'll be here tomorrow. Promise."

"How do you do that?" Roger said against John's neck.

"Read your mind?"

Roger laughed and pulled John through the doorway. "Goes both ways, I think."

"So what am I thinking now?" John's eyes were warm, inviting.

"You're thinking you want me to undress you." Roger reached for the top button of John's shirt and made his way down until he could push it off his shoulders. He leaned over and nipped at John's shoulder and continued upward until he reached John's ear. John sighed as Roger took his earlobe between his teeth and pulled, then licked it. The rise and fall of John's shoulders became more pronounced as his breaths stuttered in response to Roger's mouth.

"Smart man."

Roger took John's pants and underwear off, then watched as John untied his robe with shaking hands.

"You look good." John pushed off the robe so they were both naked.

"Thanks." He'd been exercising more the past few years, trying to stay in shape. He was glad John noticed. He lay back on the bed with his hands supporting his head, reveling in his nakedness.

"Lube?" John asked.

"In the nightstand."

"Condom?"

"Same place." Roger grinned, then said, "You sound like a surgeon, you know."

John pulled a condom and lube out of the drawer. "I sound like a conductor. Dealing with musicians can be a bit like herding cats." John narrowed his eyes and turned his head to one side in an obvious attempt to appear miffed.

"Am I a cat?"

"No. You're...."

Roger thought John looked a bit embarrassed. "I'm your best friend?"

"Much more than that." John straddled Roger and glanced down at him with a softness and warmth that took Roger by surprise. "How… what do you want me to do?"

Roger chewed the inside of his cheek for a moment, then said, "I want you inside of me."

"Really?" John looked stunned. In all their time together, Roger had never bottomed.

"Really." No more joking around this time. Roger was completely serious. He'd wanted this for so long. "Seems like you're the guy for the firsts."

"You haven't…?"

No more pretense. "I've never been with any man but you." He felt vulnerable to say it, but that vulnerability felt strangely good.

"I… I didn't know." John appeared stunned to hear this. "All those years… there was no one else?"

"Nope." He'd never have cheated on Dorothy, and when they'd split up, he'd only wanted to be with John. Roger saw how John's expression had changed. He looked genuinely pleased, even though Roger saw how he tried to hide his pleasure. "Just no jokes about butt virgins, okay?"

"Shut up." John glared at him. "It's not something to joke about. It's…. It m-means a lot to me. I don't know what to s-say."

"How about just kissing me?"

John brushed his lips over Roger's and Roger inhaled the crisp fragrance of John's cologne. Their tongues tangled and danced, teeth tapping when they got too carried away. Awkward and wonderful at the same time. Like coming home to a place you could barely remember, but that felt so familiar it was as if you'd never left.

"Show me what to do," Roger said as John latched on to his left nipple and flicked it with his tongue. "Oh, holy shit!"

John smiled his approval, then looked up at Roger and nipped this time.

"Ahhh, fuck!"

"Turn over." John's expression was tender and encouraging. "I promise I'll be gentle."

Roger rolled onto his belly, and a moment later John licked a line down Roger's back, pausing from time to time to feather kisses.

"You look amazing. Taste even better." John kneaded the muscles of his ass as Roger closed his eyes and reveled in the feel of John's hands on his body. He was so gentle, so loving. A different John from when they'd been together after college, but just as wonderful.

He was just about to say something clever—he still felt the urge to do that when his emotions threatened to get the better of him—when he heard John pop the cap on the lube and felt something cool and slick between his ass cheeks. All clever thoughts vanished as he felt John's finger glide across his hole. He closed his eyes and sucked in a deep breath.

"Feel good?"

Roger could only nod.

"Pull your knees under you." Roger heard both need and desire in John's voice. "I want this to feel good for you. It'll be easier like this."

Roger tried to remember a time they'd been together when he'd felt this vulnerable, but couldn't. John didn't touch him immediately, and Roger knew he was watching. Looking at him. Roger shivered and a moment later felt John's hands on his back, reassuring and gentle. A sensual, not-quite-sexual touch.

"Beautiful," John murmured as he skated his warm hands over Roger's lower back. "You called me that once."

"I remember."

"*You're* beautiful, Roger." John traced a single finger over Roger's hole again, then circled it once more.

"John."

John stilled his finger. Roger felt John's lips on his lower back as John pressed the tip inside of him just a bit. "Still feel good?"

"Yes." Roger was surprised he could speak even that single word. But when John reached around him with his other hand, clasped his cock, and squeezed, all Roger could do was whimper.

John pressed farther inside. Roger fought the urge to tighten around his finger. John began to stroke his cock at the same time he slipped it all the way inside. And fuck, but that felt so damn good! Too good. If John kept it up, Roger was sure he was going to come.

"Want you," Roger gasped.

"Not like this, you don't." John released Roger's cock and poured some more lube on his hands. "I'm not anywhere near fitting in there yet."

John pushed a second finger inside and Roger had to inhale to counter the burn. He was just going to ask why John liked this when John brushed what Roger knew must be his prostate. "Holy mother of.... Ahhh." Okay. So maybe he understood a little better now.

John continued to stretch him, stopping from time to time to roll his balls and squeeze his cock.

"Last one." John nipped at Roger's ass. It stung both inside and out as he pressed a third finger into him.

"Fuck."

"You're almost there." John found his prostate again, and Roger realized he'd keened to meet John's hand this time.

"Please, John. I'm ready. Fuck me, for heaven's sake!"

John laughed, and the next thing Roger heard was the sound of the foil wrapper on the condom and click of the cap on the lube. *Finally!*

Breathe. Just breathe. Why was he even nervous about this? He didn't have much time to think about it before John pressed against his entrance, slippery and hard. John. *His* John.

John leaned down and kissed him between his shoulder blades, a reassuring gesture that helped oh so much. Roger took comfort in the way John could gentle him and how John knew he needed it.

The tension in Roger's body eased once more as John pressed inside just a bit, past the tight ring of muscles. And holy fuck, but did it burn! Roger panted and tried to relax.

"You're doing great. And you feel amazing," John said as he pushed farther inside. And just when Roger thought the burn was too much, he brushed that spot inside.

"God. Feels incredible."

John pushed inward until Roger could feel his thighs against his ass. "You really are beautiful. So fucking beautiful." John's voice quavered a bit as he spoke, maybe from emotion, or maybe because he was feeling some of what Roger did now.

His John. Inside of him. Holding his hips. Moving, slowly at first, then picking up the pace. And the pain faded into hunger and need that seemed to start in Roger's belly and flooded his body with heat.

"John... yes... more... please." Roger could hear John's breathing as he moved.

"I don't know if I can hold back. You're so tight, and it's just too good."

"Then don't. Just do it. And tell me what it feels like."

Roger heard John's inhaled breath as he reached around and clasped Roger's cock again, then slid his fist up and down in rhythm with his thrusts. "It feels hot, like you're sucking me inside. Like I can't ever get deep enough. Like I can't ever get enough of you. Like... I... never... will."

Roger's orgasm took him by surprise. "John. Oh, fuck. John."

John's body shuddered a moment later and he cried out his release. Roger thought he could almost feel it when John came. A wonderful feeling came over him—a sense of sameness, of belonging, of *knowing* that this was the best fucking thing in his life and he had finally, *finally*, figured out where the hell he was meant to be.

ROGER CRADLED John's head against his chest. They'd showered off the sweat and lube before sliding naked between the sheets. John's eyes were open, but he'd been silent since they finished in the shower.

"What's up?" Roger asked.

"Tell me what you see." John's voice sounded surprisingly tentative.

"What?" Roger studied John's face but for once didn't find the answer there.

"Tell me what you see when you look at me." John's cheeks colored as he said this. "I... I need to hear it. I need to understand."

Roger knew John needed the reassurance that things really *were* different this time. "I'm not very good at it," Roger said after a long moment. "Telling you what I feel."

John smiled. "You're better at it than you know. A year ago you told me, and I wasn't ready to hear it. I'm ready now. God, I'm so sorry for walking away from you then."

"You asked what I see when I look at you." Roger reached out and touched John's chest with the tips of his fingers. His hand still ached when he straightened the fingers, but he'd long since gotten used to it. "I see John." Roger smiled and took a deep breath as thought deepened into emotion. "The kid who blew me away in high school. Made the whole damn world turn upside down. Showed me I wasn't who I thought I was.

Or maybe that I wanted to be someone else, but I was just me. Fucked-up Roger."

John took Roger's hand between his own. "Not fucked up. Just Roger."

"Yeah. Just Roger."

"Anything else?" John's expression was serene, peaceful, even happy.

"Just that I like to look at you." He felt his cheeks heat with the admission. *Like a fucking kid!* "Shit, it's so corny."

"I like corny sometimes. Besides, I promise not to tell anyone you're not always cool."

Roger laughed this time. "Right."

"Go on." John wasn't letting him off the hook.

"Fine. You asked for it." He took a deep breath, then said, "I see my life in you. From when I was a kid until now. My future, if you'll stick around."

John's eyes filled with tears, which he blinked away. "You're right. It *is* corny. But it makes me feel good. It makes me love you more."

CHAPTER 52

JOHN OPENED his eyes and grinned to realize he was lying in Roger's bed. Roger was snoring softly. For a while John just watched him sleep. Then the slight headache from drinking too much the night before began to get worse. He'd find something for the headache and then make them both breakfast.

He slipped out from under the comforter and pulled on his jeans and undershirt. He walked barefoot into the bathroom, relieved his overly full bladder, then splashed some water on his face. The reflection that greeted him in the mirror was tired but happy. *He* was happy. Hopeful too.

He opened the medicine cabinet and peered inside. Two of the shelves were lined with prescription medication, none of the usual cholesterol or blood pressure meds he figured he'd see in a forty-two-year-old man's stash. None of the sleeping pills he'd gotten used to seeing when he visited his mother, either. *It's none of your business.* He rubbed his mouth with a hand, then shrugged the thought away. He found a bottle of Excedrin on the top shelf and popped two of the pills.

An hour later Roger stumbled into the kitchen as John was pulling a dozen popovers from the oven. He laced his arms through John's. "Hey! Watch it. I've got to put this pan down."

Roger kissed his ear, then let John go before settling into one of the chairs at the breakfast table. "Looks delicious."

"I used to make these when I was a kid." John shook his head. "At least until my father decided I shouldn't be spending time in the kitchen. Too gay."

"I was sorry to hear about your mom."

"I know it sounds terrible, but it's really better." He set one of the popovers on a plate and handed it to Roger, then slid the jam his way. "The last few years, she didn't know where she was or who I was." He paused, then added, "Thanks for the flowers, by the way."

"You're welcome." Roger pulled off a piece of the popover and began to chew on it. "So why now? Why did you decide to take another chance on me? Why did you decide not to go back to Boston?"

John swallowed hard. Why not tell him the truth? "Before my mother died," he said, "she talked about you." He laughed softly. "How you were a 'good boy' and you made me happy. She was still thinking we were in college, but I realized it was still true. I *am* happier when you're in my life."

"Even with all the bullshit?" Roger pressed his lips together and the lines around his eyes appeared more pronounced.

"Yes. Even with all the bullshit." John nodded. "But it's more than just what she said. It's also because you're different. I guess I'm different too. Doesn't mean I'm not afraid I'll lose you for good this time." He couldn't help it—something still niggled at the back of his brain. Something he still didn't quite understand about Roger.

Roger set his mug down and settled into his chair. "I told you last time you were here that I'd changed. You just didn't believe it."

"You really *have* changed." John grinned outright. "Ten years ago you'd have told me what a stubborn ass I was."

"Yeah. I probably would have." He grinned and added, "This time I just thought it."

John sighed theatrically. "I love you, you know."

"Yeah." Roger grinned again. John grinned back. "I know."

"So are you going to tell me what this is all about?" John went back to work on his popover, chewing slowly but not really tasting it. He wasn't going to let Roger off the hook that easily. It might have taken him two long years and a cup of coffee to put it all together, but it wasn't going to take him that long to get an honest answer.

"What do you mean?"

"Something happened. Three, maybe four years ago? Something that made you realize you needed to change direction."

"I don't know what you're—"

"What's going on, Roger? What's with all the meds? Are you sick?" God, just the thought that there might be something seriously wrong with Roger made him dizzy.

"I'm fine." Roger smiled reassuringly at him. "Look at me. Do I look sick?"

"Not good enough."

"It's nothing really. We can talk about it later."

"No. Not later. We'll talk about it now or we won't talk at all." John steeled himself. "If you've really changed—if *both* of us have changed enough to make this work—you have to be honest with me."

Roger pressed his lips together but said nothing.

Fuck! Was he going to have to walk out now, when they'd come this far? "If you're not going to be entirely honest, this isn't going to work. Remember what you said about you and Dorothy not talking? How it reminded you of us? This is where you come clean and tell me the whole truth."

"It's not what you think. Or maybe it is… I don't know. I want to be honest with you. And you have a right to know. It's just… I don't want you to treat me any differently. I don't want you to be with me for the wrong reasons."

"Then let me make that call. Because if you don't trust me enough to do the right thing, there's no point in this."

Roger looked completely miserable. Frustrated. Confused. Scared. *Shit.* He'd never seen Roger look scared, and it frightened the hell out of him.

"You're right," Roger said. "I need to trust you. I *do* trust you."

John pretended to sip his cold coffee.

Roger only hesitated a moment, but it felt like an eternity. "It probably started somewhere around six years ago, except I didn't realize anything was going on back then. But then about three years ago, I was shooting hoops with a few work buddies and I fell." He paused and took a deep breath. "Weirdest thing. I didn't trip on anything. I didn't land wrong. I just… fell. Like I landed on my feet and suddenly my feet didn't feel like my feet—they felt like someone else's feet." Roger ran a hand through his hair and added, "I know. Sounds really weird, doesn't it?"

"A little, I guess." John felt the tension slowly build throughout his body. He didn't like where this was going at all. Not at all.

"I didn't get hurt, just a bunch of bruises," Roger continued. "But then a few weeks later, I had this tingling in my hand. My right hand. The good one."

John couldn't miss the faraway look in Roger's eyes as he glanced at his hand and flexed it. John had a vague recollection of Roger rubbing that hand when they'd painted the shutters together. He swallowed hard and forced himself to breathe slowly. He needed to be patient, even though he wanted to scream for Roger to get to the point because he didn't think he could handle waiting and worrying about where this was going.

Roger shrugged. "Doctor said it was nothing. Carpal tunnel from all the time I spent at the computer. I figured he was right. I'd overdone it. He gave me some exercises to do and sent me on my way.

"Then a month later, I tried to play the violin. I still like to play when I can sometimes." He smiled sadly, then continued, "I always loved to play. But this time, I picked up the bow and I couldn't hold it. I dropped it on the floor. Thank God it didn't break. And then when Dorothy and I went on vacation that last time, I fell again. I finally went to see a neurologist." Roger combed his fingers through his hair and shook his head.

"Roger. Please. Tell me what's wrong before I lose my mind."

"I've got multiple sclerosis," Roger said in a gentle voice. "MS."

"MS," John repeated as Roger's words began to sink in. *No. Not now.* Not when they really had a shot at happiness.

"It's okay. Really. It comes and goes. Mostly it goes." Roger took John's hand and squeezed it. "The doctor says it's the best kind, if you're gonna get it."

"There's no best kind of sick." John thought of Nate and he could barely breathe. Sick was pain. Death. Loneliness.

"Most people who get this live a long time. Maybe not as long as someone without it, but it's not a death sentence." Roger got up from the chair and walked over to the window, then turned around. "But it made me think about my life and what I wanted."

"That's why you quit your job." John hoped his voice didn't sound as flat as he thought it did.

"Yeah. I'd been teaching on the weekends for a few years. I kept thinking about teaching full time, but I never had the nerve to just pick up and take a chance on it." He shrugged. "Seemed like a good a time as any. A wake-up call. And things with me and Dorothy hadn't been good for years. Hell, they were never very good. And what you said years ago about not needing to give up music? That I should teach?"

"Yes?" John was surprised to hear Roger bring it up; he didn't think Roger had really understood at the time. And maybe he hadn't. But now....

"After you left the last time—when you said you couldn't do this again—I went to hear you conduct." Roger smiled now, and John saw none of the bullshit he'd seen before, just a newfound confidence that seemed to radiate from Roger. "I realized I could handle it. That I could be close to music and not play. I figured out that I really liked to teach. That I was good at it, just like you said I'd be. And when I figured that out, I realized teaching was enough for me. It made me happy."

"Roger...." John couldn't find the words.

Roger grinned. "I've got a bit of a confession to make. I've been going to most of your CSO concerts. I knew you didn't want to see me, but I needed to see you."

John wasn't sure how to respond to that, but he *was* sure that if he thought too much about it, he'd cry. Instead he asked, "Why didn't you just tell me you were sick when you said you wanted us to be together?" John stood up and walked over to him, then wrapped his arms around him and held him close.

"I didn't want you to say yes because you felt sorry for me. I wanted you to stay because you knew we should be together."

John knew Roger was right, though it cut him to the quick. He blinked back tears. "Damn you. You're making me cry again. You're the only one who can make me do that."

"I'm sorry." Roger brushed John's tears away with his thumbs before kissing him sweetly on the lips.

"Don't apologize." For once, he didn't need an apology. "You were right. I would have stayed for the wrong reasons." He took a long breath.

"And now?" Roger's eyes were wide. Hopeful.

"I told you last night I'd be here in the morning. Nothing's changed. I stayed because I love you and I want us to be together." He leaned in and kissed Roger. "But please, if there's something more I need to know—whatever it is—just tell me and get it over with."

"There's nothing else. Except telling you I love you." Roger smiled. "But you already knew that."

PART 5

December 15, 2006

AFTER MORE than ten years as music director of the Chicago Symphony Orchestra, Maestro John Fuchs passes his baton to rising star conductor David Somers at the end of the current season. Maestro Fuchs has agreed to return as a guest conductor for the symphony in future seasons.

CHAPTER 53

Late Spring 2006

JOHN WATCHED David Somers squirm in his seat. He was quite pleased with himself—David rarely let anything or anyone ruffle him. He had to give Roger at least part of the credit, though.

"I…," David began, clearly struggling to regain his composure. His dark-blue eyes were so obviously focused on a point on the wall over John's shoulder that John was tempted to laugh. "I think it's probably time for me to retire." Then, perhaps realizing that his choice of words wasn't the best, he added quickly, "For the evening, that is."

Roger laughed. He'd pretended to drink an entire bottle of a perfectly lovely Brunello di Montalcino Riserva by himself, although he'd only drunk half a glass. The rest they'd dumped unceremoniously down one of the toilets—they only needed David to *believe* Roger was drunk to make this work.

"I fail to see what's so amusing." It was as close to a glare as John had ever seen from David.

"That's because you haven't had enough wine." Roger slurred his words slightly. He was a better actor than John gave him credit for. "I was thinking it was funny because John's retiring"—Roger pointed at John and grinned—"and you're being stubborn."

They were a pretty good team. A variation on the good-cop, bad-cop theme: sober musician, noisy drunk musician. Not that John was completely sober—he had a nice warm buzz going.

"I've told you both," David said, ignoring a particularly loud hiccup from Roger, "that I'm flattered, but I'm just not interested in the CSO. I've got plenty of work to keep me busy."

"YOU READY for this?" John asked a few hours later as they stood on the edge of the vineyard next to David's villa, bottles of expensive wine in hand.

Roger, now dressed in nothing but his boxers and a T-shirt, winked at John. "This was *your* idea, remember?"

"I think I suggested something along the lines of creating a ruckus. Nudity was *your* idea."

Roger huffed. "I am *not* nude. And it's fucking freezing out here. I'm going to need a dip in the hot tub or my junk's going to be permanently shriveled up."

John laughed and shook his head in mock disgust. "I saw the housekeeper blush. Poor woman. I think you've traumatized her."

Roger ran a hand over the flat surface of his abs and smirked. "I think she was enjoying the view."

Roger's body looked damn good, although he wasn't going to say it.

"Show time," Roger whispered with a nod in the direction of the house. David wore silk pajamas with a robe thrown over his shoulders and was making his way toward the row of vines where Roger and John were standing. With a grin at John, he hiccupped loudly as he turned to face David and pulled off his T-shirt, then made as if he was going to pull off his boxers.

"Stop!" David's voice echoed throughout the vineyard.

"I think we've broken through the force fields, Captain," Roger said in his best approximation of a Scottish brogue. "The enemy is considering surrender."

John laughed and rolled his eyes at the *Star Trek* reference. "The threat of you running around with nothing on was enough, apparently."

Roger turned around and mooned John, who covered his eyes in mock embarrassment. The show was meant just for him, but John half hoped David had seen it. He wanted to see if they could make him blush.

"*Please* stop," David said again as he walked down the row between the vines. "Half my staff is threatening to quit." He did not look at all pleased. John was pretty sure he'd seen Roger's little display.

"Your turn," Roger said with a nod in John's direction. John held up his bottle of wine and took a quick swig. They'd dumped half the wine out of this one as well. It was a pity too. David's wine cellar was amazing. He'd chosen the least rare vintages for their little stunt, and still he felt guilty for having wasted such good wine.

John lifted the bottle and said, "To Bacchus!"

Roger snorted and whispered, "Once a nerd, always a nerd."

"You have to know your audience, o half-naked one," John said with a wave of his free hand.

"To Bacchus!" Roger said as he took the bottle from John's hand and pretended to drink.

John looked directly at David and smiled, then proceeded to unbutton his shirt and toss in onto the grass. He was almost happy that David was being obstinate—it gave him an excuse to revisit a bit of his wilder past. Still, he was bound and determined to find a replacement he trusted before he headed for Costa Rica with Roger.

"Don't you think that you're fooling me, either of you. I know what's going on here." David set his face in a scowl.

"And what would that be?" Roger asked as he slipped out of his boxers and hung them delicately on one of the nearby vines.

"You're trying to wear me down." In the moonlight, John saw that David's cheeks had pinked.

"We're just having fun," John countered. "Haven't you ever fantasized about running naked through a vineyard in the summer?"

"Never." David's face appeared grim, although he was still blushing. "Besides, it's spring and it's barely sixty degrees out."

"Roger's just letting it all out. What with the moon"—John gestured to the nearly full moon above the horizon—"the warm spring air, and the beautiful scenery, it's hard to fault him."

"I fault him." David looked as though he might actually be enjoying this. Good. The guy needed to be pulled kicking and screaming from his self-imposed exile.

Roger grabbed the bottle from John and started singing. "Ninety-nine bottles of beer on the wall, ninety-nine bottles of beer...." At least he sang on key.

David looked at John and shook his head. "Please make him stop."

"Not happening. He's having too much fun." John clapped David on the back and walked him between the vines. "Why don't I walk you back to the house? You can play something for me. A new composition, perhaps?"

David frowned in response.

JOHN WANDERED into the sitting room at nearly two in the morning and poured himself some cognac. David always stocked good cognac. John settled into one of the leather chairs and smiled as he heard footsteps from the hallway. This was it. The last step in their plan. John sincerely hoped it would work.

"Where's your cohort?" David eyed John warily as he entered the room.

"Taking a shower. He slipped and fell. Landed in a puddle." John sipped his cognac and watched the flames dance in the fireplace.

"There's something you're not telling me about all of this."

So David had figured it out. Good. This part of their plan would work better if David knew the truth, even if Roger had asked him not to talk about it unless it was absolutely necessary. John figured it was necessary. He also knew Roger would forgive him.

"There are plenty of things I don't tell you." John watched the cognac glimmer gold in the firelight. He really wanted a cigarette, but he'd quit when he and Roger moved in together nearly ten years before, and he'd made it this long without one.

"If you'd just tell me the truth, I might actually listen." David settled into one of the leather chairs after pouring himself a drink.

John looked up to find David's gaze fixed on him. He took another sip and closed his eyes as the alcohol warmed his chest. "You'll consider making your interest known to Doris and the symphony association?"

David's jaw appeared tense. "I might. As it stands, though, I see no reason to take over for someone who is at the height of his career. It makes no sense."

A bit of a roundabout way of saying it, but John understood. David wasn't hesitating to apply for the job out of lack of interest, he was hesitating because he wanted to understand. John could work with that. "Are you concerned that I'm making a bad decision?"

David straightened in his chair. "It isn't my place to question your decisions."

"That isn't what I asked," John pointed out. "I asked if *you* were concerned." He smiled.

"Why are you smiling?" David narrowed his eyes.

"I'm smiling because sometimes I'm a bit dense."

"Dense?"

"Somewhere along the way, I forgot that you weren't my student anymore." John exhaled and relaxed into the chair.

"I haven't been your student in some time."

"No. But I still treat you like one." John raised his glass to his lips but did not drink.

David frowned.

"Somewhere along the way, David, you've become a friend. You deserve to be treated like one."

David's lips parted and his eyes widened almost imperceptibly. "I did not mean to complain," he said in a low voice. "I merely want to understand."

John offered David another smile. "There are more important things in life than a career. Sometimes you need to step back and enjoy what you have while you still have it." John took another sip of the cognac, allowing it to dance on his tongue for a moment before swallowing it down.

"Roger is ill."

This time David had surprised John. He nodded, then asked, "How did you know?"

"There's only one thing you love more than your career."

"I've underestimated you again, haven't I, David?"

David inclined his head and smiled. "I've learned a few things since my wife died." He watched the fire and did not meet John's eyes.

How long had Helena Somers been gone now? Five years? Six? John could still imagine her here at the villa. Helena had helped David find this beautiful place, and it had become David's sanctuary. Before her death, *she* had been David's sanctuary.

"Roger has MS. He could live a long time." John finished his cognac. "Or he might not. I don't want to waste whatever time we have." *We wasted too much time already.*

For several minutes David was silent. Then he inhaled an audible breath and asked, "If I agree to apply for the CSO job, will you give me something in return?"

"Something?"

"A promise of sorts." David wore an almost playful expression.

"All right. What do you want from me?"

"I'd like you to conduct at least once a season." David pressed his lips together, his gaze slightly wistful.

"You'll miss me." John grinned.

"Of course not. I just appreciate good conducting." David's smile belied his words.

"I promise."

David lifted the crystal carafe, and John held out his now-empty glass.

"Thank you, David."

"Any time."

"WELL?" ROGER was sitting in bed, waiting for him.

"Done deal. Assuming he impresses the symphony association—and I've no doubt he will—David Somers will be the next artistic director of the CSO." John shed his clothing and slipped into bed beside Roger. "Thanks for your help."

"My pleasure." Roger's eyes twinkled. "Although dumping all that wine really made me sick."

"You're not supposed to drink."

Roger ignored this and snaked his arms around John's waist. "Are you sure you're doing the right thing, though? We could live in Chicago and you could keep your job—"

"I'm sure." John brushed his lips against Roger's neck and felt him shudder in response. "I told myself if we ever figured out how to make this insane relationship work, I'd spend as much time with you as possible."

"Insane?"

"Don't look at me."

Roger buried his head in John's shoulder and sighed. "Am I that bad?"

"Horrible." John shuddered as Roger nipped at his earlobe. "Pure… ahhh… torture."

"Good."

"Just… oh Christ… no more… nghhh… insanity, okay?" It was always so hard to think with Roger around. Talking was even worse.

"Got it. No more insanity."

"Other than the usual, I mean." John sighed as Roger traced a line over his jaw and down to his neck. "Because I'm used to your insanity now. Your insanity is addictive. I couldn't go on without it."

Shira Anthony was a professional opera singer in her last incarnation, performing roles in such operas as *Tosca*, *Pagliacci*, and *La Traviata*, among others. She's given up TV for evenings spent with her laptop, and she never goes anywhere without a pile of unread M/M romance on her Kindle.

Shira is married with two children and two insane dogs, and when she's not writing, she is usually in a courtroom trying to make the world safer for children. When she's not working, she can be found aboard a 35' catamaran at the Carolina coast with her favorite sexy captain at the wheel.

Shira's Blue Notes Series of classical-music-themed gay romances was named one of Scattered Thoughts and Rogue Word's "Best Series of 2012," and *The Melody Thief* was named one of the "Best Novels in a Series of 2012." *The Melody Thief* also received an honorable mention, "One Perfect Score" at the 2012 Rainbow Awards.

Shira can be found on:

Facebook: https://www.facebook.com/shira.anthony

Goodreads: http://www.goodreads.com/author/show/4641776.Shira_Anthony

Twitter: @WriterShira

Website: http://www.shiraanthony.com

E-mail: shiraanthony@hotmail.com

The Blue Notes Series

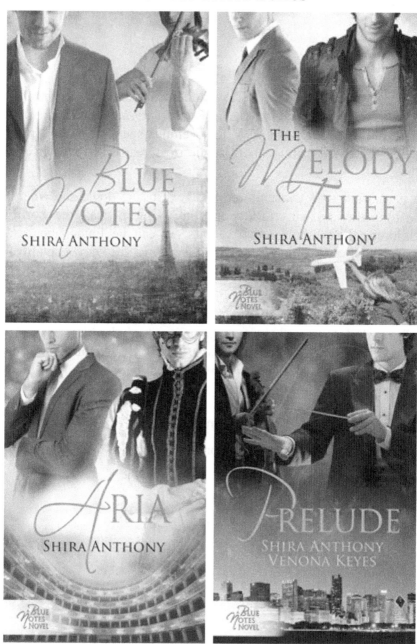

http://www.dreamspinnerpress.com

Also from SHIRA ANTHONY

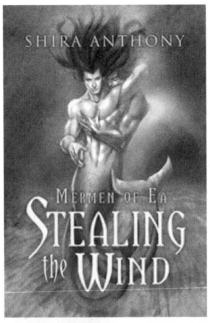

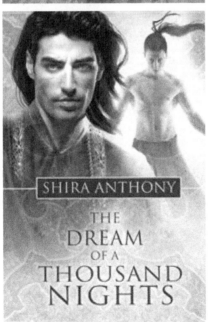

http://www.dreamspinnerpress.com

From SHIRA ANTHONY & EM LYNLEY

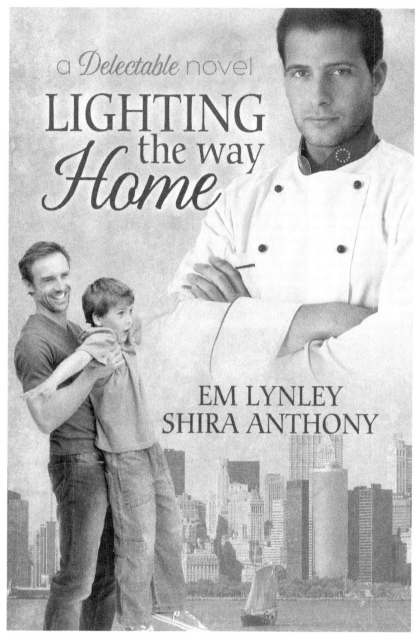

a *Delectable* novel

LIGHTING
the way
Home

EM LYNLEY
SHIRA ANTHONY

http://www.dreamspinnerpress.com

From SHIRA ANTHONY & VENONA KEYES

the trust

Shira Anthony
Venona Keyes

http://www.dreamspinnerpress.com

CPSIA information can be obtained at www.ICGtesting.com
Printed in the USA
LVOW05s2111150115

422989LV00035B/2314/P